VERY BAD THINGS

Seraphim George

Copyright © 2025 by Seraphim George

All rights reserved. No part of this book may be reproduced, distributed, or transmitted in any form or by any means—electronic, mechanical, photocopying, recording, or otherwise—without the prior written permission of the publisher, except in the case of brief quotations used in critical reviews and articles.
This is a work of fiction. Names, characters, places, and incidents are products of the author's imagination or are used fictitiously. Any resemblance to actual events, locales, or persons, living or dead, is entirely coincidental.

Published by Quo Vadis Press
Boston, MA
Cover & Interior design: Seraphim George

ISBN: [979-8-9998878-7-0]
First Edition
Printed in the United States of America

*To all the good people who tried to fix the bad ones.
And to all the bad people who made sure they failed.*

PART ONE

CHAPTER ONE

Lester Filch is a very bad man. If the saying "Bad things happen to good people" were true, then he'd never experience bad things. On the contrary, he'd experience very good things. In fact, Lester Filch experienced so many bad things that he should have been a very, very good person.

This wasn't the case, as any of his contemporaries in West Lemon, New Jersey—where he lived—or 25th Street, New York, NY—where he worked—would tell you without question. Lester Filch was just plain bad. He didn't start out that way. He had a very good beginning for about eight months while still inside his mother's womb. From the day of conception there was silent, comfortable bliss within, wrapped in warm blankets of flesh and blood, soothed by his mother's heartbeat.

There was no way he could know that his mother, when the pounding of her heart increased, was hard at work doing what she did best to pay the bills, and hating every minute of it. But it was no matter to Lester. He lived within a cavernous suite, in which the world outside—and his mother's sorrows—couldn't touch him, and very bad things were very foreign to him indeed.

What he couldn't know was how close he had come to

danger. Though, he might have told you later, it would have been better had his mother scraped him out of her belly and saved him the trouble of living. On the day she made her decision, the rhythmic beating of her heart pounded in his developing ears, drowning out the conversation, sheltering him from the knowledge that just outside those fleshy walls, in the sanctuary of St. Matthew's church, his fate rested upon a knife's uncertain edge.

"I can't keep him," his mother told the priest. "He sorta ruins my aura, you know? Gets in the way of business."

According to Father DiCenzo—now bent with age and sallow-skinned—there was nothing physical about her he could remember, though their conversation remained alive in his mind. There were a lot of prostitutes in New York then, just as there are now, and to remember a face among so many was impossible.

"I never got a good look at her face anyway," he said to me, dragging a wraithlike hand across shrunken lips to clear a reservoir of spit pooling at the corner of his mouth. "The only thing I remember about her now is how she chewed her gum while she told me her plight. After a few minutes, it began to drive me crazy."

"Father, listen," she had said, "to be honest, I was on my way to the clinic across the street. But if anything's gonna stick with me from my childhood, it's my religion, and I wanted to do what's right by the Church and the man upstairs, you see. So I decide, maybe I don't wanna do this.

"But see, I haven't been to church since confirmation. So since you were in the area, I thought I'd stop by before I eject the little sucker and see if you can't convince me not to."

Father DiCenzo was shocked by her brazen attitude toward such a monumental decision, with little remorse for even the idea of the child's loss, as if he were a very bad thing. But she came to him, and that was something.

Every theological argument he had ever heard—from Plato to the Gospel—embroiled his brain cells in a desperate attempt to say what might convince her. He fired missiles of faith, truth, hope, cosmic absolutes that had brought down empires. She dismissed them with a shrug and a "Who cares? How does it affect me?"

Even when he pressed on her guilt—forcing her to admit she felt bad even thinking of killing the life inside—she appealed instead to her own pain. She was dealt a lot of bad cards in life, and there were high rents, violent pimps you didn't wanna owe, the drug-use, not to mention the ordeal of childbirth, the tearing and ripping she dreaded more than death. It would be less cruel, she argued, to throw the baby into a garbage pail than for her to have to push it out. Selfish, yes—but practical.

Finally, Father DiCenzo stopped dispensing theology and descended to her bare-bones, pragmatic philosophy. "I'll give you five thousand dollars to have that baby," he said. He thought he was starting low and planned to work his way up. After all, he was doing the Lord's work in style, never needing for anything thanks to Rome and a few good investments.

But in her mind the price was right. "I'd push you and all of St. Matthew's choir out of my you-know-what for five thousand bucks. You've got a deal, padre."

It was a good deal. Twenty-five hundred up front. Twenty-five hundred when the baby arrived at the parsonage. Save a life, make five thousand dollars. Cheaper, really, than an indulgence in Luther's day.

Though Lester Filch would, in later years, wish the price had been too low, his mother did exactly as the priest asked—though not everything went according to plan.

Around eight months into his stay at the Hotel InUtero, Lester was threatened with lynching if he didn't vacate the premises fast. He hadn't missed any rent, he hadn't skipped payment. But on the thirteenth day of the eighth month his luck ran out. His umbilical cord looped around his neck, choking him, and life for Lester—rather than end—had only just begun.

He had almost cost his mother five thousand dollars, and you can bet she was relieved to see him alive despite his cries. She wasn't so relieved when the nurse thrust him into her arms, when all she wanted to do was leave that hell-hole of a hospital room. Instead, she was forced to feed her inconvenience as he attempted—one month premature—to suck her absolutely dry.

She lied to the nurses, told them the father was in Korea and couldn't pick them up. She'd walk home and wait until his return. But the staff refused to let her out alone and procured her a ride anyway.

Home, she told her driver, was in the apartments next to St. Matthew's Church. The man chauffeured the woman and her screaming, no-name baby to the address. He watched as they entered the foyer. Then he drove away.

She backtracked to the church.

Father DiCenzo was nowhere to be found. So she laid the darling child—whose screeches ricocheted off the church ceiling—inside the baptismal font. He thrashed like a fish out of holy water. She threw a blanket over him, tried to hush him, but there was no pleasing it.

With a pencil and offering envelope she scrawled a note:

HEY PADRE. HERE'S THE KID. HE KICKED HIS WAY OUT AND SCREAMED THE WHOLE TIME. GUESS I'M NOT THE MOTHERING TYPE. THANKS FOR SPARING ME THE GUILT. THANKS FOR THE CASH. I'LL BE BACK LATER TO PICK UP THE REST.

She never signed her name. She also never came back.

The priest became convinced something had happened to her, as bad things do happen to bad people. None of that silly whining about evil men avoiding justice and good men dying young. That was atheist nonsense from beatniks—questioning everything with nothing better to do than smoke pot.

For Father DiCenzo it was simple: if a good man died young, he wasn't good at all. Questioning this meant questioning the fear of God itself. Bad men get damned. Good men get blessed. Case closed.

The news confirmed his theory the next day.

A prostitute had solicited a man through his car window when a runaway Peter Pan bus careened out of control. Its first point of impact was, unfortunately, the very car she leaned into. You can only imagine the shock of the potential customer, finding her head exactly where she had promised it would be—between his legs—but without payment or an accompanying body.

For the priest, it was a satisfying explanation for why she never came back for her money. There was no doubt in his mind that the head in that man's lap belonged to Lester's mother.

"Served her right," he muttered uneasily as he watched the news broadcast. A twinge of guilt gnawed at him, threatening his clean-cut theory, but he didn't amend the comment. Instead he coughed, "Poor thing," and changed the channel.

A week later, on newsstands across Manhattan—beside porn magazines the priest usually avoided—blared a headline:

NEW YORK CITY PROSTITUTE WINS STATE LOTTO FOR $100,000.

Below it was the photograph of a woman who bore an uncanny resemblance to little Lester Filch. And she was smiling. The exact kind of smile that says the universe has been conned, and it will be conned again.

CHAPTER TWO

Every day thousands of babies are born. Where they are born can certainly differ. Some babies—lavished with nurses, adequate supplies, proper clothing—are born in high-end homes; you know, hooked up right from the beginning. Others are practically dropped in the mud. And there are thousands of circumstances in between.

Whether wrapped in swaddling clothes and laid in a manger or set upon the Nile in a basket, babies are born in as many different situations as their personal appearances.

But despite the discrepancies in their placement, all children can be divided into two types of people: those who are wanted and those who are unwanted. This has nothing to do with location or class. Countries that provide their citizens with health care and therapy still produce mothers who toss their screaming babies into plastic bags and throw them in a dumpster like yesterday's leftover meatloaf.

In contrast, countries that cry out with war, famine, or plague and make you want to write a check to the next big charity still produce mothers who will die for those they give birth to. They will starve so their little ones can eat.

Lester Filch, as previously discussed, was one of those unwanted babies born inconsequentially. His birth, for that unknown woman, was a very bad thing.

Across the country was his very different—and very good—opposite. Like Lester, this child had her good eight months, but unlike him, she never let them go, perpetuating her good fortune through the birth canal and into a warm and welcoming world.

Beatrice Goodie was born in San Perfecto, California, to two doting parents who planned the blessed event for quite a long time. Beatrice's mother was unable to have children of her own for the first ten years of her marriage. In fact, infertility was the only unfortunate thing in Mrs. Goodie's life.

Wherever she went, Mrs. Goodie struck a stunning feminine figure. She was a classic beauty admired in her high-class neighborhood by men and women alike, though always with a hint of jealousy from San Perfecto's band of wealthy women.

She never had to work. Her husband was a doctor and did so well in his job and in the stock market that she would never have to work again. But she didn't need a professional job, as everything she did turned to gold, especially her art, which was as exquisite as the artist. Every time she sold a painting, Mrs. Goodie invested the money, helped it grow exponentially, and gave it all away to charity.

Through all this, she and her husband prayed for a baby, and they never gave up trying. God knows they never gave up. The neighbors knew too, come to think of it. Finally, to the neighbors' eventual relief and the couple's utter joy, Beatrice was conceived in the lush gardens of their estate—in between two rhododendron bushes in bloom, underneath a perfectly full moon, and surrounded by fireflies. It was the perfect conception.

As unfortunate as her prolonged infertility was for Mrs. Goodie (though she never complained of her situation, for that would be an utterly disingenuous thing to do given all she *did* have), it proved not so unfortunate as she might have thought.

In the same spirit as the rest of the child's life, Beatrice's late arrival was a very good thing. For ten years, persevering as she was to conceive, Mrs. Goodie's love and desire for the unborn child grew deeper. When her daughter inhaled her first breath, there was no other woman in the world that wanted her baby as much as Mrs. Goodie.

Beatrice grew up in a home that Martha Stewart would have envied. The goodness seeping from its walls and draperies, the absolute perfection of her surroundings, crafted her into an equally sickening beauty.

Sometimes, those of us who are more run-of-the-mill and unlucky in life see someone who looks better, has more talent, owns an abundance of material possessions, or was dealt a better lot and feel the unmistakable urge to slap them. That wouldn't be so with Beatrice Goodie. For that exquisite specimen of feminine life, you would want to backhand her across the face and then maybe give her a few kicks while she was down. She was *that* good.

While most humans seem to struggle with their original sin, Beatrice lacked even the propensity to do evil. No one has ever had to teach a child to do bad; no one, that is, until *she* came into the world.

She didn't even cry when the doctor slapped her behind to kick in the automatic functions. The only time she did cry, as far as her parents can remember, was when a commercial came on television for one of those charities for overseas degenerates—the kind of commercial people long to change but usually can't reach the remote on time.

The little girl gazed into the television and the staring eyes of the starving little boy—skin stretched tight as paper over his bones, stomach bloated, flies wrestling for a place inside his eyes—and a loud wail broke from her normal silence.

Such uncanny compassion didn't fail to affect the course of her future childhood and found its way into even the most mundane aspects of her life. For example, sweet oatmeal made with milk and sugar was her favorite food growing up, but during one week in the sixth grade, Beatrice experienced a revolution.

It was on a day when a fellow student presented a report on Cuba's poverty and political unrest. The one fact that stood out more than any other was the pittance made by Cuban workers who picked sugarcane and then processed it. They were practically slaves, and no product made with the sweat of the disadvantaged should be supported and eaten by truly good people.

So Beatrice swore off sugar—to her dentist's delight, though she never had a cavity before.

Coincidentally, two days later, a boy twisted one of her nipples during recess in a flirtatious but painfully out-of-place gesture. It hurt quite a bit. She forgave the boy because, through that traumatic experience, she learned the torture that cows must go through every time they were milked. From that week on, she had her oatmeal plain and enjoyed it. Her future veganism was inevitable.

Beatrice Goodie won every possible prize for scholastic achievement, reaching a number of accolades far beyond that of her classmates. And just so there could be no accusation that she was not a well-rounded student, through middle school and high school she was sure to win trophies in soccer, track, and field hockey.

She joined the San Perfecto High School cheerleading squad to become the only student to make captain during her sophomore year. There never seemed to be enough time in the day—but always just enough time to get done exactly what was needed.

Like her mother, she managed to gain enemies from among her female colleagues, most likely due to her magnetic pull for the opposite sex and—in some cases—the not-so-opposite sex (a rumor that never reached her innocent ears). How she would have reacted to that particular controversy isn't known, though she would have had a good response, no doubt.

Every man that knew her loved her and wanted her not only for her perky, well-formed breasts and chiselled behind, but also for her wit—or so they claimed. And she let them have their fun, though she never gave in to their advances.

She liked those boys and was thankful for the continual affirmation of her beauty that they provided. But she preferred her state of independent chastity and kept in the company of a few women she could truly call friends.

Not only that, but—as she put it—the idea of dating seemed too preferential to be fair. And what wasn't fair wasn't good.

It could be said that the amount of possessions she owned wasn't fair, especially in light of so many who live in a constant state of destitution. The only outdated item she ever owned was a toothbrush she used for far too long.

She never wore clothes for more than one season, and her bedroom's interior design changed about every five years. But all this overabundance wasn't because she was selfish. Neither did she lack gratitude for everything she had.

Her parents were to blame. They insisted on providing for their daughter the new and improved. Every desire had to be fulfilled, and they were able to give her everything because they had everything to give. When, for example, on her sixteenth birthday she received a green Camaro and, after thanking her parents profusely, made the casual comment that green was very close to yellow—her favorite color—they immediately decided to purchase a yellow Camaro for her as well.

Beatrice begged them not to and to do their best to believe she was really happy with the green Camaro. The second car was never bought, but that one mistake lingered on Mr. and Mrs. Goodie's minds as a dark and unfortunate miscalculation in their lives as parents.

CHAPTER THREE

When Lester Filch was ten years old, he lost seven pets in seven days. It was uncanny, and by far the worst week of his childhood—though not the worst day. (The worst day was when his parents named him Lester, after Lester Cole, an infamous communist writer.)

His adoptive father—Redd Filch, a good man contrary to the suspicions of a certain Joseph McCarthy—always tried to give his son everything he needed. What he needed, however, was better luck.

It started on a Sunday when Mr. Filch, far from coming home from church, returned instead from his local chapter of Marxists for a Uniform Metropolis (the MUM Club) with a goldfish named Alice. This was unusual, since Redd had just been blacklisted and lost his job—his MUM Club membership being the last straw. His boss had been a staunch American, a no-compromise democratic fighter, and there was no overlooking Redd Filch's commie ways.

Despite the financial difficulties, money was the last thing on the man's mind. His son worried him most. Lester never seemed to smile, and his father couldn't understand why. There was barely enough time in his day to ask Lester how school was going or what he did with his friends. What he didn't know—and what Lester felt too ashamed to share—was that there were no friends, in or out of school. His son was lonely, and therefore unhappy, and though he didn't know why, Redd knew unhappiness when he saw it on Lester's face. He believed there was no amount of money that wasn't worth a smile on that usually pallid demeaner.

The answer wasn't toys or food. Toys were too noisy, too complicated. The few times Lester accepted them as gifts, the little gadgets inevitably broke under his rough, heavy hands. Rather than cry, he hurled the playthings across the room in fits of rage. After several episodes, he nearly shouted at his father, "No more toys!"

So Redd stopped buying toys.

Sweets were no good either. They made Lester's teeth hurt. What he did enjoy were celery sticks. Upsetting as it was for Redd to see him gnaw them without salt or peanut butter, it was at least something. Mr. Filch often left the room, grated raw by the crunching—slow crunching, fast crunching, a mixture of both—that Lester seemed to revel in. The boy would sit and listen to the crunch, mesmerized, slipping into a catatonic trance.

Eventually beets made it onto his short list of favorite snacks. They lacked crunch but turned his teeth blood-red with juice, and he would stand at the mirror for long stretches, making faces at himself, delighted at the image of a vampire staring back.

And beside celery and beets, there was one other thing Lester wanted above all else: a pet.

His child psychologist was alarmed by the obsession. She felt no compunction in telling Redd she feared the boy, in his misery, desired another life upon which to inflict his inner pain. A puppy, she warned, could end up vivisected in some perverse scientific experiment.

His schoolmates agreed in their own cruel way.

One day his teacher asked the class what they wanted most in the world. Lester, beaming at her—a rare occurrence—confidently answered, "I want a pet."

Snickers rolled across the room like a wave, crashing over his psyche.

"What is it, Filch, looking to finally get a girlfriend?" a classmate jeered.

"The creep will probably kill whatever he gets," another chimed in. "We should call Animal Control."

"For his pet or for him?" added a third, and the laughter grew to humiliating proportions.

Lester never spoke up in class again. He buried the desire deep, hoping one day it would come to pass.

Despite his odd, isolationist tendencies, there was no malice in the longing—only the simple desire to love another living thing. When he flew into rages, throwing objects about, he always wound down in the arms of his teddy bear, Poofy, curling up on the bed, petting its fur, wishing it were alive and capable of something other than a blank, soulless stare.

Redd agonized for eight years over granting his son's wish before he brought Alice home. From the day Lester could talk, he had begged for a pet. Most fathers would have given in, but Redd held back—not out of fear of his son's supposed psychopathy, but because of what had happened two weeks into Lester's arrival in West Lemon, New Jersey.

It should have been a wonderful day for both Connie and Redd Filch, who fought and paid dearly to adopt him. They already had a surrogate son of sorts: a small lovebird named Dolt. Being good people, they never neglected Dolt once Lester arrived. In fact, he and the three-year-old became fast friends. Connie and Redd often found Lester toddling around with Dolt perched peacefully on his shoulder.

There was one rule: by seven o'clock, Dolt had to be in his cage. Connie insisted she didn't want to be surprised by flying animals after dark, and she certainly didn't want Dolt disturbing Lester at bedtime.

That rule became important two Mondays into Lester's stay, when a series of malevolent circumstances conspired against Mrs. Filch. The first was Dolt catching a cold two days before. Drafts in October left him weak, so the vet prescribed some strong medication. Birds and colds don't mix.

They should have let him die.

The second circumstance was that Lester, having settled into his new surroundings, entered a rebellious stage, testing his boundaries.

The third was that Connie had done laundry that morning and stacked towels neatly in the upstairs hallway closet. When she turned away, the door was left ajar.

That night, around 7:30, Lester climbed from his crib to explore. Instinctively, he knew it was wrong, but he also knew his new parents were tucked away in their bedroom. His first stop was the closet. Usually locked, secured with a childproof knob, it was inviting him in. He rummaged through boxes and soon found a toy: his father's old roller skates. Instantly fascinated, he rolled them along the hall, making motor noises, winding them up before shooting them forward.

Minutes later, bored, he crept downstairs. His next stop was Dolt's cage. The bird, upon seeing his simian friend, paced on his perch frantically. Dolt flapped so violently feathers snowed down and the cage rattled. Lester laughed, clapping his hands with delight. He opened the cage.

Instead of the usual chirp and hop onto his shoulder, Dolt—doped up on medication—launched into a manic flight. He disappeared through the house, shrieking with his newfound wild freedom. Unconcerned, Lester clapped happily again. Dolt had never flown away before. He would come back.

But Dolt's cries of ecstasy caught Connie's ear. She opened the bedroom door, peering into the dim hall. She heard only the flapping of wings, which reminded her of bats—the creature she feared the most.

Perhaps it was the white of her eyes. Perhaps her voice calling out Lester's name. But something drew Dolt upward. He shot up the stairwell like a green bullet and careened into her face, clawing and flapping at it, frantic and disoriented by nerves and medicine. Connie shrieked—not in pain but in fear. She waved her arms, struggling to push her attacker away. Had the roller skates not been left at the top of the stairs, she might have succeeded.

There is no need to wallow in the gruesome details. Only a passing note about a broken neck, her wide-eyed stare of surprise, and her body twisted like a broken marionette on the first floor.

It was a very bad thing for everyone involved—least of all Connie Filch, whose last thought was a childhood memory of roller skating along Lake Champlain with her father. The image was pleasant, and, coupled with the fact that she had no time to comprehend her own death, soothed her into eternity.

Lester never forgot the sight of his dead mother, nor the cry that echoed through the house for years. Redd never forgot either. He did not blame the bird or the boy outright, but his broken heart could not forget that together they had caused his beloved's demise. He swore off animals, vowing never again to see his son in the presence of a pet, lest the nightmare return too clearly.

And what happened to Dolt, the lovebird? Either from guilt, disease, or a convenient overdose, the bird died a few days after Connie.

The tragedy pressed its hellish footprint into Redd Filch's mind for eight years. The very fact that Lester continued to demand a pet seemed a cruel joke. But time, as it does, eventually washed the print away, leaving only a faint outline in the mud. And not enough of it to keep his only child from what he most desired. So Alice the goldfish came home to an ecstatic ten-year-old and to her inevitable demise.

CHAPTER FOUR

When Beatrice turned two, she received her first pet: a very rare Persian cat she called Fuff, which was two-year-old for Fluffy. The butchered name stuck, even when she learned to pronounce words correctly.

Fuff wasn't something she asked for. Her parents assumed she wanted a pet since the child held an abiding love for stuffed animals. During one Christmas season, Mrs. Goodie realized her daughter didn't have a stuffed cat, though every other animal she could think of filled two bedrooms. Natural instinct suggested that Beatrice needed another stuffed animal, this time to fill the cat-shaped hole in her heart. But as Mrs. Goodie browsed Ted E. Bayer's stuffed animal emporium, inspiration struck. Everything in the store was too expensive—the cheapest doll, a stuffed penguin the size of her hand, cost forty dollars—and none of it looked right. They were cartoonish, absurdly disproportioned, and biologically inaccurate.

So she decided only a real cat would do. Beatrice deserved the best, and perhaps a living, breathing one would offset the psychological damage of having lacked a stuffed one for so long.

Fuff was—at least to Beatrice and Mrs. Jane Goodie—a delightful, good-natured creature. She was downright childlike: begging for food when the refrigerator opened, flipping her water dish when displeased, knocking over pans when no one was around. She was spoiled to the point of being cute. It was uncanny.

Every morning at six, Jane Goodie woke to feed Fuff her portion of filet mignon, cooked medium rare and sprinkled with tarragon and sesame seeds. She cleaned the litter box until it was spotless, a porcelain throne fit for feline royalty. One morning she dared to load the washing machine before tending to the litter on schedule. Upon entering the kitchen, she gave a small cry of horror. Diarrhea covered the linoleum like a milk chocolate film. The carpet leading into the dining room did not escape either; faeces smudged into the fibers like a finger painting from the bowels of hell.

Fuff sat in the middle of it, her flat face arranged into a look that said, *Don't* ever *be late again.*

Mrs. Goodie only shook her head. "You silly kitty. Are you angry because mummy didn't change your litter box? I'm sorry, sweetheart. I'll never do it again."

And after their cleaner, Lucía, scrubbed it all away, she never did.

Johnathan Goodie, however, saw through the delicate fluffy exterior to the Mephistopheles within. Despite all the attention lavished upon it by the women in the household, the cat latched onto him like a demon, tormenting him, and only him, every day. At five AM it meowed or scratched his face until he woke up. Then, with utter satisfaction, it would curl up at the end of the bed and go back to sleep—as if its only purpose had been to wake him.

The little devil took pleasure in a myriad of other activities: ripping keys from his typewriter, shredding the upholstered Togo couch in his office (and only his office), playing with his glasses until they broke.

When John complained, no one listened. His wife mounted a spirited defense of the cat's misunderstood nature. Even Beatrice, though occasionally swiped at, believed Fuff deserved love and tolerance. After a while Johnathan stopped complaining and prayed instead—though not a religious man—for the cat to die.

His prayers went unanswered. Fuff lived for twenty-six years.

She even outlived him. Mr. Goodie allegedly died of a heart attack in his mid-forties despite being a marathon runner with a stalwart heart. People murmured about the mysterious circumstances. His wife found his body with the cat perched triumphantly on his chest, glaring as if to claim a victory.

On the death certificate: heart attack. In the cat's eyes: checkmate.

Perhaps Fuff's need to torment Mr. Goodie came from Beatrice's growing indifference. To the cat's horror, she had developed an obsession with horses. Johnathan Goodie, partial to dogs, even considered bringing in a canine assassin to dispatch the feline. But Jane refused. "I will not have a mangy, smelly, flea-bitten mutt in this house, especially at poor Fuffy Wuffy's expense." She cradled the cat as she said it. Fuffy Wuffy glared back at John defiantly. There would be no dogs.

But with Beatrice's love of horses, Johnathan saw his opportunity for revenge. He would abandon the cat by pushing all their attention to its rivals. Jane Goodie fancied the idea, too.

One day four horses came home.

They consumed the family's time, as horses do, but the Goodies insisted on caring for them themselves, to feel connected to their new companions. With each hour in the stables, John noticed a depression seep into the feline, a sulking misery that never lifted. It was a small victory, but one he savored.

Now, we might wonder how a declaration by Beatrice that she loved horses so easily led to the decision to buy four. That was how it was in the Goodie home. Many spoiled children need only say, *jump*, to make their parents jump. Not Beatrice. She was never spoiled—meaning, that in her very nature she remained untouched and never desired to act spoiled, though her parents always tried to spoil her. Rather than having to say, *jump*, to cause them to jump, Beatrice only had to express how much she enjoyed watching people jump. So her parents assumed on the day she said, *You know, one day I think I'd like to ride horses*, that she really meant, *I want a horse… Now!*

By now we know that the Goodies' parenting skills were always over-the-top, so what would their little girl like better than one horse but four! They only stopped there because they couldn't fit more in their back yard. Beatrice was certainly surprised to see them and very pleased, but the thought did cross her mind that this may have been a bit excessive.

The horses were all female, christened Abigail, Annabelle, Agatha, and Alice. Two were stunning Arabians—Annabelle (black) became John's; Agatha (grey) belonged to Jane. Beatrice chose Abigail, a Hanoverian of breathtaking elegance, on which she won ribbons and trophies. But Alice was the odd mare out: a mixed breed, common, head drooping. The ranch couldn't sell her and convinced the Goodies to take her for free. She became a fixture at the fence line, resting her head on the post as her companions rode off without her.

But she wasn't unhappy. Life at the Goodie household was still better than ending up as a bottle of Elmer's Glue. She had food, shade, and a warm barn. And in the end, when all the other horses dropped dead, Alice was still standing.

CHAPTER FIVE

Lester Filch and Alice the goldfish got along very well, at least for as long as the fish remained alive. Unfortunately, that wasn't long at all. In fact, very bad things conspired against her.

The first event was an open window in Lester's bedroom. Through it came Kimchi—the neighbor's orange tabby—looking for an easy snack while Lester was in school. The glint of sunlight on the goldfish bowl drew him in. After a moment's consideration, he slid under the sash and sat gazing thoughtfully into the water. How best to do it? Kimchi didn't like getting wet, but he did enjoy the taste of fish. Sacrifices had to be made.

Alice seemed quite aware of the difference between friend and foe. She kept to the back of her bowl, trembling at the thought of a claw raking her into oblivion.

But that moment never came.

Kimchi's paw had just broken the surface when Redd Filch entered the room. With a yell, he lunged at the startled cat, who bounded around the room screeching like a banshee. Redd grabbed a heavy textbook and chased the beast with it, swatting it like a fly. Kimchi finally ran headlong into the window, bounced back, stunned, and then squeezed under the windowpane to freedom. Outside, he attempted to retain some dignity, grooming himself a few feet from Redd's exasperated glare as if nothing had happened.

Peering into the fish bowl, Redd half expected to find Alice dead from fright. Instead, she swam around in a flurry of short-term-memory bliss. What he didn't notice, however, was that Kimchi's attempt on her life had pushed the bowl to the bureau's very edge.

That night, as Lester slept, Redd decided to do a little work around the living room. In a rickety house, vibrations travel. Each nail pounded into the wall sent tremors upstairs. Slowly, Alice's bowl inched closer to disaster. With one last hammer strike, the bowl tipped over, shattering on the floor, and leaving Alice scrambling for her life in a shard of glass containing just enough water to keep her alive.

An hour later, after his father had gone to bed, Lester awoke to use the bathroom. That's when he found Alice gasping in her own shallow hell. He ran to the kitchen, arms outstretched, water sloshing over the jagged glass. But the darkness betrayed him. The area rug slipped from beneath his feet, and he pitched forward, sending Alice flying into the sink.

Lester scrambled up, fumbling for the light switch. He flipped the switch, but the light did not come on. It didn't need to. The sound of grinding metal against bone was enough to let him know that it was all over. Seven days after Alice arrived in West Lemon, New Jersey, she was reduced to so much pulp and flesh.

The experience accosted Lester's mind for the rest of his life. He finally got what he wanted—something to love—and it was taken from him. After Alice, he never smiled again. Redd tried desperately to right the injustice, buying pet after pet in the following week. What followed became the stuff of legends.

The next day, Lester's father brought home two tree frogs in a terrarium. Lester was wary but grateful, offering only a meek "thank you." That night, after feeding them their dose of crickets, he forgot to secure the mesh cover. He searched the whole house: moved furniture and prodded every nook and cranny, but he couldn't find the tree frogs until the next morning when he glanced up at the garage ceiling.

The two amphibians were glued to the flypaper that dangled from the rafters, like little green postage stamps. He didn't cry when he saw them, as he did when Alice died. He only turned around and went to his room in a daze. The mist in his son's eyes told Redd the gist of what had happened. He ran into the garage and found the remains. Unlike his son, he *did* cry.

The rest of the week fared no better. On day three, Lester's dad arrived with two adorable kittens. The boy didn't smile or even thank him, but he did run up to the little basket and began to pet them. He disappeared into his room with his new friends. They lasted all of two days.

On the second day, as the two little ones were wrestling together in the living room, Lester decided to pour a little milk into saucer for them. He left them to fight it out on the rug. But when he left, the slightly open door to the back yard proved too inviting for them to resist. They say curiosity killed the cat. This time, it killed two.

Mr. Filch hadn't mowed the lawn for four weeks, and the grass was knee high. The only silver lining, if there is such a thing as a silver lining in cases such as these, was that neither Redd Filch nor his son heard the screech of death over the whirring of the mower blades. And there were no gruesome remains. All they discovered—after Lester ran at his father, waving his hands and yelling over the noise of his father's machine—was a small tuft of hair that looked just like the tip of a kitten's tail.

Day six started with a black lab, about one year old, named Grimm. There was no smile for Grimm, no thank you, no excited approach, only a casual glance as his father released the dog in the house. Day six ended with the dog crushed under the wheels of their Cadillac, as Mr. Filch backed out of the garage. Both he and Lester were in the car on their way to the dentist. This time both of them heard the canine's sharp cry of pain as the car lurched over its body.

They didn't even get out of the car. Lester just stared ahead, completely unmoved.

"I think we left the garage door open," his father said nervously as the car left the scene.

"I think we did, too."

The day after that was a real stretch for Redd. It was his last attempt at hope. Finding a pet that actually survived became something of an obsession, as if doing so would prove a philosophical point. With the advent of pet number seven, a little love bird, he still clung to a shred of belief that this one would work out. It would be too uncanny, almost supernatural, if seven pets died in seven days. Life couldn't be that cruel. If there was a God (*and there probably isn't*, he thought) then *He* certainly couldn't be that cruel.

Lester was at the kitchen table when his father came home with the bird, tempting fate.

"Look, Lester," said Mr. Filch, "I know it's been hard trying to find a pet that's right for you, but give this guy a shot. It's a bird, Lester!"

He brought the little cage from behind his back and placed it on the table. "He's a lovebird, just like I used to have when you were a baby. The pet store owner said he was trained and everything. His wings are clipped and he talks and will sit on your shoulders."

As if to prove the point, the little bird gave a sharp whistle and said, "Love you! Love you!"

Lester turned his sullen face and heavy eyes to their new guest. There was no change of expression. He turned back to the window.

"Oh come on, son," his father begged. "Give this one a chance. It'll work out. It *has* to!"

The bird chirped in agreement, and said again, "Love you! Love you!"

His father gave a frustrated sigh. "Look, I'll take him out. He's tame. I'll show you."

He clicked the cage door open. "See?"

The bird waited a few seconds before realizing what happened. With a gleeful chirp, it took off and flew through the window into the great outdoors. Seeing that it was November and a storm was approaching West Lemon, the bird didn't have a chance.

Lester didn't budge. He stared out the window as a single snowflake drifted down from the sky and delicately came to rest upon the sill. He hated snow.

Red Filch just stood with his mouth open, gawking after the bird and completely at a loss. There was no denying it now. Whatever God or gods exist, his son was cursed. Lester Filch was doomed to be the most miserable human being alive.

CHAPTER SIX

Beatrice Goodie—by senior year and to nobody's surprise—was the San Perfecto homecoming queen. It was the night San Perfecto shone with Queen Beatrice, the most radiant homecoming queen its high school ever had.

She wore an otherwise plain blue dress, but on her it was unrivalled by any gown worn by any model or celebrity. No designer could have added anything to it. Beatrice's thick, golden curls reflected the auditorium lights and held up her crown with grace. She was cut straight from a storybook. Every boy at school wanted to either marry her (for the old-fashioned types) or bed her (for those with more liberated morality). Every girl wanted to be her and simultaneously rip her to shreds for outshining them all.

With all this success, Beatrice's most amazing quality was that no matter how good she looked, she had almost no ego. In fact, she used her popularity to bring rival classes together. She was the Martin Luther King Jr. of San Perfecto High. She tried hard to befriend not only jocks and cheerleaders but nerds as well. She saw herself as a bridge over which the less fortunate dweebs could cross over into social acceptance, and over which the jocks could cross to see the other side of humanity.

At home she would host "crossover parties," inviting both the least wanted and the most wanted students. They all came. These get togethers single-handedly broke down the school's rigid class system. It caused some to raise their eyebrows—but many more to raise their glass to Beatrice Goodie.

Her greatest triumph came with the marriage of two friends from opposite poles: Elsie Clayhorn, the school's biggest nerd, and Brock Johnson, captain of the football team.

Elsie lived and breathed mathematics and literature. She was Chess Club president (in reality, a cover for a secret Dungeons & Dragons society), founder of the Math League, and starter of the Astrophysics Association. None of this, in itself, made her a nerd. Beatrice even visited the club, since she enjoyed chess and was proficient at it. When she discovered their secret, she didn't hesitate to bring her beauty to the role-playing table, to the fascination of every D&D aficionado there. Her only complaint was that they always made her the helpless princess, when what she wanted was to be a ranger or rogue.

Elsie's real problem wasn't the gaming; it was her appearance. She would often stare into her bedroom mirror at the plaid, baggy clothes that accosted her, the frizzy hair, and the oversized glasses. Elsie drowned in self-pity. She didn't like what she saw but didn't know how to fix it, and when she said she didn't care about looks, she really did.

Beatrice befriended her at one of those secret D&D meetings. She came to believe in Elsie's personality, wit, and smile. The nerd became a canvas, and Beatrice was the artist. Beatrice helped her abandon the frumpy clothes, even subsidizing the new wardrobe. She taught Elsie to dress with dignity—showing what she had without giving it away. Under her tutelage, Elsie blossomed like a rose, every thorn carefully clipped.

Beatrice made sure Elsie would keep her old friends, encouraging loyalty, and brought her onto her own "crossover team." They both began to reach across the societal river, letting others know that there was another side and that it was safe.

At one such party, Elsie laid eyes on Brock Johnson.

His description goes without saying: chiselled, dimpled, golden-haired. The typical high school quarterback. All the girls noticed him. He was like a male Beatrice in looks and popularity but was unlike her in every other way. Brock was self-serving and arrogant. It was why Beatrice had no intention of giving in to his advances. Never unkind, she kept Brock in his place, which would often drive him even more mad with lust. Around her he was like a puppy. His masculine charade melted away in her warmth.

One warm, moonlit evening in June, the two of them were walking around their neighborhood. It was a few days before graduation. "Listen Brock," she said, "I like your company. I really do. But you know I don't like you in that way. I like my life. I'm not looking for a boyfriend. And anyway, it's mean to pick and choose like that. I don't like showing partiality.

"But have you ever thought of *real* love, Brock? You just turned nineteen, and you've had all the girls you wanted, mostly trash, and how long did they last? A week, maybe two?"

The sky was clear and flecked with diamond dust. Brock didn't take his eyes off the dome above. He didn't answer her, but she knew he was listening.

"You're about to graduate," she went on, "and then what? You need a girl who's faithful, kind, and needs your love and protection. She should be attractive, yes, but what's more important are the qualities that would make her a friend for the rest of your life. Do you hear what I'm saying?"

Brock nodded in affirmation, and said meekly, "But *you're* that girl. I love *you*, Beatrice. Can't you see that?"

"Maybe. But I don't love you. I'm not the girl for you. But there are others." She paused, staring at the ground, and said, "like Elsie Clayhorn."

A scoff escaped his lips. "Elsie Clayhorn? Are you kidding me?"

"I'm serious, Brock. Remember the party I had? You talked to her more than any other girl!"

"But she's a complete nerd! She's nice and all, and yea she's pretty—thanks to you—but I don't really think it would work. I mean, she wouldn't want an arrogant guy like me anyway."

The last sentence he spoke told Beatrice there was a chance. He *did* care. She could tell.

At the end of their walk, she told him she was going over to Elsie's house for a visit and that he would be welcome. To her relief, after a moment's hesitation, he agreed. The rest, as they say, is history.

Within a year, Elsie and Brock were married. Elsie's parents thought Brock was too good for her. Brock's parents thought Elsie was beneath him. But the love bug had done its work. Beatrice was Maid of Honor at the wedding. She cried through the entire ceremony. It was the only time she ever looked bad.

Beatrice's wealth, popularity, and genuine sincerity ensured she was going to be a success. People expected she would end up stowed away like the Virgin Mary in a safe grotto, either by her parents or by a doting husband. But Beatrice didn't do what was expected. She chose instead to live for the disenfranchised and marginalized, to use her goodness for the sake of others, to be another Mother Teresa.

She was going to be a social worker.

CHAPTER SEVEN

For Lester Filch, high school was far from easy. Some might say that seven dead pets in seven days makes for a childhood that can't get worse. But Lester would tell you those cute and cuddly corpses were the least of his troubles. That particular nightmare ended after seven days. School went on for twelve whole years. Lester would have easily traded in those twelve years dealing with the worst set of peers anyone—miserable or not—could wish for, in exchange for twelve years of dead animals.

Like a rising crescendo in a symphony, the hardship in school grew louder by the year until, by the time he was a senior, he ended up skipping most of his classes altogether. It was a miracle he even graduated, though mostly it was because all the teachers just wanted him to go away.

In freshman year, a few bullies agreed to form a welcome party by beating Lester Filch up on the first day of school. High school went downhill from there. With all the school massacres that take place in today's America, Lester Filch would surely have been a mass murderer in the making. He would have worn long black trench coats and white make-up, striking fear into his fellow students. And if he grew angry enough, if they pushed him a bit too far, he would have brought a shotgun to school and blown away every smug jock face he saw (and maybe the occasional cheerleader, who wouldn't go out with him).

But these were things he only dreamed about. At the time Lester went to school, killing wasn't really an option. Maybe it was a general dread of eternal judgment that still lingered in the social conscience of the day, but it was more likely the fact that if you kill someone, you end up in prison for the rest of your life, and who knew whether that would be worse than high school.

Only during senior year was there a really positive development in his life: Lester Filch asked a girl out on a date. It was during the second week of school. Nancy Biel, a West Lemon cheerleader, broke up with her football boyfriend. Lester always had a crush on Nancy, ever since the sixth grade, but he never had the guts to ask her out. Truth be told, however, he had many crushes over the years and all were unrequited. He never took a chance, and they remained like so many burning embers.

One morning after Math Class, she was walking down the hall, holding her books up against her ample bosom.

"Nancy?" said Lester, blocking her way. He could see the revulsion in her tightened mouth and slightly raised eyebrows: a reaction he expected. At least she was being civil. He stumbled over the next words. "I was wondering if maybe, I mean, if you're not doing anything, could you possibly want to grab a coffee with me?"

"No," she replied without a bit of hesitation. "I don't think so." As she brushed past him, she said without a smile, "but thanks."

When Nancy Biel noticed tears glistening in Lester's eyes, she was sure it was because she broke his heart. *How stupid of him*, she thought with a growing sense of guilt, *that he would actually think I'd give him, of all people, the time of day. It's not my fault he's that way.*

But Lester Filch's tears weren't born of grief at all. They were born of joy. He had asked a girl out! Sure, she said *No*, but what girl wouldn't? Even if a girl *had* said yes, he would think something was wrong with her or that she was hiding some trick up her sleeve. But at least he had found the courage to ask Nancy Biel out. It was a step in the right direction.

From a list of crushes he had yet to deal with, he chose two other girls to ask out. They were all very popular and attractive, so he was sure of their denial. He wanted no disappointments and received none. The captain of the girls Lacrosse team—a girl by the name of Sarah Eliot—just laughed in his face without giving him a straight answer before walking away, still laughing.

Lester came across her in the hallway the next day, talking about it to Alice Borden, another lacrosse team member. When Lester heard his name from a distance, he backed up and hid behind a locker just around the corner, eavesdropping.

"I *cannot* believe he asked me out!" Sarah exclaimed.

"I know," said Alice, "but you shouldn't have laughed at him. At least be nice, you know?"

"Don't tell me you like him, Alice. He's the creepiest, most miserable guy in school. Everybody hates him."

"I didn't say I liked him," said Alice bashfully. "I just said you shouldn't have laughed."

"Well, maybe, but why does he have to be so creepy? His eyes, they're cold and calculating, like he's thinking of ways to make your life miserable. He's always complaining about something, too, and he never has friends because he always has an attitude. I can't go out with a guy like that."

"No, you're right. But you know, I think he would be much better looking if he would just smile. He has nice features. He's just pale and lanky. If he took better care of himself, things would be different."

The bell rang, and the halls filled with chattering students. Lester disappeared into the crowd, and the two girls were none the wiser. But when he saw Alice Borden alone after Chemistry class the next day, he took his opportunity. He believed she would be nice to him, like Nancy Biel, but there was no doubt that she would turn him down.

Lester came up beside her as they walked down the hall to their next class.

"Oh, hello Lester," Alice said with a forced smile. She looked nervous, darting him uncertain glances but never losing her stride.

"So it's been going around that I asked Sarah out, but it was only for coffee."

"Yeah, I heard." She never turned her head towards him.

He saw her clutch at her books a little tighter.

"Well, she was kind of mean about it. She's not as nice as you."

Alice came to a halt and turned to face him. They were standing in the middle of the hall.

"Lester, are you going to ask me out?" she asked. "Because you have to do better than that, and you have to stop shooting out invitations like a machine gun."

Heat rose to his face. That was unexpected. Her large, blue eyes, like perfectly round drops of water; her taut, red mouth; her dainty nose; topped off with an air of kind self-assurance, melted away his stubborn resolve to be rejected. There was no room for disappointment. It had become a game for him, a way to make other people uncomfortable, but suddenly he realized it could no longer be a game. He wanted her to say *yes*.

"Yea, I'm sorry. What I mean is, yes, will you go out with me?" He braced himself for the expected rejection, like a man under the murderous stare of a firing squad, awaiting the certain *rat-a-tat-tat* of death.

"Sure. Where?"

Lester opened his eyes in surprise.

"I said yes." Alice smiled. Then she was somber, as if giving a speech to a battalion of men about to enter the fray of battle. "Now that doesn't mean there's anything between us, got it? You and I aren't in it for anything other than a friendly chat. You may call this a date if you want to—only because you have no friends to talk to about it—but it isn't, in fact, a date. I'm doing this to be nice. And anyway, maybe a date with a girl would do you good."

They made plans for next evening: Friday. Dinner at Charlie's Pub.

The next night, when his father walked in on him putting on a dress shirt and asked what he was up to, Lester beamed for the first time in years.

"I'm going on a date!" he said.

Mr. Filch tried unsuccessfully to suppress his disbelief. "A date!" he exclaimed. "Lester, that's wonderful! I mean, you haven't . . ."

"Gone on a date?" Lester finished sarcastically. "No. So wish me luck." On the verge of being late, he gave his Dad a passing smile and ran out of the house. It was one of the few times he wished he had a car.

Charlie's Pub was a twenty minute walk downtown. When he walked up to the front door, a young brunette wearing black capris and a black shirt stood at a podium. "One tonight?" she asked.

"Two, please," he replied, smiling. He never said please. "She isn't here, though."

They wound their way through the restaurant to a private, dim booth at the far end. It was a good seat. When he sat down, complaints began to crowd out his excitement. There were too many people. The lights weren't dim enough. He was overdressed, and everyone was looking at him. The food was too expensive. He didn't bring enough money to cover both meals.

An audible *No!* escaped his lips. Lester whispered through gritted teeth, "This is supposed to be a *good* night, probably the best thing that ever happened to me. I can't let myself be like this. She'll never like me."

A waitress came over, and Lester ordered a Coke. He sipped it as he studied the menu. He tried deciding between the stuffed cabbage or the corned beef and cabbage. Cabbage was his favorite food, and he hadn't been to Charlie's in quite a long time.

By his third glass of Coke, he checked his watch: 6:45. They had agreed to meet at six. *She probably got held up*, he thought, thinking positively for the first time in his life. *Aren't girls usually late to these kinds of things?*

Two glasses later, he could no longer be positive. It had been two hours. The waitress stopped coming by to ask if he wanted anything. He already told her he was expecting a date. She was either too embarrassed for him or too frustrated that she probably wasn't going to get a tip that night. After all, the Coke cost him only seventy five cents. And there were free refills.

Lester finally conceded defeat and left his seventy five cents on the table before walking dejectedly out of Charlie's, head down, refusing to meet the hostess' knowing glance. It took him an hour to take the twenty minute walk home.

His father looked up from his newspaper and asked expectantly, "How was the date, son?"

Lester ignored him, moved like a zombie into his room, and shut the door to the world.

CHAPTER EIGHT

If life is a mountain, then the night of senior prom was rock bottom for Lester Filch. And there was no reason to look up. Everyone expected him to stay there.

The only good thing about that night was that Senior year was mercifully ending. For most kids, the end meant parties, family gatherings, and tossing caps into the air. For Lester Filch, it meant freedom: after graduation he would never have to set foot inside West Lemon High School again.

He planned not to attend. Graduation struck him as a hypocrite's event—enemies smiling beside one another in forced camaraderie. He wanted no part of it. He hated them all.

If anyone had begged him to attend, he would have laughed. But no one begged him.

In History class, he overheard a boy announce that he might skip the ceremony. Immediately three classmates protested: it wouldn't be the same without him; how could he possibly skip graduation; and what would Sheila think?

The next day a teacher asked the class who was planning to attend. Every hand went up—except Lester's.

"Oh. Lester. You're not going?" The woman sounded relieved.

"No," Lester answered darkly. "I don't want to."

"Okay, then," she replied, moving on to the implications of Nixon's resignation. Behind him, a girl whispered, "I'm glad he's not coming. The last thing we need is rain."

Lester smiled. For once, their dislike gave him an idea: maybe he *should* attend. If it would ruin their day, it might be worth it. He even daydreamed of sabotaging the sprinkler system. *That'll give them rain.* But if he got caught, he would never graduate—and graduation was the only thing he wanted.

If graduation held no interest for Lester, prom night was definitely out as well. He expected to spend it as he spent most nights: reading alone, watching television, or wandering the streets of West Lemon.

But the day before prom brought a surprise: Molly Fishburn asked him out.

Any other boy would have reasonably said no. Molly Fishburn was Lester's female counterpart: the least popular girl in school and the most miserable. She was voted "Ugliest Girl" three times in an unofficial poll, until senior year when her sudden supply of breasts spared her. That year she won Biggest Rack. Progress.

Her appearance was a patchwork of disasters: a pig-snout nose, mismatched eyes, cross-eyed on top of that, a crooked smile caged in braces, freckles, and a tangle of unkempt frizz. Her knees cracked with every step. Her shoes squeaked. And a pickle smell followed her, though she swore she never ate them.

This vision of fright placed her lunch tray down across from Lester Filch as he sat contemplating his Salisbury Steak.

"I've got a proposition," she squealed.

"What?" Lester muttered without making eye contact.

"A date. Obviously you don't have one." She glared at him with her crossed eyes in contempt.

He was about to throw out his rejection when he glimpsed a vision of his future: forty years old, still wandering Main Street alone, living with his Dad. Maybe life was handing him a lemon he could squeeze for once.

"Okay," he said begrudgingly.

Molly blinked in surprise. "Well, then, fine. I'll call you. Wear something nice."

That night Lester and his father went to Mr. Dressy's Tuxedo Shop. Redd nearly skipped down the street, brimming with sickening enthusiasm. "You're going to have so much fun!" he said, patting his son on the back. "Makes me happy to see you happy. Pick any tux you want. Expensive, too! I don't mind."

But they were late. Only one tux remained: shabby black pants and a jacket frayed at the edges. It cost fifty dollars—a fortune for Redd—but he didn't flinch.

Lester tried to share his father's excitement. Fifty dollars meant that this truly was special, and for once, he felt something like hope.

When prom night came he was waiting in his room, smoking a cigarette, admiring his reflection in the mirror. Pale and lanky, yes, but maybe not so bad. Alice Borden's words came back—he did have some good features, if only he would smile more. *Maybe college will be different*, he thought. *Maybe I could try a little harder.*

The phone rang.

"Lester!" his father called. "Telephone! It's for you!"

It had to be Molly. Maybe she was late.

"Hello?"

"Lester, it's Molly," said the gruff female voice on the other line.

"Hi, Molly," Lester greeted her as pleasantly as he could, swallowing down the urge to be sick. It would only be one night, and this was a good thing. *Don't blow it.* "How are you doing tonight, Molly?"

"Cut the chit-chat, Lester. I'm sorry to tell you, but I'm not going with you tonight."

The blood drained from his face. He peered around the wall that separated the kitchen from the living room. His dad was on the recliner reading his newspaper. Hopefully he couldn't overhear.

He hissed into the phone. "But why?" Then he changed his tone, to sound more accommodating. "Are you sick or something?" *Please let her be sick*, he prayed. *At least lie to me.*

"No, I'm not sick, thank God. Jacob Josselyn asked me out about an hour ago. That bitch he was going with really *is* sick. I got the hots for him. I'm sure you understand. I figured you wouldn't have any fun anyway."

Lester couldn't open his mouth to respond. The ugliest, least popular girl in school was ditching him for someone else, someone who was known for being a player. Jacob Josselyn didn't want to dance with Molly Fishburn that night. He wanted to dance with her right and left breast.

"You there?" she growled. "You still there?"

"Yeah, I'm here," he said quietly. Where was the anger when he needed it? Where were the insults, something that really hurt, something that would make her cry? It was all gone.

"Well, so long, I guess." With that she hung up.

"Everything okay?" his father asked from the living room.

"Yeah, Dad," he replied, voice cracking. "Everything's fine. I'm gonna go now."

"Okay, son! Have a great time! Can't wait to hear all about it!"

His father's enthusiasm stung worse than Molly's rejection.

Halfway down the driveway, his father's voice rang out again. "Lester! Don't you want to use the car tonight?"

Through tears, Lester waved back with a fake smile. "No, Dad, but thanks! We'll walk."

"Okay! I love you!"

The words darted across the lawn, stinging like bees. Lester wanted to run back, collapse into his father's arms, weep until nothing remained. But he couldn't. He wouldn't break the man like that. All Lester had to do to make his father happy was to have one good night, and he couldn't even manage that.

Lester didn't respond, but he waved again and his father disappeared from view.

Two houses down, he stopped, pulled his coat, bow tie, and cummerbund off and shoved them under a rhododendron. In just a shirt and pants, he could at least walk Main Street without every passerby staring at him, knowing he was a failed prom night date.

There was nothing else to do but sulk. He would have to wait until his father went to sleep before coming home, and then prepare his story for the next morning.

It fit very nicely in his head already, like a well-scripted movie. He and Molly, a very popular and beautiful female, strolled together to school, conversing the whole way about what they were going to do with their lives, philosophizing about the meaning of life, trying to figure out how best to change so as to make useful citizens of themselves. Once at prom, Lester became rather shy, so he and Molly hung around the hors d'œuvres table, chatting lightly and observing their fellow students. Every once in a while they would steal a glance at each other, then look down again in embarrassment. He hoped she would take the lead and press him to dance. When she was obviously too timid, he miraculously plucked up his courage and asked her out on the floor.

They danced beautifully. It surprised him, and he wondered whether it was some innate ability he had never known, or if she was pulling him along to float across the dance floor. Then their lips met under the refracting light of a disco ball, and as they kissed, the other students gathered around them in shock because he, Lester Filch, had gotten to first base with Molly Fishburn. His date was not named prom queen, but he was happy nonetheless. The walk home was reserved, but they held hands, talking through touch.

Lester came to when he bumped into a tall, high school jock escorting his date down Main Street. He scowled at them when they shoved by. Lester had been carried away by useless fantasizing. It wasn't what happened, of course, but it was the story he would tell his father the next morning.

Then came the urge to go to prom anyway.

He found himself making his way to High Bridge Road and turning into the school parking lot. There was a lot of internal argumentation. Why would he want to see that? The slow dancing, mock attempts at romance, the laughing and cavorting around in fake displays of solidarity, the photos being taken. It was all a waste of time.

So why *did* he have to see it? Why this addiction to torment? He couldn't answer, but he kept moving anyway until the growing din of conversation met him on the road.

Lester peered through the gym window. The lights, the disco ball, the couples, all of it seemed beautiful and disgusting at the same time. And there, in the center of the dance floor, was Molly Fishburn and Jacob Josselyn. Her braces were gone. Her hair was straightened. Glasses vanished, and somehow, in the dim light, she looked less cross-eyed.

Maybe going in there was a bad idea. He looked at his watch and saw with surprise it was already ten o'clock. He spent two hours wandering the streets. His father would expect him home later, but there were excuses that could be made. Molly's parents were strict. They gave her a nine o'clock curfew. Molly felt sick and tried to stick it out as long as possible. There was a drug bust at the school and police broke up the dance. That had happened in Little Pickering, the town next door. It could happen in West Lemon.

The first excuse was what he decided on. Her being sick could seem like an excuse to get away from him, and he didn't want his father to think that. The third excuse slightly pushed the limits of belief.

It took a while to walk from school back to his neighborhood. There was no rush, and if he could push his arrival home another hour, his story would appear more credible. He would have had three fictional hours dancing in the arms of the lovely Molly Fishburn.

The Main Street stores were either closed or closing. Through open doors, Lester heard cashiers, cleaners, and vendors shouting instructions at one other, the clanging of chairs being placed on tables. There was something soothing in the commotion. He sat down on the curb lit by the warm glow of a street lamp. Few cars were on the road. He stared blankly at a firetruck that passed him, unaffected by its blaring, ear-piercing scream. After a few more minutes, the cold set in. It was time to admit defeat. The night was over, and he would rather be in bed or smoking a cigarette.

The sky seemed lighter as he neared his street. There was usually a red haze on the nightly horizon around West Lemon, especially in the direction of New York City. But that night it seemed redder.

Lester wondered if it was going to rain. A cloud—very low to the ground—was gathering fast and, along with the crimson glow, blotted out the stars. *That's funny*, he thought. *The sky was clear a minute ago.*

As he turned onto his road, the acrid smell of burning wood and rubber filled nose.

"Oh no!" he exclaimed, breaking into a trot. "Someone's house is on fire." The image of the firetruck rushing past came back. He hoped it wasn't anywhere near his house. Fires that were too close could sometimes spread fast. His trot became a run.

The smell grew thicker, along with the raining flakes of ash, and the red glow from the tongues of fire licking the sky. He couldn't see the exact house because the blaze still raged beyond his view, but it seemed a lot further than he thought. It would be close to home. Too close for comfort, he worried.

The sight of his own house engulfed in flames, twisting up around it into a cloud of smoke and ash, was the only thing that convinced him of the truth. Lester stood petrified in front of the hellish scene, his skin searing in the heat. He was frozen in place. Two policemen saw him and ran over. They probably guessed from the shock and horror on his face that he lived there. They both pulled Lester away, and turned his body around to face them.

"Do you live here?" one of them asked, shaking him by the shoulders.

"Yes," he said weakly. "I'm Lester Filch."

Both of their expressions turned to grief.

"I can't tell you how sorry I am," the other officer said, "especially on a night like this, when you should be having fun with your friends, but your father, Mr. Redd Filch, died in the fire tonight. I'm so sorry."

Lester stared blankly at the cop, then turned to look at the fire, then turned back towards the cop as if waiting for something more. It couldn't really be happening. He was dreaming. That's all. It was a dream, and his father would wake him up and tell him it was the day of the prom.

"How?" he muttered.

"A cigarette, we think."

Lester began to hyperventilate, but the policeman went on. "Your father called the emergency line and said the house was on fire. Seemed he thought someone was smoking upstairs. Damn things have caused a lot of trouble. He was about to go up there with a fire extinguisher, said he wanted to try to salvage a few things. The operator told him to get out. Again, I'm so sorry."

The world around Lester, the crowds gathered in front of the house, the whirring lights of firetrucks and police cars, the inferno, all spun around him until he collapsed onto the ground on all fours. He wept and screamed at the same time. He clutched at his face and then his stomach, feeling in that moment that he wanted to claw at his eyes, to hurt himself, to dash his head against the cement. His stomach clenched and he dry-heaved, because there was no food in him.

This was all his fault. The cops didn't say it, but the logic was clear. For a moment, he thought he was going insane. He cried out for his Dad. Then for his mother. Then he cried for himself as everything that really mattered to him was turned to ash: his house and his father, both burning together in one final act of humiliation.

PART TWO

PART TWO

CHAPTER NINE

Lester Filch had a simple life, but every day he never failed to complain about it. If it was raining, well, then he could complain right along with the rest of the world. The day was grey and depressing. He would invariably get soaked to the bone on his way to work, and he would probably catch a cold, which would probably turn into pneumonia, which would probably bring on the inexorable approach of death. It was unavoidable, these bouts of disease, when it was raining like a curse from Heaven.

During winter, the low temperatures motivated similar complaints. Usually they were accompanied by the lament that every coat he had wasn't thick enough to withstand the biting cold. This led to laments over the fact that he didn't have enough money, that he was underpaid and underappreciated, and that quitting his good-for-nothing job would be the best thing for him to do. This he never did, of course, because as bad as his job was, there were worse jobs out there, and he knew they would find him, and then he'd end up being worse off than before. So he simply complained.

If it was a sunny day, there'd be no praise from his lips about the warm, bright light of life coming from the sky. The sun would be too blinding, and its ultraviolet rays the source of eventual blindness unless he wore his sunglasses, which were uncomfortable. But if he took them off, he'd probably be blinded by the sun's glare off the puddles in spring, the windows in summer, and the snow in winter. He would trip and break a leg. And if he broke a leg, he'd be the victim of the health care system, with all its rigged shortcomings to benefit the rich. If he wasn't overlooked by doctors and ignored by nurses, so that the infection in his leg (that would develop from whatever cuts and bruises he sustained in the fall) would worsen, then he'd be misdiagnosed, so that instead of having a leg broken, they'd tell him he had cancer as well. This would afford the system more opportunities to bleed him dry, so that the little money he kept would go into making him recover from maladies he never had. And what about insurance? The insurance company covering the employees of Borr Dun Inc. would find some excuse not to cover his medical expenses.

He never broke his leg, of course. Not in real life. But in his mind, over the forty years of his life, he had broken his leg, along with several other parts of his body, several hundred times.

And it wasn't just outdoors that made him complain. His West Lemon apartment gave him plenty of opportunities to vent his interior frustrations to the landlord, Alan Meeks.

Mr. Meeks was a fifty-eight-year-old, large and imposing man, who owned two apartment complexes, one in West Lemon and one in East Lemon. The mere size of his frame could have been enough to cower even the toughest of men. The money he amassed only added to the aura that this man could do, buy, or break anything or anyone he wanted. His rotund midriff didn't hide the muscular foundation that in youth must have shone forth like a chiselled sculpture by Michelangelo.

But the man's intimidation stopped as soon as he opened his mouth. In fact, most of his money came from investments rather than renters, because if payments made to him were late or missing, he'd never go after anyone to collect and never threw anyone out. He was, in fact, quite shy and soft spoken, never asserting himself or giving his delinquent renters a hard time, well-deserved as it might have been. If Mr. Meeks hadn't been so lucky in finance, even if he'd owned ten apartment buildings, he would have been a very poor man.

This made him an easy sponge for Lester Filch, who almost every day called him up to complain, for at least five minutes, about what went on in his apartment building. Mr. Meeks, who never hung up on anybody, sat stone still with the receiver glued to his ear and listened. Once the landlord decided to take a stand against the constant deluge of complaints by not answering his phone. It was a mistake he didn't repeat. The next morning, taped to the door of his house like Luther's Ninety-Five Theses, was the following:

> Since you were not home when I called, I thought I might write. For the rent I'm paying, I expect better than this.
> - cracks in the ceiling (which could fall on my head any moment)
> - faucet leaks
> - toilet doesn't properly drain
> - when it rains, one corner of the bathroom ceiling drips
> - the front door creaks when it opens
> - (so does the second step on the stairs to the second floor)
> - the pipes are far too noisy for peace of mind

- drafty windows don't help with the flu epidemic that's going around
- the thin walls are atrocious. While I don't expect you to put in new walls (though I certainly deserve it for what I'm paying), I expect you to take care of the noise pollution:
  - my neighbors to the right have parties that are too loud and go on for far too long
  - my neighbors above seem to enjoy having sex when I can clearly hear them
  - the people below me yell too much (I have threatened to call the police a few times, not that they would do anything about it)

These are only a few of the problems I encountered this week. Please fix what's wrong, tell my neighbors that they should have parties and do their fornication elsewhere, or I'll find myself another place to live.

LF

For some reason Mr. Meeks couldn't explain, the sound of the man's growl over the phone was less vexing than this list posted on his own front door, and he decided then that listening on the phone for five minutes a day was worth avoiding a humiliating note. So every evening he would nod, mumble nervous promises to try and make the situation more accommodating to his renter, then hang up with a heavy sigh.

The only man Lester Filch never complained to was his boss, Bor Dun's manager, Austin M. Tatioussian, an Armenian man who seemed to enjoy tormenting and firing unruly or disagreeable employees.

On Lester Filch's first day, Mr. Tatioussian strode into the office like Goliath on his way to meet King David and called the new data enterer into his office, just so he could tell him off before their relationship even got started. There was a pecking order to the factory's hierarchy, and Lester Filch, if he wanted to keep the job, had better know about it.

Throughout the less-than-comforting speech, Lester tried not to look nervous, a sign of weakness, but was quickly losing the battle. He had reason to be anxious. He had to keep this new job.

Lester's cubicle was wedged between the copy machine and the men's bathroom, which meant his daily soundtrack was a mix of flushing toilets and the paper jam alarm. His job as "data analyst" was little more than entering numbers from inventory sheets into a terminal that still ran on green text. He knew exactly how many paper clips Bor Dun Inc. produced in a given day, week, month, and quarter. He also knew exactly how much that fact didn't matter.

"Filch!" Mr. Tatioussian's voice bellowed across the cubicle farm. Conversations died. A junior accountant ducked behind her monitor. Lester stiffened.

The manager's shadow appeared over his desk. A tall man with shoulders like a wrestler, his face was a permanent grimace, as if chewing on gristle. He slapped a spreadsheet onto Lester's keyboard.

"What is this?"

Lester blinked at the sheet. "Um...numbers?"

"Wrong numbers," Tatioussian barked. "You entered 750,000 paper clips produced last month. Do you know what happens if corporate sees this?"

Lester swallowed. "They'll...uh...be happy we're producing so many?"

"They'll know you're a moron!" The man's spit flecked onto Lester's screen. "We produced 75,000. You added an extra zero. Do you know what that means? It means corporate thinks we're a factory the size of God!"

Lester stared. "Is that...bad?"

Tatioussian leaned down, inches from his pale face. "You make me look like an idiot one more time, Filch, and I'll see to it you're counting paper clips by hand in the warehouse, up to your neck in rust."

When the man stormed off, the accountant peeked over her cubicle. "Don't worry, Filch," she whispered. "Happens to everyone."

Lester turned his hollow eyes toward her. "No. It happens to me."

When Tatioussian finally stormed off, Lester tried to sink into the anonymity of his cubicle. But anonymity was impossible in an office where every sneeze, cough, and sigh carried through the partitions like a broadcast.

That afternoon, in a misguided attempt at "team building," a junior supervisor invited everyone to gather around the breakroom table for cake. It was someone's birthday—Lester never caught whose, nor did he care. A sheet cake sagged under too much frosting.

"Come on, Filch," said the accountant across from him, "have a piece."

Lester stared at the cake as though it were a loaded gun. "I don't eat cake."

"Not even a sliver?"

"No. Too much sugar. Diabetes runs in my family. So does obesity. And heart disease. Also, there could be salmonella in the eggs, or rat droppings in the flour. I read about that in a study once."

The supervisor laughed nervously. "Oh, Lester, you're such a kidder."

He wasn't.

Everyone ate in silence after that, glancing sideways at him. Lester folded his arms, satisfied. He had successfully drained the joy from another celebration.

He should have quit. It was no skin off his back to ditch these losers. But he was already in trouble financially, and this job came on the heels of the last job he was fired from. Lester had been the manager of a fast food restaurant called *The Wurst Place*. He drove home from work one Tuesday night after his usual dinner: a liverwurst and sauerkraut sandwich, their specialty.

The rain, the old lady, the hourglass-shaped Chevrolet Cavalier — it all happened so fast. He wasn't hurt by the accident, but the lady broke her leg and he made the news, which made The Wurst Place's manager mad.

Providence or dumb luck had spared his life but not his job, and he had to pay out a bit. Fines, insurance hikes, and new car payments sent him into a downward spiral.

And so he found himself here: trapped at Bor Dun Inc., a paper-clip counting hell.

For Lester, every good thing in life—the acquisition of a patient landlord, the forgiving warmth of the sun, the seemingly miraculous escape from death—had attached to it a catch. He coined the saying, EVERY SILVER LINING HAS ITS CLOUD. And Lester Filch had a unique talent for finding the worst cloud and blowing it along through clear open skies for everyone to see. If he met someone truly happy, for any reason, then he knew they weren't really aware of the true meaning of life, denying its sobering and depressing reality. And Lester Filch was hell-bent on making those happy-go-lucky do-gooders think twice about smiling again.

CHAPTER TEN

Misery loves company. It's another saying invented by the uninitiated in the world of very bad things. Whoever wrote this proverb only studied the exterior of misery, not the inner workings. They must have seen a group of people stuck in a rainstorm at a bus stop, or passengers roasting on a grounded airplane with no A/C, or motorists jammed together in rush-hour traffic with bladders full to bursting. Anyone who observed such situations might think, *misery loves company*. But they'd be dead wrong.

Lester Filch was truly miserable, and I can tell you that he absolutely *hated* company. He hated the bus station strangers, the fellow passengers, the fellow drivers. Anyone who got too close and tried to strike up conversation received narrowed eyes, a growl, or—if he really disliked them—both barrels at once. Lester Filch's entire existence was dedicated to solitude, and anyone who intruded on it did so at their own peril.

It was no wonder, then, that the moment Lester met Beatrice Goodie was destined to be both uncomfortable and thoroughly miserable. She was, after all, only trying to be neighborly.

A new position at a home health aide clinic had brought Beatrice to West Lemon, and more specifically, to Alan Meeks' apartment complex. It was pretty low income, and she, like the Buddha she was, had left her riches to dwell among the common folk. Her pay made sure of that. But the Meeks apartments were good enough, and as always, she would make the best of it.

On her very first day, she attempted that old-fashioned ritual of goodness: bringing a pie to her neighbors. Not too difficult. Just an easy recipe from a book she unpacked first thing, and there you have it: a nice cherry pie. The elderly woman on her left wasn't home, so she fatefully went to her right. And there it was: the moment Beatrice Goodie—after nearly forty years of good fortune—came face to face with a very bad thing.

She had never hated anyone before. Without cause, it's easy not to hate. But when her clear blue eyes met Lester Filch's grey ones, she suddenly discovered that goodness wasn't a static moral condition. Goodness could curdle. Her lips tightened, her eyes widened, and she took half a step back before she could stop herself.

Lester, for his part, was not surprised. He expected to sour everything he touched, like mildew spreading across pristine bathroom tile. If he didn't spoil someone's mood, he considered it an unnatural departure from the order of things.

"Hello," Beatrice said timidly, thrusting out the warm pie. "I'm Beatrice. I thought I'd bring you a pie, since we're neighbors now."

Lester stared into her eyes as though into a void, saying nothing. Beatrice began to fidget, her arms trembling under the weight of pie.

"I thought you were the mailman," Lester finally muttered. "Or rather—I *wish* you were the mailman. He has a check for me. But you're no mailman. And that's no check. So if you don't mind—"

He began to close the door. She stuck her foot in the gap.

"But your pie!"

"I've got a peanut allergy," Lester said flatly.

"There aren't any peanuts in it."

"Then I've got a dairy allergy."

"It's dairy-free."

"I'm allergic to gluten."

"It's a gluten-free crust!"

"Then it's probably disgusting."

And with that, Lester Filch slammed the door. Beatrice stood there, pie in hand, as unwelcome as she had ever been in her life. Truth be told, she didn't even like cherry pie.

In the wake of that encounter, Beatrice found herself second-guessing her arrival in West Lemon. Boston had been her original plan. When she shunned her parents' California kingdom—her mother's tears, her father's thunderous threat of disinheritance—she had imagined the East Coast as a place of grit and honesty, a place where life wasn't gilded.

"Well if I'm making a mistake," she told her father quietly in the wake of his protests, "it's *my* mistake. Finally. Something that's my own."

Boston had seemed everything she wanted: quaint and historic, but busy and modern too. Haphazard colonial streets ran between granite churches and glass skyscrapers. For a Californian, the East Coast's three hundred years of history was practically ancient. She devoured it. She took duck tours, culinary tours, bought discount passes for museums, gave away most of her spare cash to panhandlers, and revelled in the sense of having escaped perfection.

She enrolled in social work at Boston College. Her first year was filled with tours and charity projects; her second year brought internships at shelters. She discovered, painfully, that her radiant goodness wasn't always welcome.

At a shelter for battered women, no one wanted to talk to her. At a homeless shelter, the clients recoiled from her earnestness. She had the look and smell of privilege, and all her sincerity only sharpened the contrast. She couldn't help being Beatrice Goodie—beautiful, privileged, and terribly good—and for the very people who needed help, that made her intolerable.

She turned to work at a suicide hotline, where anonymity might save her. She memorized the scripts, spoke gently, followed the rules. But statistics soon betrayed her: Beatrice had the highest suicide rate of any operator: thirteen suicides in one week.

Her supervisors couldn't understand it. She was perfect on paper: punctual, responsible, rule-following. They finally tracked down a caller who had *not* gone through with his suicide after speaking with her.

The man was blunt. Beatrice's voice—so good, so serene, so unearthly—had nearly driven him to pull the trigger. It reminded him of the girlfriend who abandoned him, of all the women who seemed too good for him, of a world where he would never measure up. Death felt preferable to being judged by perfection.

Only the accident of having no bullets, and the intrusion of his best friend at the right time, saved him. His friend had hung up the phone, shaken him, and convinced him that if goodness could drive you to despair, then maybe "goodness" wasn't the right standard at all. But Beatrice never heard that part. She only saw the tally of the dead. And so she quit.

CHAPTER ELEVEN

The day Beatrice Goodie quit social work was a very bad day, indeed. But it wasn't because she was too good for social work and the many bodies she had left strewn across New York. It was because she ran into Lester Filch again.

Not that she recognized him at first. He had filled out—or more accurately, filled down. His torso sagged, his face sagged, his pants sagged; even his socks sagged in ways gravity had never intended. He didn't wear clothes so much as he stored himself inside them. Gone was the hollow-eyed, lanky teenager who was once stood up at Charlie's Pub. In his place stood a forty-year-old man who looked as if a subway rat had eaten him and then thoughtfully regurgitated him into a rent-stabilized unit. In a way, it had. Two decades in West Lemon's apartment complexes can do that to a body—especially a body so aggressively opposed to sunlight and joy.

And now, to Beatrice's horror, he lived right next door.

The day she quit should have been a day of righteous pivoting, of fresh air and clearer purpose. Instead, it began in fluorescent light. Her resignation unfolded in an office that smelled like wet wool and burnt coffee: the social services center on Fifteenth, where well-meaning posters yellowed on the walls and the water cooler bubbled like a bout of acid reflux. The carpet had been vacuumed so many times it developed a crop circle the size of Saturn around the supervisor's chair. On the corkboard hung a laminated chart titled HELPFUL PHRASES FOR CRISIS CALLS, as if salvation could be ordered à la carte:

"I hear how much you're hurting."

"Let's take this one breath at a time."

"Have you tried taking a walk?"

Beatrice had used all the phrases in her arsenal, in the kindly voice that had lulled thirteen people into oblivion. She learned the hard way that her comfort sometimes killed. The previous night's caller—the one slightly unhinged caller with the choked laughter who said he could "smell the ocean in the bathroom tiles"—had hung up after she gently recommended a cup of tea to calm himself. Tea. It was not her fault, precisely, that he chose the Brooklyn Bridge over chamomile, but she could not bear the thought that her goodness had greased the skids.

So she signed her resignation. A graceful, looping signature, a little flourish at the end. The supervisor dabbed his eye with a paper napkin as if she were a donor and not a liability. "We'll miss your light," he said.

Light. She slotted the word into her pocket like a bent penny. Outside, the day had the color of dishwater. On the bus home, she gave up her seat to a man who had two perfectly good legs and a moral limp. He did not say thank you.

When she got home, Beatrice climbed the steps to Alan Meeks' building with the tender determination of someone who believes in fresh starts and thinks a decent meal might fix the world. She set a freshly baked loaf of banana bread on the counter, cut out some thick slices, wrapped them in wax paper, and wrote a note in her neat hand: HELLO, NEIGHBOR. I MADE EXTRA. Then she knocked on the door of 2B.

The door opened and Lester Filch grabbed the package without a word and opened it. He sniffed the offering, packed it into his mouth with the heel of his hand like a gambler stuffing a chip into a rigged slot, chewed so loudly she could hear his molars praying for death, and said, through pulp, "Too moist. It'll give me gas." He thrust the package back into her hands and shut the door with the soft finality of a coffin lid.

She smiled at the wood only inches from her nose, because it would have been impolite to snarl. It was not, she told herself, a bad day. It was merely a day with a bad man in it.

The laundry room of Alan Meeks' complex sat in the basement like a slow, dying heart. Pipes veined the low ceiling, sweating. The washers—three boxy veterans—hunched along a wall, enamel scabbed, lids dented, coin slots gummed with soap and sin. Each machine wore a handwritten warning taped to its face, a rosary of ailments:

> DO NOT USE HOT—SQUEALS.
> LID SNAPS. WATCH FINGERS.
> LEAVES RUST ON WHITES (SORRY).

A scent rose from the floor drain that suggested a stew of old socks, rainwater, and the final desperate thoughts of unfortunate insects. Fluorescents buzzed like lazy wasps. Someone had once tried to cheer the place with a potted plant. It had died, dried, and stood there as a reminder of what all life was heading towards.

Beatrice arrived at ten in the morning on a Tuesday with a canvas bag and the optimism of a woman who believed stains came out if you apologized to them. She sorted with the care of a nurse preparing an operating table: towels here, sheets there, whites in a pure little pile. Her detergent was measured like a chemistry experiment to the line. She folded between cycles, her hands skilled at gentleness, laying blouses into rectangles so tidy even the wrinkles gave way on their own.

She was humming when the door banged open and Lester slouched in with a mesh sack that looked damp even when it wasn't. The sack sighed on the floor, and so did he. A wave of odor rolled out: locker room, cabbage, cigarettes, and something sweetly sinister, like a pastry left under a radiator.

He did not sort. He did not separate. He did not show mercy to his reds or his whites or to the eyes of anyone who had to witness what happened next. He opened Washer Two, which wore the SORRY note, tipped his entire life into its mouth, and poured in a glug of detergent big enough to baptize a mule. Then he fetched a jug of bleach the size of a toddler, unscrewed the cap, and kept pouring until Beatrice finally found her voice.

"Careful!" she said, in the way one might address a sleepwalking toddler balancing on a balcony railing. "Bleach can eat at fabric."

"Good," he said. "The fabric started it."

He threw the cap on top of the heap, slammed the lid, and sat on the dryer opposite her. It growled beneath him. He stared at her socks on the folding shelf as if they had personally offended the municipal code.

"If you add a capful of softener," she tried, "it might make things—"

"I don't need softener," he interrupted. "I need normal neighbors."

She folded a towel—square, precise, a small defiance—and smiled as one smiles at a barking dog.

A minute later, a grey slurry frothed out from the bottom of Washer Two and dribbled across the tile, erasing the dark brown outlines of ancient spills dried on the linoleum. A mouse skittered out of the corner, reconsidered, and retreated faster than how it came in.

"Accidents happen," Beatrice sang cheerfully, fetching a mop in the utility closet.

"Yeah, right," replied Lester as he jumped off the washer and stepped over the growing puddle. "Accidents happen."

When Beatrice came back with the mop, he was gone.

Mail arrived at four each day like clockwork. The alcove was a narrow throat lit by a bulb that wore a dusty halo of faint light. A hand-lettered sign read PLEASE DO NOT SLAM—IT WAKES THE BABY, which was sweet and useless. There was no door to the mailroom. It had been removed.

Beatrice believed in mail the way children believe in fairy godmothers. Letters changed lives. Envelopes held checks and apologies. She unlocked 3B and found only flyers: PIZZA, YOGA (flex your truth), and a postcard that said YOU'VE ALREADY WON!!! which is how the Devil says hello.

She rolled her eyes when Lester walked in with a butter knife. Next to her, he began to pry at 2B with it. His key, it seemed, had a political objection to locks. "They changed the slot widths," he muttered. "It's always the slot widths."

"Maybe the super can give you a new key?" she offered.

"Maybe the super can shove that new key up his—" he said with a grunt as the door opened so violently a fan of pre-approved credit offers fire-hosed his chest. He read one as if it had personally cheated him. "'Dear Valued Applicant,'" he sneered. "I'm valued now. That's rich."

Beatrice, for her part, gently re-delivered three misdelivered letters to the right slots. Lester watched, mouth pursed. "They'll only throw them away," he said. "People never want what comes for them."

"Sometimes they do," she said. "Sometimes they're waiting."

"For what?" he said.

"For good news," she said simply.

He flicked a credit offer into the communal trash and brushed by so close she could smell him: old cigarettes, cabbage, damp wool, and that strange sweetness, like a pastry that had learned despair.

It was apparent that the Meeks' apartment complex had a plan for Beatrice. That plan was to break her. Within its walls were a myriad of opportunities for her and Lester Filch to get more and more acquainted. It didn't end at the laundry or mail rooms.

The garbage chute, for example, lived at the end of the hall behind a steel door with a handle that had seen more bacteria than a hospital. A sign above the hatch implored: TIE BAGS. NO LOOSE FOOD. CHUTE CLOGS EASILY. Below the sign someone had written in Sharpie: SO DO SOME OF US. Someone else had crossed it out. Yet another had written a rather nasty confession about their ex that had nothing to do with garbage and everything to do with what he liked to suck.

Mrs. D'Angelo—the old Italian widow from 3C—was inching a bulging bag down the corridor when Beatrice, born to relieve suffering wherever it lurked, swooped in with the grace of a pelican and hoisted the bag. It was warm. Warm is not a temperature one hopes for in refuse. A brown liquid kissed her calf. She smiled anyway, because kindness atrophies without use.

"You're an angel," Mrs. D'Angelo wheezed. "My back, you know."

"Of course," Beatrice chirped. "I've got it."

The elevator dinged. Out of it lurched Lester, lugging a bag tied with dental floss and hope. The bag had a mournful, bulgy quality, like a beanbag chair with secrets.

"We were here first," Beatrice said, in what she thought of as her firm voice (it sounded like a soft voice in heels).

He pushed past her anyway and wedged his bag into the hatch. He shoved harder. The bag moaned, split, and revealed the inner lives of half a week: coffee grounds like grave dirt, chicken bones, a slick of something once lasagna, now archaeology. The first wave slopped across the floor and toward Beatrice's shoes with unhurried purpose.

She pivoted, saving her shoes but not the hem of her pants from splatters. Mrs. D'Angelo crossed herself. A meatball balanced precariously on the hinge. The smell unfurled, warm and personal.

"Bad design," Lester declared, wiping his hands on his pants. "Small throat. Needs a wider mouth. Write a letter."

"I'll write a note," Beatrice said, because that was what good people do; they write notes to the void. She knelt with paper towels and began a tender triage.

Lester blinked at both of them. "I hate this building," he said, almost tenderly, as one might say *I love you.*

CHAPTER TWELVE

Two days later the elevator died, which is what elevators in old buildings do when they've reached the age of Methuselah. The CLOSED FOR REPAIR sign was affixed with tape. Someone had drawn a sad face on the sign; someone else added a moustache.

Beatrice carried a box upstairs to a woman who ran the local shelter: a donation of blankets, because goodness is a habit you do not simply quit, like caffeine or belief. On the landing between floors she met Lester, descending, dragging a suitcase that had seen better owners. They were trapped in the narrow switchback of the stairwell in that particular intimacy of strangers who must negotiate past each other with items they cherish differently.

The stairwell smelled of damp concrete and a memory of pea soup. The walls sweated faintly from the humidity. Their shoulders brushed as they passed each other. Her box corner tapped his suitcase and left a polite dimple.

"What's in there?" he asked, nodding at her box, because curiosity is a rudeness that sometimes passes for conversation.

"Blankets," she said. "For women who need them."

He sniffed. "Women always need something."

"So do men," she said sharply, stepping past him. "They just call it something else."

"Rent," he said.

Lester's suitcase zipper snagged on the splintered wood from a broken railing. He yanked; it resisted. He yanked harder; it gave way, flopping open to disgorge a sad parade: two shirts the color of dishwater, a rolled magazine, a packet of saltines, a plastic grocery bag full of absolutely nothing (the safest way to own plastic grocery bags), and a framed photo face-down.

He scrambled, swore, snatched the frame. She pretended not to see.

"Do you need—" she began.

"I need space," he said angrily, and she gave it to him, climbing on as he re-contained his life with the brusque efficiency of a man who has re-contained himself a thousand times.

Saturday morning brought a handbill slipped under every door: SAFETY INSPECTION—FIRE ALARMS, EXITS, GENERAL HOUSEKEEPING, 11 A.M., signed MEEKS.

West Lemon tenants treat "safety" the way sailors treat omens: with polite dread. People put on pants. People hide their candles. People kick errant shoes under beds and hope mice will do the right thing.

By ten fifty-eight the hallway smelled like collective exertion. Doors cracked. Hair was smoothed. Lies were readied.

Beatrice stood at her door with a plate of oatmeal cookies in case the inspector had blood sugar issues. Lester hovered at his, a cigarette angled from his mouth like a middle finger given fire. He misted his threshold with a spray bottle of something that smelled like lemon and denial.

Mr. Meeks appeared with a contractor's tape measure hooked to his belt like an ornament. Despite his size he moved gently, as if apologizing to the air. Behind him, a city inspector wore a vest with reflective stripes and an expression that made the reflective stripes feel underdressed. Clipboard in hand, she radiated the calm menace of a person who knows which squiggle on her form could cost you money you do not possess. None of the tenants would have to fit the bill for whatever was wrong, but they all feared it would be taken out on them with rent hikes.

The two of them inspected smoke detectors. They asked about extinguishers. Lester insisted he had one. Meeks asked where. Lester said "in the area." Meeks sighed the sigh of one who has lent many extinguishers to people who cannot remember where they ended up.

The inspector opened the stairwell door and frowned. "No obstructions," she said, pointing to a bicycle chained there like a sacrificial goat.

"That's not mine," Lester said quickly from his doorway, which was true in the narrow, lawyerly sense and false in the broader, communal sense, because all sins in the hallways belonged to all tenants. Meeks unhung the bike and rolled it into the hall with the gravitas of a man moving a body. The inspector wrote something on her clipboard. The clipboard made a small, pleased sound to itself.

In 3B, Beatrice's smoke detector emitted a polite single chirp every ninety seconds, an automated stutter-step of mortality.

"Battery," the inspector said. "Replace."

"I will right away," Beatrice said, mortified that a device had accused her of laxity. She thrust the cookie plate toward the inspector, then toward Meeks, then—what was she doing?— toward Lester, who had followed them into her apartment. The inspector declined. Meeks took one and looked moved. Lester took two and looked victorious.

"Garbage chute clogs," the inspector noted when she about to leave Beatrice's unit. She was reading a prior complaint from the clipboard.

"Design issue," Lester offered, speckling crumbs across his shirt like culinary dandruff.

"The note said it was attributed to tenant behavior," the inspector corrected, and with the clean economy of a guillotine, checked a box. Somewhere deep inside, Beatrice's conscience flushed hot. Lester just smiled.

That night decided to be an opera. The baby upstairs had been practicing scales for a week: hunger, gas, existential dread. These cries were the kind that divide the soul with an axe. The walls thrummed with it. The radiator took up the note, made it metallic, and sent it through the building's guts.

At eleven, Beatrice baked. Flour calms babies by a transitive property of goodness, she believed. She mixed by hand, folded in blueberries because blue is holy, lined up muffins like soldiers of mercy. The timer dinged. The baby screamed. She put on her shoes. A poor single mother (she assumed) would appreciate a nice warm muffin on a chilly night.

At the same moment, Lester got up too, less to help than to stop the mouth of hell. He snatched his complaint from the table:

YOUR BABY IS A PUBLIC NUISANCE (underlined twice).
THIS IS A BUILDING OF SLEEPERS.
DISCONTINUE.

They met on the stairs like opposing weather systems: she with her muffins, he with his grievance. Their fingers brushed on the buzzer; she felt a slug, cool and resistant.

The door opened. The mother, twenty-five going on fifty, hair in frazzled monuments, baby screaming on her hip, stood in the light. The apartment behind her looked like a triage, smelled of panic and plastic.

"I brought muffins," Beatrice said, breathless with compassion.

"I brought a complaint," Lester said, breathless with triumph.

The mother's lips thinned. "Lady, if I wanted muffins, I'd have called my mother. And don't lecture me with those eyes. You don't know the first thing about raising a kid alone in this dump. You look like you've never even had a pimple."

Beatrice's face opened, stricken not by the insult but by its truth. "I—only wanted to—maybe I could hold her while you—"

"While I what?" the mother snapped. "Slept? Move to a planet where the walls don't breathe? No thanks. Last time I let someone 'help,' my baby smelled like perfume for two days and wouldn't latch. You people with your clean hands and your clean shoes—"

"I live here," Beatrice whispered.

"Barely," the mother said, and the baby shrieked in punctuation.

"And you—" she turned on Lester—"you knock again, I call the cops. I know she's crying. I'm not deaf."

"I will file a report," he said firmly.

"File it in your ass," she said.

Even Beatrice almost laughed.

The baby ratcheted higher. A neighbor banged the wall in protest.

"Please," Beatrice tried again, arms out. "If I could just—"

"No," the lady said flatly. "No holds. No muffins. No saints. I don't need your goodness. It makes me sick. And I don't need your threats. Close your mouths."

She slammed the door. Lester wedged his sneaker. She pushed harder. He stumbled backwards, cursed. Silence returned like a punishment. At least the baby had stopped its racket.

Beatrice's muffins cooled uselessly in her hands. Something inside her cracked and would rattle from now on when she walked.

Lester, rattled hollow long ago, felt a mild, oily satisfaction spread through him like a margarine of misery.

"See?" he said, almost pleased. "Nobody cares."

After that night, the building recalibrated. Beatrice moved more quietly, as if apologizing to the floorboards. She timed her showers to the baby's pauses. Her shampoo began to smell faintly of defeat.

Lester became bolder. When he saw her at the bodega, he explained the fraudulence of bananas. When they met on the sidewalk, he lectured her on the city's rat problem (apparently, it was worse than New York).

And yet, one afternoon when they met once again in the mail alcove, Lester found his butter knife missing. He sniffed around, muttering to himself God knew what swear words, and despite it all, Beatrice felt bad. She left her mail on the counter, jogged over to her apartment and grabbed a butter knife. When Beatrice returned, she silently handed it to him. He took it, studied it for a moment, and then returned it. Not kindness—just a ceasefire.

That night Beatrice lay awake, raw and flayed, staring at the ceiling trapezoid of streetlight. For the first time since childhood, she asked aloud: "What good is all your goodness?"

The night held no answer.

Next door, Lester stubbed his cigarette into his WORLD'S BEST DAD mug and smiled his particular smile—the one that always looked like the first half of a wince. He stared at a crack in his living room wall, listened to the cars driving by, the honking, the swearing. There would be mail at four. There would be laundry at ten. There would be a baby at nine, one, and three AM. There would be Beatrice next door. There would be him, alone. This was life: an existence so meaningless, one could only wonder if there was even a point to getting up each day.

And so the days, so very bad indeed, just kept on going.

CHAPTER THIRTEEN

Beatrice Goodie had never thought of kindness as a weapon before. A tool, yes—like a mop meant to clean a room. But after the crying-baby incident, she could not shake the memory of Lester Filch's grin—yellowed, smug, sinister in its confidence. He had claimed victory that night. It itched inside her like a rash.

If goodness had failed softly, perhaps it was time to make it fail loudly. She would kill him with kindness. Smother him with smiles. Drown him in decency until he either choked or—God willing—coughed up a scrap of humanity.

It was not the Goodie way to hate. So she decided to start a project.

The mail room was a common meeting point. Both of them liked to get their deliveries at the same time. Usually it was just a reminder of unwanted responsibilities wrapped in envelopes: bills, summonses, glossy lies from credit card companies promising a better life for a high-interest fee. Still, that day Beatrice was hopeful when she walked into that room of potential bad news. She arrived early. She polished Lester's mailbox with her sleeve until it gleamed. When he shambled in, butter knife ready, she was waiting with a smile that nearly cracked her jaw.

"Good afternoon, Lester," she sang. "I saved you a spot."

He squinted. "You polished my slot."

"Isn't it nice?"

"Keep your hands off my slot," he said, jamming the knife into the lock. The metal screeched like a violin being tortured. "Now I'll get fingerprints on it."

"I thought you might like some help," she said.

He recoiled. "I said don't touch my slot."

"Just being neighborly."

"You're being criminal."

The lock gave, and his mailbox vomited an avalanche: three overdue notices, five pre-approved cards, and one jury summons. The papers fanned across the floor like feathers shed by a dying bird.

Beatrice pounced. "Oh! A summons! Civic duty is so important. You'll make a wonderful juror."

Lester snorted. "They'll put me in jail just for thinking."

"You might save someone's life."

"I might vote guilty to get home quicker."

She gathered the papers, stacked them with maternal precision. He tore one in half while looking her dead in the eye, then let the halves flutter to the tiles. She crouched, pressed them together, and murmured, "Everything can be mended, Lester."

The neighbors who happened to gather—Mrs. D'Angelo, the young couple from 1A, even Alan Meeks himself—watched with fascination. They were trying to get into the mail room but Lester and Beatrice were putting on a show right in front of the door. Lester smirked at the audience. "You see? She thinks I'm her project. Get some Elmer's. Paste me back together."

He ripped up and dropped another envelope. Beatrice scooped it up and smoothed the pieces against her chest. She smiled harder. The smile was beginning to ache.

"She's like a fungus," Lester announced. "She won't go away. Won't die, keeps spreading."

"Fungus feeds the forest," Beatrice replied, voice bright but eyes brittle.

The neighbors snickered as they looked on. The jury, it seemed, had already been sworn in.

If Lester Filch would not accept words, he might accept food, thought Beatrice. Nobody hates soup, she reasoned. Soup is primal. Soup heals.

She made a vat of lentil and carrot, fragrant with cumin, tender with bay leaf, steaming with motherly intent. She carried it down in a gleaming pot, oven mitts on her hands like gauntlets of righteousness, and knocked.

Lester opened the door in his wife-beater tank top, cigarette clamped to his lips, smoke curling through stale air. Behind him, his apartment lay dim and cluttered: towers of newspapers and what might once have been a recliner before it evolved into a compost heap. The carpet bore stains that reminded her of a world map. The air smelled of old cabbage, forgotten socks, and still the faint, sweet rot of something that refused to name itself.

"I brought you dinner," she declared. "It's full of vitamins."

He peered inside the pot. "It's full of vegetables."

"Exactly."

"I hate vegetables."

"You'll love these. They're organic."

He took the pot, turned, walked to the sink, and with the casual grace of a man watering weeds, dumped the entire steaming contents down the drain. Lentils gurgled like drowning pilgrims. Carrots bobbed, whirled, vanished. A puff of steam fogged the tile, carrying away the last of her hope.

"Thanks," he said, handing her the pot, and shut the door.

Beatrice stood stone-still, mitts still on, her hands holding a pot of emptiness. It's what she felt inside at that moment: empty. For the first time in her life she considered soup an instrument of humiliation.

One week later, the elevator trapped Lester and Beatrice between floors. The box shuddered, then froze with the sigh of old machinery surrendering to entropy. The emergency light blinked red like a heart monitor.

Beatrice clutched her grocery bag. "Well," she chirped nervously, "at least we have company."

Lester leaned against the wall, lit a cigarette, and said nothing.

"You know, Lester, they say strangers in elevators make the best friends."

He exhaled. Smoke coiled into her face.

"Perhaps," she coughed, "we could... play a game? Twenty questions?"

"Fine. Question one: why am I stuck with you?"

"Because the universe wants us to learn something."

"Lesson learned," he said, and farted—long, unapologetic, echoing in the confined space. "Universe make me do that, too?"

Beatrice pressed her lips together until her teeth ached. She inhaled through her nose. The air was thick with cigarette, cabbage, and now something more primal.

After twenty minutes, the elevator jolted back to life. Beatrice bolted out gasping. Lester stayed inside, leaning against the panel, looking pleased with himself as the doors closed and swept him from her view.

Enough was enough. If kindness failed privately, perhaps it would succeed publicly. Beatrice organized a "Good Neighbor Committee," posting hand-lettered flyers with smiling suns and the slogan TOGETHER WE CAN MAKE WEST LEMON BETTER! She reserved the basement laundry room (scrubbed for the occasion) and brewed pitchers of lemonade.

Half the building came: widows, students, young couples, the chronically curious. They sat on plastic chairs, sipping lemonade, nodding politely. Beatrice stood before them with notes and a vision.

"We can address noise, garbage, even friendship," she announced. "A building is a family if we let it be."

The crowd murmured, half-sceptical but intrigued. And then Lester arrived. He slouched into a chair, arms crossed, and declared, "This is a cult."

"It's not a cult," Beatrice said sweetly. "It's community."

"Same thing," he said. "One leader, free drinks, promises nobody really believes."

Snickers spread. Beatrice pressed on, showing a chart she'd drawn about recycling. Lester raised his hand.

"Yes, Lester?"

"Why separate glass from plastic when it all ends up in the same landfill? That's like separating your shit from your piss before you flush."

Laughter rippled. She flushed.

She tried to talk about noise control and ways to improve it. Lester cut in: "Maybe the noise is life around here. Maybe silence is worse. Ever think of that? Silence makes you hear your own thoughts. Does anyone want that?"

Heads nodded, mutters agreed. The room tilted toward him. He had turned her meeting into his stage. Beatrice's lemonade sat sweating, untouched. Her handout leaflets drooped like wilted leaves. She watched as goodness, once again, collapsed under the weight of Lester's rot, and she felt for the first time the sour taste of rage.

Her last stand came in the lobby that afternoon, in front of witnesses. Beatrice caught him mid-cigarette talking to Mr. Meeks and two neighbors. Even the city inspector was there, returning for a follow-up.

"Lester," she said loudly, "I wanted to thank you."

He froze. "For what?"

"For teaching me patience." Beatrice raised her voice, theatrical. "Your outlook really stretched me. You've shown me that goodness can survive even in adversity. I want you to know that I see you, Lester Filch, and I believe—even you—deserve kindness."

The lobby went still.

Lester stared, then let out a coughing laugh. "See folks? Little Ms. Perfect here thinks that people like us are her homework. She thinks we're her project. Newsflash, Blondie— I'm not your makeover. I'm the mold on your ceiling, and I like it there."

The inspector smirked. Mr. Meeks coughed. The neighbors chuckled. The judgment was clear: her sermon had failed. Beatrice's smile cracked, a hairline fracture she couldn't hide. Lester crushed his cigarette on the floor with his foot and walked into the elevator.

"See you upstairs, Mother Teresa," he said, as the doors closed on him again.

That night, Beatrice sat on her bed, muffins cooling on a plate, untouched. For the first time in her life she wondered if goodness itself might be a fraud—she hated him. She truly hated him.

Downstairs, Lester drank from his WORLD'S BEST DAD mug again, this time grinning. He had survived soup, mail, committees, speeches. Goodness had flung itself at him and shattered like a wineglass against a sewer grate. And nothing made him happier than the sound of breaking glass.

CHAPTER FOURTEEN

Some wars are fought with bombs, some with treaties. This war was fought with mildew, noise complaints, and the smell of boiled cabbage. The war, of course, was Lester's war against Beatrice Goodie. She had tried her best and now it was his turn for an offensive. If you asked her, she was on a crusade for decency. If you asked him, it was just another game. And if you asked the building itself—its cracked pipes and rotting floorboards—it would groan that neither side had clean hands by the end.

For a few weeks after her attempt at bringing the tenants together, Beatrice tried to recommit herself to her original creed: patience, tolerance, muffins. But each day spent next to Lester Filch was like living beside a swamp. His smell crept through the vents and crawled under the doors—fried onions, cigarettes, cabbage—while his voice oozed through the walls in muttered complaints about television reruns, the mail, or the "idiots upstairs."

She resolved to resist. Goodness, she told herself, isn't passive; it's an active force. But the building had other plans. If goodness was a river, West Lemon Apartments was a clogged storm drain, and Lester Filch the rotting corpse wedged inside. The pressure was bound to build.

It began, as many catastrophes do, in the bathroom. Beatrice had drawn a bath, a ritual of cleansing both body and spirit. Lavender bubbles frothed around her like halos, candlelight played upon the tiles, and for one brief moment she imagined the world was orderly again.

Then the water turned brown.

At first a tint, then a swirl, then—horror—an entire spaghetti noodle bobbing to the surface like a snake. Coffee grounds floated up next, little islands of bitterness. A sausage chunk bobbed up to say hello.

Beatrice shrieked, leapt out of the water, and clutched her towel around her as if modesty mattered to an invading pasta tide.

The culprit was, of course, Lester—experimenting with what he called "Tuesday stew" with macaroni, cabbage, bacon grease all poured down the drain when it went wrong. He almost never used the garbage disposal for some reason. But when he tried this time, it backfired into Beatrice's sanctified bath.

Moments later, the hallway filled with other neighbors who had similar visits from past meals. Beatrice barged into the hallway just in time to hear Lester say, "Oh, come on, folks. You never been to Carmine's before? That's good stuff!"

She confronted him, dripping and furious. "You've ruined my bath!"

He squinted at her towel. "You smell funny. You should try it again."

Laughter echoed down the hall. Beatrice retreated, humiliated, lavender bubbles still clinging to her calves. Now she was convinced that the building had chosen sides, and it wasn't hers. Maybe they were all rotten. Maybe they tolerated Lester

Filch because they were all just like him. Maybe all this God-forsaken trash heap had was miserable, rotten people.

The plumbing battle might have been dismissed as an accident, but fate rarely stops at one humiliation. Two weeks later, exterminators came for the basement. Roaches had colonized the laundry room. Rats had laid siege to the stairwell. Flyers announced SPRAYING ON FRIDAY; the whole building buzzed with dread.

Beatrice saw an opportunity. She baked cookies, determined to show the workers that kindness, not poison, was the true antidote to vermin. She didn't believe in extermination. Animals lived together all the time in the wild, and unless they were eating one another, they wouldn't just exterminate each other for no reason. Why couldn't they all coexist?

When the men arrived, sweat shining under fluorescent light, she greeted them with a plate as they made their way through the lobby.

"Don't eat those," Lester muttered from behind, emerging from a cough of smoke. He was sitting in one of the leather couches next to the stairs. "She bakes with rat poison. Vegan crumbs. You'll die noble but unsatisfied." The exterminators laughed uneasily but took the cookies anyway.

The spraying began. Hissing clouds filled the corners. At once, the walls broke open: a flood of roaches poured out, antennae thrashing, a black tide scuttling across linoleum. She shrieked, then fell to her knees, flapping her hands. "Don't hurt them!"

The exterminators came out from the stairwell and stared at her. "Lady, that's... literally what we're here for."

She scooped at the insects, guiding them toward safety. A rat stumbled into view, poisoned, belly bloated. It collapsed at her feet with a squeak like a deflating balloon.

Beatrice gasped, cradling it. "It's okay," she whispered. "You are loved."

The rat convulsed, then emptied its bowels onto her skirt.

Even the exterminators bent double with laughter. Beatrice dropped it quickly, and the carcass skidded down the hall, streaking the floor, until it bumped against Lester's boot. He nudged it with theatrical disdain.

"Another satisfied tenant," he announced.

The exterminators' laughter followed her upstairs like vermin.

If humiliation comes in threes, Beatrice should have known her time was up.

At midnight a few days after the pest control incident, Lester attempted to boil sausages in his coffee pot. He fell asleep, and the water boiled off until the sausages smoked, hissed, and blackened. At 12:47, alarms shrieked awake. The building convulsed with panic. Neighbors poured into the halls, the baby upstairs screamed, sirens wailed in the distance.

Beatrice, seizing her moment, became a shepherd to the flock. "Stay calm!" she said, wrapping herself in her robe as she came into the hall. "Let's everyone get out!" She corralled old women, guided the drunk guy from 5C, soothed a couple sleepy but frightened children. She pounded on Lester's door, which was still closed, as were his eyes. He opened one of them.

"If it's real, let it take me."

He forced himself to get up and open the door. Beatrice almost banged on his chest. The smoke poured from his doorway. "The smoke!" she yelled. "You'll die!"

"Good."

She pulled him into the hallway, neighbors gawking as he pushed her away.

"See?" he shouted, "She won't let me burn! She'll drag me to heaven if it kills us both!"

The laughter started again. People were suddenly not so keen to move into the stairwell. They saw whatever it was came from his apartment.

"Anyway," said Lester, "It's a false alarm. Burnt sausages."

Something cracked then. Lester had contaminated her air, her bath, her dignity. Even her muffins—her last fortress—had become a joke.

"You miserable, rancid, cabbage-soaked troll!" she screamed. The tenants who remained in the hall quieted down. "I've tried kindness, patience, mercy—but you don't want help! You want filth! You want everyone as rotten as you! Well, congratulations—you've won! You're poison, Lester Filch! And I hope you choke on your own smoke!"

The hallway froze. Even the baby upstairs hushed. Then she was gone, slamming her door behind her, determined to pack her boxes and leave that place as soon as she could. He *had* won, and she no longer had it in her to care.

The day she moved, Lester was leaning on the stairway railing, mug in hand—WORLD'S BEST DAD, half-full of tar-black coffee. He watched her struggling with her boxes. Nobody helped, and that made him happy.

When she passed with her final box, he asked, "Going somewhere, Goodie?"

"Anywhere you're not," she spat.

He raised the mug. "Safe travels."

She climbed into the van, slammed the door, and was gone.

Silence settled in around him. Lester shuffled back upstairs and into his apartment, sat in his recliner, and lit a cigarette. For the first time in weeks, the air felt clear. He had driven out goodness itself. Beatrice Goodie had snapped. He sipped from his mug, smiling to himself.

Even goodness, it seemed, had a breaking point. And he was it.

CHAPTER FIFTEEN

Lester Filch woke with a start. He was being chased by a goldfish in the sewers underneath New York, which flowed into a giant food processor. As he looked up from the sinkhole, his dead adoptive mother walked up to the switch and flicked it on. Just as he felt the grinding pain of metal on metal crushing his body into a pulp, he woke up.

He lay there sweating, staring into the dark until his eyes caught the red blink of his alarm clock: 12:00. Flashing. Mocking. The power had gone out again.

"Figures," he groaned. "A run-down dump can't handle a breeze without dying."

He fumbled for his watch on the nightstand, squinting at its cloudy plastic face. 3:10 a.m. He didn't doubt it, though he knew the thing ran about ten minutes fast. It always had. Fixing it meant holding down two buttons at once for some absurd ritual of beeps and numbers, and Lester had never bothered. "Close enough," he said every day for the past fifteen years. By now "close enough" was gospel.

Groggily, he heaved himself out of bed and stuck his face up against the window, shivering at the curtain of cold air clinging to the glass. Snow fell in thick drifts on the sills, and from what he could see by the streetlight, there was already a foot on the ground.

Lester grunted with frustration. He had gone to bed early that night, because he heard a winter storm was on the way. Closing his eyes was an easy way to avoid seeing the snowflakes, which reminded him of dandruff and Christmas—two very bad things. Plus the next day he would drive through snow and sleet and walk over a parking lot of ice, a daunting prospect turning his forty-five–minute commute into a two-hour hassle. He needed sleep. The thought crossed his mind to call in sick, but what would he do all day anyway? Watch TV? There was never anything good on. He had no books to read.

No, he would go to work and at least get paid.

Having made his decision, he reached over, pressed the buttons on the alarm clock, and set it to 3:10 to match his watch. "Done," he muttered, satisfied.

Lester fumbled back to bed and quickly fell asleep again.

What he didn't bother to remember—what Lester Filch never bothered to remember—was that in reality it was only 3:00. Those ten phantom minutes, shrugged off for years, would soon matter very much. But he had been too tired to care. To anyone else, those ten minutes of added time could hardly be called tragic—easily remedied by buying a semi-descent watch at the Boscov's down the street—but for Filch, who had a knack for finding the worst possible outcome in any given scenario no matter how trite, the oversight proved no less catastrophic. Those ten minutes—vanished like snow into gutters—would one day mean all the difference in the world.

CHAPTER SIXTEEN

Arthur Medlar was a forty-five-year-old man who would rather be doing anything else except visiting his fiancée in West Lemon, New Jersey. The night Lester Filch went to bed early to avoid the snow, Arthur was driving back to Manhattan, having endured another dinner at Beatrice's new apartment.

He sped past grey slush and tacky Christmas ornaments that overstayed their welcome, the kind of overblown suburban decorations that made him shiver with revulsion. Every minute away from New York—where the real fun happened—was a minute wasted. His only consolation was his Hummer, the gas-guzzling giant he loved more than his own mother. In fact, he had occasionally imagined running her over with it, a thought that amused him more than it should have.

Still, in West Lemon the car had its charms. In Manhattan, it blended into traffic. Out here, it gleamed like a chariot of fire on its way to Heaven. People gawked. Arthur preened. Whenever he passed a storefront with glass panes, he slowed down just to admire his reflection—the man and his machine in perfect union.

Arthur had always had a flair for style. Back in high school he dressed better than anyone else, which prompted rumors he might be gay. The rumors, he knew, mostly came from jealous boys; after all, he was just as successful on the field as off it, lettering in soccer and football. Women never failed him, and he never failed to pursue them. Appearance was everything, and Arthur had mastered the art of turning it to his advantage.

At Amherst College he built the persona to match: sharp dresser, strong athlete, top grades, and always on the social circuit. He was the kind of man who made sure he was at every party, never without an audience. Later, after NYU Law, he briefly impressed as an entertainment lawyer before tiring of the grind. Business school came next. Then ICU Media, where he climbed the corporate ladder until he became CEO, pulling in $1.5 million a year—a figure he considered modest.

Now, in his mid-forties, with wealth and reputation secured, he had finally agreed to marry. It wasn't his idea—marriage was, in his opinion, a trap of nagging, boredom, and eventual divorce—but his parents had leaned on him for years. They wanted grandchildren, though secretly Arthur found children distasteful. He smiled at them when required, which was enough to fool his parents into hope. Eventually, after he turned thirty-nine and still had no fiancée, they gave up on the grandchild fantasy. They decided, instead, to simply demand respectability. A married son. A respectable match. Nothing more.

He mentioned these doubts to his mother once, asking her what the point of marriage actually was, and he received a lecture.

"Arthur, we own three estates across this country, we've given you the ability to do everything you wanted, to make a name for yourself, and beside that, we've left you an inheritance. Do you think that comes free? We pay a price for our position in life. We must be respectable."

"But that's antiquated, Mother," he argued, "like, a hundred years antiquated. And you don't care about reputation. You're in Michigan most of the time or California. People don't know you have an unmarried son unless you tell them. I don't want to get married. Lie to them, if you have to."

She gave a grunt of exasperation. "You know nothing. You think only of yourself."

"You're damned right I do. This is *my* life. I can't just get married because you want me to."

"So you're going to just die alone? Don't you want love? Don't you want commitment? Are you happy with those tramps you bring home? No better than whores. Yes, I've heard the rumors of your so-called high life in New York."

"And what difference would marriage make?" he asked bitterly, "when Dad's just as happy with his own whores?"

She slapped him hard, leaving behind the stinging reminder of his disrespect.

That conversation hadn't gone so well. But he laughed about his comeback now. That would teach his mother, the hypocrite. As was his father. Whores. He could live with whores. At least they didn't entangle him in drama. He was a free spirit: rich and free. Then came Beatrice.

She was unlike anyone he'd ever dated: reserved, moral, unspoiled. The type of woman who deflected his advances instead of succumbing to them. Castles surrounded by moats of morality had always turned him on. They were challenges, and Arthur Medlar never lost a challenge. He told himself he would eventually "open" her, mold her into the kind of woman he preferred—compliant, indulgent, willing. For now, her innocence only heightened his anticipation.

But she bored him. That was the problem. She talked endlessly about her career, her ideals, her causes: health care, the homeless, civil rights. None of it interested him. They weren't his problems. They weren't problems at all. People were poor or sick because life—or God—made them that way. The way she spoke, with conviction and sincerity, made him want to yawn. He would nod, smile, and drown her out.

The engagement itself had been almost inevitable. Mrs. Medlar, upon hearing that her husband's business partner had a daughter in her forties that was still unmarried, orchestrated the match with ruthless precision. Beatrice's reputation as a saint—part social worker, part would-be Mother Teresa—made her tolerable. She was no hussy, no trophy wife, no genetic liability. The Goodies, relieved to have a potential wealthy son-in-law for their eccentric daughter, encouraged it. They hoped maybe he would snap her out of this obsession she had with poverty. Within a year, Arthur had talked his way into Beatrice's life enough to secure a ring.

On their wedding night he planned to be an artist with a blank canvas, molding her into the women he usually played with, the kind who liked it rough, who allowed him total control. She was so elegant now, even at forty, so destined to be clay. And when he was done with her, she would still complement him perfectly, satisfy his parents, and be the doting wife the world expected him to have.

The night of the snow storm that woke up Lester Filch, Beatrice made Arthur chicken parmesan. He would have preferred a meal at a restaurant, but he was polite and told her it was good. The dish wasn't terrible, really, but as always she ruined it further by talking. He tried to steer the conversation back to himself, and she listened with interest. She always did. Still, it was so much *work*.

After dinner, they watched a movie on television. There was a moment when he was struck by the need to force himself on her as she curled up next to him. It passed quickly, but the impulse scared him a little. When he felt the warmth of her body pressed up against him and the curve of her breasts nestled there, a shirt's breadth away from his skin—just to get comfortable, he was sure, nothing more—he became excited. In his mind, he was pushing her down on the couch, ripping off her clothing as she struggled to push him off, forcing apart her legs. The image lasted only a moment. It left his heart racing. There would be time enough, he told himself, on their wedding night.

By the time he left her place, he was still restless. He thought about stopping at Jasmine's—Jasmine never talked much, and that was a gift. But he was tired. The road back to New York would be distraction enough in a snow storm. He turned up the radio, headlights slicing through the curtain of snow. Just outside East Lemon, a barricade forced him onto a side road. He cursed and slammed on the brakes. A tree trunk was sprawled across the pavement.

Arthur stepped out and inspected the trunk. Big enough to kill someone, for sure. On a slick night like this, a smaller car would be crushed. He even considered moving it. But then he thought of his shirt, his coat, his shoes. All imported, tailored, pressed. He wasn't about to ruin them wrestling with bark.

There was always the police. He could call. But when he got back into the Hummer and reached for his phone in the glove compartment, he saw it was dead. He could plug it into the charger and wait, but that would cost time. The night wasn't getting any younger, nor his bed any closer. Plus football was on tonight, and maybe he could have Jasmine come over his place instead.

He frowned at the tree, weighing the scale. When it came to a contest between safety and inconvenience, safety lost. It always did. He eased his car onto the snowy shoulder and swung around the trunk with room to spare. "Problem solved," he muttered, brushing his hands as if he had accomplished something.

He never did call the police. Beatrice, the long drive, the detour, the tree, they all slipped his mind in the midst of shouts and football cat-calls that night. And in the midst of Jasmine's cat-calls, too. At least he made it home.

CHAPTER SEVENTEEN

Lester Filch woke for the second time that morning, weary as usual but relieved to hear his alarm blaring at seven. He dragged himself from bed, dreading the outdoors where the storm had calmed down but wind still rattled the windows. Then he remembered the power outage and muttered curses. If a snowfall could kill the power there, what would a real blizzard do? He reset the other clocks in his apartment with bitter care, not remembering the lost ten minutes.

Breakfast that morning was cottage cheese and eggs, eaten to a soundtrack of complaints. Shower, clothes, grumbles—it was his ritual. Normally he left at 8:15 on the dot, timed to slide into his desk chair at 8:59, a science he had perfected. But the storm, the outage, and a nagging anxiety convinced him to head out early when the clocks turned 8:00.

The roads were slushy but passable. He flashed middle fingers and shouted curses at every driver who dared delay him, though none could hear through sealed windows. Snow plows slowed him down further. By the time he reached the outskirts of East Lemon, his was right on schedule. Then came the barricade: ROAD CLOSED. DETOUR LEFT.

He cursed aloud. It figured. Things had almost gone smoothly that morning, despite the snow, and now this. The detour promised at least thirty wasted minutes. A police cruiser was idling on the other side of the barricade, so there was no chance of simply driving around. With a groan, he turned left, tires hissing onto the wooded back road.

Even though the snow was over, mist closed in around his car, as he spend down the street. Each bend he took was a disappointment. The main road wasn't showing up anytime soon. His phone, a luxury in those days, had no signal. Reception was still an imperfect science. He stewed with paranoia as he clutched the steering wheel. Coworkers would rat him out if he was late. His boss would fire him. No severance, no job prospects, no apartment—he could already see himself in the gutter, and in some small way, thought perhaps he might even prefer it. But fear still grabbed at his guts. He was more attached to his life than he was willing to admit.

Then came the tree. He had barely a second. Lester swerved, slammed on the brakes, skidded. Screeching filled his ears. The sudden whoosh of splintering wood. His car shrieked into the trunk, flipped, rolled, and wrapped itself like foil around another oak. At sixty miles an hour the impact tore the engine apart. Fire erupted, swallowing steel and memory alike.

Less than ten minutes later—at 8:30 sharp—the barricade at East Lemon was pulled aside. The construction crew, having finished enough work to reopen the main road, waved traffic through toward I-95 and New York City. Had Lester Filch set his clock correctly that morning, he would have arrived ten minutes later and just in time to see them open up the way to work. His life would have remained very boring and very bad, indeed.

CHAPTER EIGHTEEN

Lester Filch came to three days later. He had no family (and if he had, they'd surely have found an excuse not to visit him in the hospital), so it came as no surprise that he woke from his coma greeted by no one.

Waking to a white room with ghostly figures flitting back and forth, heaven would have been the easiest explanation—except he didn't remember dying. In fact, he didn't remember anything at all. As far as his mind was concerned, Lester Filch was born that very moment.

His first thought: WHITE. Everything was so white. He tried to scoot up, but agony shot through the base of his skull, followed by a pulsing throb in his forehead. Worse still, when he commanded his legs to move, nothing happened. Panic seized him. His breath quickened into ragged gulps.

My god. Where the hell am I?

I know this looks like a hospital. I am in a hospital.

I am... who?
I am a man. That's it. A man in a white hospital that looks like heaven.

A scream welled up, then broke into a whimper, followed by a gurgle of spit that dribbled down his chin. He tried to wipe it, but his arms were strapped down. An IV sprouted from his left wrist. His scalp itched beneath a helmet of bandages. Hot tears spilled and stung his face.

A nurse entered, and Lester grunted desperately. She gasped and ran out, only to return with a tall, broad-shouldered doctor in a white coat.

A doctor, Lester thought with relief. *I remember doctors.*
"Hello, Mr. Filch," the man said, cheerful but taut around the edges. "Welcome back. I'm Dr. Leonard. You've had quite an accident. Do you remember what happened?"

"No," Lester croaked, trying to see his face but realizing with horror that everything looked a little blurry. "I can't even remember who I am. You just called me Filch... is my first name Leonard?"

"That's my name," the doctor said, studying him. "I'm Dr. Leonard. You're Lester Filch." The doctor bent down even closer. "Can you recall anything else? Your parents? Where you were born?"

"No. Faces, maybe. But no names. Nothing sticks." He groaned. "What happened to me?"

"Well, you've been unconscious for three days."

"Three days!"

"I'm afraid so. And it seems you have retrograde amnesia. It affects long-term memories more than short ones. The good news is that it's almost never permanent."

"Almost never?"

Dr. Leonard fiddled with his clipboard. "We must leave room for extraordinary cases. But chance is on your side."

The doctor explained the crash on the snowy road, the fire, the broken legs and hip, the fractured vertebrae, the skull injury that scrambled his memory and blurred his vision. A glass shard had sliced open the left side of his face. Another one had pierced his neck, puncturing the artery and sending out blood in all directions. The doctor didn't explain it quite that way, but Lester was able to imagine it enough. By rights, he should have bled out, but the flames which burned forty percent of his body, and mostly his top half, had cauterized the wound. "Quite miraculous, really," said Dr. Leonard. "That fire ended up being a very good thing indeed!"

"Miraculous?" Lester muttered. "What's the use of living if there's nothing to come back to? I don't know who I am, Doctor."

The nurse came in and began fussing at his chin, wiping drool, arranging his pillows as if she were a mother pampering her first born. Lester gave up resisting. His eyes brimmed again with tears.

Dr. Leonard looked down on him with sympathy. "It'll be a long road, Mr. Filch," he said gently. "Three weeks at least in the hospital, probably closer to five. Months of therapy. Lots of monitoring to make sure you're being put back together well."

"Great," he muttered.

"Well, think of it as a second chance. The world is your oyster, Mr. Filch."

"Yeah," Lester sighed. "But I lost the pearl in the last one."

As the doctor padded him softly on the shoulder, Lester repeated the few sticks he was given to build his life back: *I'm a man in a hospital. I had a car accident. I have amnesia. I think I work at Bor Dun Inc. That came back to me okay. Something about paper clips.* An image of a paper clip flashed before his eyes. *Paper clips? What the hell does that have to do with anything?*

Hospitals run on gossip. Sterile walls, sterile food, sterile sheets—but the chatter of nurses kept the place alive. As Lester Filch drifted in and out of his happy place, hopped up on morphine, he heard two of them talking outside his room.

"Did you go in there yet?" one of them asked the other.

"God, yes. Smells like somebody left a hot dog on a radiator."

"More like kielbasa," said the other "Burnt on one side, raw on the other!"

They both snorted with laughter into their masks.

"Poor thing," said the first, though her pity seemed more for the sausage than the patient. "Looks like a bratwurst that lost a fight."

"Don't say bratwurst. I'll never eat lunch again."

From inside his room, Lester rasped, "I can hear you, you know!"

A pause. Then the first nurse, sweet as poison, said, "See? Even sounds like a grill."

Their laughter squeaked down the hall, leaving Lester stewing. He glared at the ceiling. "I'm not meat," he muttered. "I'm a man." The fluorescent lights flickered indifferently, disagreeing.

In the middle of the night, the door creaked open again. Lester was awake, unable to sleep because of how uncomfortable his body felt and because the pain medication was losing its grip on his nerves. A new figure shuffled into the dark room. It was Father Mulrooney, the hospital chaplain, a squat man almost as round as the vial of holy water dangling from his neck. He squinted at Lester's chart, nodded gravely, and advanced like an undertaker with a quota.

"My son," he intoned.

Lester cracked one eye. "Who the hell are you?"

"I am here to prepare you," the priest said, dabbing his fingers with the blessed liquid. "The Lord waits for all men."

"Tell him to keep waiting."

Mulrooney ignored him, pressed wet fingers to his forehead, and began: "In nomine Patris, et Filii, et Spiritus Sancti—"

"Hey!" he yelled, moving his head away from the hallowed hand. "Get your Latin hands off me! I'm not even Catholic!"

"All men are Catholic, in the end," the priest said serenely.

"Not me! I'm a Lutheran! And I'm not dying!"

The chaplain paused for a moment, looked down at the chart in his hand, and frowned. "Room 214? Mark Delgado?"

"I'm Lester Filch, you moron!"

They stared at each other. Silence thickened, broken only by the squeak of the janitor's mop just outside the room in the hallway.

"Well," Mulrooney said at last, pocketing the vial, "you look half-dead anyway. Consider it a trial run." He departed with the dignity of a man who had botched many blessings before.

Lester lay there, head bandaged, body broken, faintly smelling of lavender holy water. "A man can't even rot in peace without somebody sprinkling him like parsley," he said, trying to wipe his forehead but remembering he couldn't move his arms. So he let the blessing stay. But deep down he was glad to keep it. He knew he needed all the help he could get.

CHAPTER NINETEEN

Three months is enough time for a season to change, for a wound to scab, for hope to curdle. For Lester Filch, it was three months of surgeries and indignities; for Beatrice Goodie, three months of rehearsing sainthood in strangers' living rooms. Both thought they were crawling toward some new version of themselves. Neither realized they were merely being wound tighter for the inevitable conflagration.

Doctors carved and pasted Lester like a school project. Skin grafts from his thighs were stapled to his chest; staples from his chest were yanked and replaced with stitches; stitches dissolved and left him looking like a roadmap of bad decisions. His reflection in the bathroom mirror became a grotesque geography: mountains where flesh puckered, valleys where skin collapsed, rivers of scar tissue winding in improbable directions.

Surgeons praised their handiwork. "You're healing beautifully," one said, though Lester suspected the man had never seen beauty outside a medical diagram. The only beauty Lester could confirm was the curve of his morphine drip, which he eyed like a lover.

Physical therapy was worse. He was marched up and down hospital corridors by nurses half his size but twice his determination. They spoke in tones reserved for golden retrievers and toddlers: "Good step, Lester! Just two more!" He rewarded them with a cold look that often turned sad toward the end of their walk—angry at the very people trying to help him, though he couldn't say why.

The therapy rooms smelled of sweat, disinfectant, and despair, punctuated by the wet wheeze of old men straining on stationary bikes. The worst was the food. Each tray arrived lukewarm, beige, and accusatory, with mashed potatoes that slouched like they had given up and chicken breast so dry it might have been sanded. Dessert was usually gelatin that wobbled with an unnatural equine confidence. Lester often refused to eat, declaring that starvation was preferable. Staff told him resilience was key. He told them resilience was a myth invented by people who weren't hungry.

And yet, Lester limped out of the hospital after those three months, stitched together, bitter as bile, his body a monument to medical persistence and human stubbornness. But he was still clueless as to who he was and why he was so miserable. It was more than just the accident—he knew that in his soul, but he had detached emotions floating around with no memories to land on.

Meanwhile, across town, Beatrice Goodie was being broken in gentler, quieter ways. She abandoned social work's phones and paper trails for the more tactile misery of home health care. After her initial training, she thought it was going to be practical, grounding, full of visible good and far less suicidal. But instead, she found herself juggling bedpans and loneliness in apartments that reeked of mothballs, grease, cats, and dying plants.

One old woman demanded she rearrange the canned goods alphabetically every visit, convinced soup labels were government codes. Another insisted Beatrice test her urine with litmus paper before flushing, "just to be sure it's Christian." A half-deaf veteran mistook her for his wife daily and accused her of infidelity with a mailman Beatrice never met.

And always, the food. Patients insisted she eat with them. She swallowed grey porridge, reheated casseroles from the Reagan era, and Jell-O studded with mysterious fruit. She smiled through every bite. Her patience grew muscles she hadn't known she possessed. Beatrice learned to hold silence like a cup of tea. She learned to coax pills down unwilling throats with tricks of honey and applesauce. She learned that some people would never say thank you and that goodness offered without applause is the only kind that counts—or so she reminded herself each night before collapsing into bed.

Yet cracks appeared. More than once she left a visit trembling, her saintly composure rattled by cruelty disguised as confusion. A man slapped her hand away when she tried to help him dress, snarling, "Keep your charity to yourself." Another accused her of stealing his teaspoons. She bought him a new set out of her own pocket. The next week, he accused her again.

She kept at it. She folded towels, washed hair, whispered reassurances, but sometimes, when she looked in the mirror, she wondered if her smile was still real or just another uniform.

And so, by the end of three months, the stage was set. Lester Filch, patched and scarred, smelling faintly of smoke and antiseptic, shuffled back into his dingy apartment like a ghost who had refused exorcism. Beatrice Goodie, polished by suffering into a quieter, harder version of herself, arrived at the apartment complex with her kit, ready to perform kindness on demand. Fate, smug as ever, had wound the clock. All that remained was for the two hands—Good and Bad—to meet again.

The day Beatrice Goodie re-entered the Meeks apartment complex in West Lemon, she shuddered. As she climbed the stairs (because the elevator was broken, of course) and entered the floor she used to live on, she trembled. As she approached Lester Filch's door, she practically fainted. It could not be. It had been a year. Her supervisor had given her the address but never once mentioned his name, so standing by the door, she pulled out his file from the manila envelope and stared in horror at what she saw. It was true. Lester Filch was her patient. *Oh God, if you exist, you really are a jerk.*

Three months earlier, she would have marched away from that door with a self-justifying grimace of determination. Now she stood with a clipboard, a tote bag of medical supplies, and the brittle patience of a woman who had cleaned one too many bedpans. *Whatever. This is gonna happen, so let's get it over with.*

Beatrice knocked once. The door opened with a groan, and her own personal Lucifer appeared.

But Lucifer had a walker. Other than that, the first thing she noticed were his eyes. He was still Lester, but slightly repurposed. There was something slightly off about them. Of course, she quickly noticed the rest of him as well. His chest bore a jagged scar that rose above his collar like a cracked riverbed. His face was stitched in seams, puckered in patches, and one eyebrow hung lower than the other. He looked like a jigsaw puzzle someone had solved in the dark. Burn scars melted the left side of his face, and she saw they probably made their way down his back. The faint odor of disinfectant clung to him, poorly disguising the smell of smoked meat baked into his pores.

Beatrice put on a professional smile to mask the shock, one she practiced often in mirrors: half warmth, half armor. "Mr. Filch. What a surprise."

But, those eyes. He only squinted at her. She could tell he didn't know who she was. "What are you selling?" he asked with suspicion.

"Not selling. Home health. I'm here to help with your recovery."

"I don't need help. I need quiet."

He could have barked this at her—indeed, the old Lester would have. But he stated it flatly, as if she ought to know better, and what he wanted, what he *needed* in fact, was peace. Behind him, his apartment sagged with neglect. Newspapers still slumped against the wall like fallen soldiers. Dishes fossilized in the sink. A smell rose from the carpet that could not be fully named, though bleach had tried.

Beatrice stepped inside anyway, determined. "Do you remember me? I used to live here."

He shook his head, and a sad look crossed over his face. She should have read his file.

"We'll start with changing your bandages," she said, changing the subject.

He crossed his arms. "They changed them at the hospital."

"Yes, but now you're home. Burns can keep oozing. Maintenance is important."

"Maintenance is for cars."

"Well, *you* haven't changed, have you?" She set her bag on the counter, pulling out gauze, tape, antiseptic. The smell of rubbing alcohol spread, clashing with the cabbage-and-smoke perfume that filled the atmosphere. She turned towards him. "Shirt off, please."

Lester scowled, muttered something about indecency, but peeled his shirt off away. The scar that almost severed his throat gleamed, angry and jagged. For a moment—even Beatrice, so full of duty—felt a flicker of pity. Then she unwrapped his torso and saw the pattern of burned skin on his stomach and back. The pity set in a little more. She washed his burns with more antiseptic, firm but careful. He squirmed but didn't resist.

"Just keeping you alive," she said.

"Alive is overrated."

"Not for me."

Their eyes met briefly, hers steady, his darting. For the first time in years, Beatrice Goodie and Lester Filch occupied the same room not as neighbors but as patient and caretaker.

She finished wrapping the new bandage around his body, neat as a Christmas present, and packed her supplies. "I'll be back Friday, and then three days a week after that," she stated. "This was just a start."

"Don't bother," he grunted.

"I *will* bother, Mr. Filch" she answered, with the conviction of a woman who had outlasted worse. "Bothering is my job."

As she walked out the door, he said her name, and she turned around.

"Do you know me?" he asked. "You talk as if you know me."

Beatrice studied his face for a moment before turning away. "Good evening, Mr. Filch. I'll see you on Friday."

As he closed the door behind her, the living room lamp flickered, as if even the electricity knew that this connection would prove to be a very bad one.

CHAPTER TWENTY

That Friday Beatrice Goodie came back with gauze, tape, and the quiet determination of a woman who decided to professionalize her mercy. She knocked once. The door didn't open.

"Mr. Filch?" she called.

There was a shuffle from inside, and the sound of a chain sliding in its place. Lester appeared, shirtless and dishevelled. His bandage from the other day had been artfully ruined—half peeled, the adhesive freckled with lint.

"New rule," he said. "No mornings."

"It's eleven thirty."

"Still morning."

She let herself in. Social work taught her to walk through thresholds; home health taught her to do it without apologizing, privacy be damned. She set her tote down, pulled out a clipboard, and clicked to business.

"Pain, one to ten?"

"Philosophically or locally?"

"Locally."

"Seven. Philosophically? Eleven."

"Noted," she said, and didn't bother writing it down.

Beatrice then cleaned the scar again and reapplied ointment, wrapped it up tight, and logged it in her form: EDGES HEALING. PATIENT HOSTILE. HUMOR MALIGNANT.

By her third visit she found the first pill graveyard: two pink tablets and a white one shoved underneath the farmer's almanac. She scooped them in her hand and presented the evidence to a somewhat bashful looking defendant.

"You hid these under there on purpose. Was it right before I came? Didn't have time to get to the trash on that walker?"

Lester eyed them with a look of feigned surprise. He said nothing.

"You have to take them," she continued. "On schedule."

"Truth is, I prefer to suffer organically. I hate swallowing those things. Why can't I have an IV drip anyway?"

"Your suffering isn't organic. It's stupid."

His head cocked, intrigued. "You called me stupid."

"I called your plan stupid," she corrected. "But yes. You are also stupid."

Beatrice made him sit down at kitchen table and take the pills with a glass of water. She stood over him until he swallowed them all, then made him open his mouth like a delinquent child hiding contraband. He did it with theatrical offense, showing her his tongue, breath sour, eyes gleaming with mockery. She handed him another glass of water. He swallowed and pantomimed a death scene, one hand to his forehead and the other reaching for a pack of cigarettes.

"Oh, no," she said, plucking them away. "Smoking is *not* going to help you get better."

He watched the pack vanish into her tote, calculating the distance between virtue and theft. "You steal like a nun. I'm not in Catholic school, you know. I'm a Lutheran."

"I only take the harmful things."

"Which is to say, everything."

Beatrice didn't dignify that with an answer. She logged: NICOTINE RESTRICTED. ANTAGONISM—BASELINE.

The following week, she broached his hygiene. After all that time, both living as his neighbor and as his nurse, she couldn't pinpoint the cabbage and she couldn't pinpoint that sweet and sour smell that came from somewhere underneath his wall to wall carpet. It had to be him.

"It's time to take your first proper shower," she said, dragging him into the bathroom. "Ever. I'll change the dressing after."

"I bathe," he said, defiantly. "I don't shower. Sponge baths. Like Napoleon."

"You smell like Waterloo."

He stared, trying to decide if that was a compliment. She wrapped his bandage with plastic, put garbage bags over the cast on his right leg, and placed a folding chair in the shower. The water poured until steam rose like absolution, promising some comfort ahead. Beatrice stationed herself outside the bathroom door like a lifeguard.

Lester lasted four minutes.

"There's no way you washed everything you need to wash in four minutes," Beatrice said, crossing her arms. But he stood shivering in clean cotton, smelling briefly of a life without cabbage. For an instant Beatrice felt pity again. He caught her expression and smirked.

"Don't get any ideas," he said.

"I have enough ideas," she replied, as she taped him back together. "Believe me."

One of those ideas was chicken soup. Nothing quite so cozy, other than a warm shower to wash away the aches and pains.

She spent a lot of time that day making it, and served the soup with crackers on the side. Lester prodded the bowl without even an attempt at eating it.

"It's beige," he complained.

"It's restorative."

"It's got vegetables in it."

"Eat."

And he did, one begrudging spoon at a time. He finished in silence, which was the closest he came to gratitude.

Her eighth visit brought the insurance forms—multi-page and multi-punishment. She braced the wobbly table with a folded magazine. "Sign here, here, and here."

"I don't sign things."

"You signed for those painkillers."

"Those were a social contract."

"These are a financial contract."

"I'm a conscientious objector."

His hand shook as she guided it over to the paper. He scrawled his block letters like a punished schoolboy.

"Done," she said, sealing the envelope. "Now no one can say you don't exist."

"But I don't," he muttered. "Not really."

"You do to me," she replied, softer than she meant to. And that silence afterward—it almost felt like a prayer.

A week later, over another bowl of soup, he said without looking at her, "I can't sleep." He kept slurping his soup as he waited for a response. "It's been a week."

"You should've told me," she said.

"I am."

"Why can't you sleep?" Beatrice got up from the table and started clearing the plates.

"It's loud at night," he replied.

"Your neighbors?"

"My memories."

Beatrice paused at the sink. The refrigerator wheezed.

"I don't remember much," he said after a moment, "but what I don't remember hurts. Is that a thing?"

"It is," she said, turning to him.

"I think I used to be worse," he added, with a smile that didn't fit his scars.

Beatrice wanted to say *you were*. Instead she said, "Pain makes people say strange things." Then, surprising herself, she sat across from him again. "I'd be lying if I said I wasn't curious. Do you *really* not remember anything?"

"No," he said sadly. "Only fragments. A man I think was my father. The name Alice. A goldfish. To be honest, I don't think I had a happy childhood, but I want to remember. I'm tired of knowing I lost something but not knowing what it is."

A tear slipped down his cheek. Beatrice stared at it, fascinated and afraid.

"Can you help me?" he asked.

Before she could answer, the phone rang. When she picked it up, a furious female voice demanded Lester, then when told he wasn't available, unleashed a spray of accusations: *you ruined my life. You owe me money. You said you'd call.*

"Who is it?" asked Lester. He sat motionless, eyes unfocused.

"Wrong number," she said, and hung up.

His gaze sharpened. "Who?"

"It was no one," she lied.

By week six, small changes showed: one clear counter, a trash bag tied, a towel hung. The fighting had become ritual, the bickering almost familiar. One afternoon, Beatrice walked into his apartment and found him sitting on his dilapidated couch with a book held upside down in his lap. She spun it right way up for him.

"Do you do this with everyone?" he asked.

"What?"

"Rescue them."

"I'm not rescuing you," said Beatrice. "You're rescuing yourself. I'm just guiding you."

"You know I didn't ask for this."

"I know."

"It doesn't make me nicer."

"I know," she repeated.

Lester nodded, and for a moment silence felt like a contract. Then he lifted a leather-bound journal. "I found this the other day. Can you read it to me?"

She hesitated. "That's not part of my job."

"Please," he said, eyes pleading. "I have no one. And you said you knew me."

Beatrice hesitated for a second before taking it from him and opening it to a random page. She read a passage.

> That damn Goodie woman... I felt, for a moment, like smashing her head in with a hammer... People like that deserve to remember they can bleed like the rest of us.

She slammed the book shut and pressed it back into his hands. "Can't you read yet?"

"No," he said, sitting up a little straighter. "In fact, I can't. Retinal detachment. The blur is still there. What, you think your chicken soup cures blindness too?."

Her breath caught in her throat. They hadn't told her, and it hadn't been on his report. This was more than just bandages and walkers and pain medication.

"I didn't know," she said. "But I'm sorry. I really can't help you with this." Beatrice walked into the kitchen and began pulling out the pots and pans to make dinner.

He lowered his head. "I'm a stranger. Even to myself."

The words were soft, almost to himself, but they pinned her in place with a saucepan in one hand. The heat of guilt caressed her face, hot and insistent.

She forced cheer into her voice: "Well. I'm here three times a week, and we've got lots of work to do to get you ready to walk again. Let's make this quick and painless, okay? For both of us."

CHAPTER TWENTY ONE

Beatrice Goodie told herself the job was simple: measure, stretch, bandage, leave. But every time she walked into Lester Filch's apartment, the air seemed to lean closer, demanding more of her than she had promised to give. His wounds were healing, yes, but the man himself—stitched, limping, half-blind—pulled at her patience the way a stone pulls at water. She wasn't there to read journals, or to listen to half-remembered dreams, or to decipher the sadness that leaked out when he thought she wasn't looking. She was there to make sure his bones didn't knit crooked and his scars didn't rot and he didn't go without food. Nothing more.

Yet she kept finding herself staying longer. She lingered by the kitchen table while he fumbled with a spoon, offered to slice his bread so he wouldn't drop it, or sat across from him while he strained to read from one of his books. Sometimes she swore she saw the old Lester lurking in the shadows of his face—a sneer ready to surface, a complaint curled at the edge of his lip. But other times, he seemed as raw and bewildered as a child. Those were the times that unsettled her most.

By the sixth week of visits, she had learned the shape of his silences. There was the irritated silence, when she adjusted his walker or insisted he swallow his pills. There was the suspicious silence, when she hovered too near his journal or tidied a corner of the apartment. And then there was the heavy silence, the one that fell after he asked a question about himself that she refused to answer. That silence lingered long after she left, clinging to her shoes like dust.

Still, routines formed. Mondays, Thursdays, Saturdays—three visits a week. Beatrice brought antiseptic, gauze, and a patience that she sometimes had to fake. He supplied sarcasm, complaints, and—on rare occasions—something close to gratitude, though it usually disguised itself as an insult.

One evening, she caught herself laughing with him. Genuinely laughing. It wasn't at anything particularly funny; Lester simply fumbled his way through an exercise, cursed at his own legs, and then, with surprising accuracy, compared himself to "a puppet whose strings were cut by a drunk." The phrasing was so random that Beatrice's laugh slipped out before she could stop it. Lester froze, startled, then gave a crooked grin. The moment passed quickly, but it lodged itself in her chest like a pebble in a shoe.

A week later, when she set down her bag after a long day, Lester surprised her again. "Stay for dinner," he said.

She blinked. "Dinner? I usually do."

Lester gestured vaguely toward the stove. "I mean, *my* dinner. You and me eating together. I've got soup in a can. You can open it without setting the place on fire. Probably."

It wasn't a grand invitation—it wasn't even polite—but something in his voice caught her off guard. It wasn't the demand of the old Lester, nor the sarcasm of the healing Lester. It was tentative, almost awkward. She almost said no. Professional boundaries. Emotional boundaries. Sanity boundaries. But she was tired, and the thought of eating yet another lonely salad in her own apartment suddenly felt unbearable.

"All right," she said softly.

The soup was terrible—lukewarm broth with the texture of brine—but they ate it anyway, sitting opposite one another at the uneven table. He slurped loudly on purpose. She rolled her eyes on purpose. For a moment, the air between them shifted from duty to something else, something she didn't want to name.

When Beatrice left that night, she carried the taste of the soup with her—salty, bland, yet strangely comforting. She also carried the unsettling awareness that she had crossed some invisible line.

The next visit he was waiting at the door when she arrived, walker braced like a weapon. "You're late," he said.

"It's nine-oh-five."

"Exactly. Late."

"You wanted me here so badly?" she teased before she could stop herself.

He stared. Then, to her surprise muttered: "Dinner again?"

This time it wasn't soup. He somehow managed spaghetti—the noodles boiled too long, the sauce watery, but he had made it. For her. She twirled a forkful, chewed carefully, and said, "It's good."

"It's terrible," he countered.

"Then it's so good it's terrible," she said, and for the first time they smiled at the same time.

After that, dinners became a pattern. Once a week at first, then two times, then almost every visit. Sometimes it was soup, sometimes sandwiches, sometimes just coffee and crackers. But it was something—an admission that he wanted her there longer, an admission she no longer resisted.

By week eight, Beatrice Goodie noticed she stopped bringing her watch inside. She no longer glanced at the clock to make sure she wasn't staying only as long as duty required.

Instead, she lingered. She asked him about his dreams. He asked her about her patients. They talked—sometimes haltingly, sometimes bitterly, sometimes with flashes of warmth she pretended not to notice.

One evening, when she rose to leave, Lester surprised her. "You know," he said, his voice low, "you're the only one who knocks on my door because you want to, not because you have to."

She almost corrected him—because technically, she *did* have to. But something in his tone made her swallow the truth.

By the end of two months, dinners were no longer accidents. They had become ritual. She sometimes brought soup or simple casseroles; he sometimes tolerated them. Lester complained less about vegetables, and she complained less about the lingering smell of smoke on his clothes. She found herself watching the clumsy determination of his hands as he fought with the lighter. He found himself listening when she talked about her other patients, though he grumbled the whole way through.

Neither of them called it friendship. Neither of them dared. But something had shifted, undeniable as gravity. Beatrice Goodie had walked into Lester Filch's apartment as his aide. She was walking out, week after week, as something else entirely—and though she didn't want to admit it, some fragile, dangerous part of her was starting to care.

CHAPTER TWENTY TWO

When they spent time together, Lester didn't bring up the journal again. Instead, he asked her questions—about current events he couldn't read in the paper, about past events he couldn't recall. They chatted through his stretches and exercises, and by the time he was finished, it would edge into dinner time.

There was no harm in it, Beatrice told herself, this comradery. It happened after her paid hours, and she felt a little bad for him. Besides—though she would never have admitted it out loud—she almost enjoyed his company. Cranky as he was, Lester had softened. The man she once despised was hard to reconcile with the one she now watched carefully preparing macaroni and cheese with hot dogs, setting the plates on the table as if it were a meal for the Queen of England.

Separating this Lester from the one she first met was difficult at first, but time wears down resolve. Hatred corrodes itself when faced with familiarity, and if she delved deep enough, she had to admit his helplessness had become... strangely attractive. Here was someone safe, someone who seemed willing to give her something in return for her help, even if it was only his attention. She had never received that before.

When he brought out dessert—ice cream sandwiches placed ceremoniously on tiny dishes—she realized something startling. All her life, she was giving herself away but had gotten nothing back. It was noble, she always told herself, to give selflessly and expect nothing in return. But now, as the years pressed in and her service yielded only exhaustion, that nobility began to look less like goodness and more like foolishness.

Her parents had given her horses, lessons, cars, education—but never as gratitude for who she was. They were bribes for conformity, for the life they wanted her to choose. That was why she had left California in the first place.

Yet there sat Lester Filch, dumb, half-blind, scarred—who seemed to want nothing more than her company. Who offered what little he had—macaroni, ice cream sandwiches, conversation—in exchange for her presence. *You can't forget loneliness,* she thought, chewing freezer-burned ice cream that caught on a lump in her throat. *You can't forget it.*

It struck her that she had never eaten a meal more lovingly prepared.

Beatrice watched him lick the sides of his sandwich first, then bite into it like a child savoring a sundae. He seemed amused, even grateful, for the little things in his life—the concrete things he didn't need to remember. Not at all like the old Lester Filch. For the first time, she thought, *here is a man I might trust. At least for now.*

It was a dangerous thought. Especially since the only other man in her life was Arthur Medlar—and he was turning out to be a disappointment.

Their engagement was more her parents' doing than her own choice. Once Mr. and Mrs. Goodie accepted their daughter wasn't going to live the life they wanted, they turned their attention to securing her future with marriage and grandchildren. Beatrice, almost forty, was in danger of becoming what they considered an "insufferable waste of good genes"—a Rembrandt sold for a dollar at a garage sale.

Arthur was, to them, a dream: wealthy, intelligent, entrepreneurial, and handsome—though Beatrice always thought "boyish" and "feminine" were closer to the mark. She agreed to give him a chance more to stem her mother's tears than out of conviction. And there wasn't exactly a line of men banging down her door.

They dated six months before he proposed. She liked him well enough, and her parents were thrilled. For her, the engagement was less about romance and more about rejecting her own lifelong prejudice—that no one was ever good enough. For forty years she measured people, jobs, even opportunities, against an impossible standard. And everyone fell short. She told herself she ran toward something higher, something greater. But maybe she had only been running toward herself.

Arthur was steady, dependable, even kind. And at her age, each tick of her biological clock reminded her that it was too dangerous to reject another chance at love, however imperfect.

Yet by the third month of their engagement, Arthur's attentiveness waned. He blamed work, money, stress, but when she finally admitted, quietly, "Arthur, I'm not happy," he exploded. His tirade startled her—clenched fists, pacing, wild accusations of ingratitude. She stood speechless, stunned that such rage lived beneath his polished exterior. For the first time, she thought of leaving him. But then he returned, contrite and apologetic, coaxing her back like a fisherman loosening the line when the catch struggled. She knew he was manipulating her, and yet she stayed. Because leaving meant facing her mother, Arthur's anger, and—most frightening of all—the possibility of being old and alone. Was it better to be used than to have nothing? She couldn't decide.

"Beatrice."

The name startled her back to the present. She blinked, realizing her ice cream sandwich had melted into brown mush between her fingers. Lester was watching her with a crooked smile.

"You alright?" he asked. "I thought I lost you there."

"I'm sorry," she said quickly, wiping her hands with a napkin. "I just... got lost in thought."

She looked at him—scarred, bitter, softened—and realized with a jolt that the man she once hated didn't seem so bad anymore. Maybe with a bit of help, he could even find his good side. Maybe she could, too. It was needy. It was self-serving. But she no longer cared. There was strength in admitting need, in recognizing the limits of coping alone.

Silently, shamefully, she prayed to the unknown god that Lester's amnesia would not go away. Because if it did, the man before her might vanish—and she already knew which version of Lester Filch she wanted to spend the next three months of therapy with.

CHAPTER TWENTY THREE

On the next visit, after dessert, she gave in.

Lester made hamburgers—a step up, she thought, from macaroni with hot dogs. Dessert was bananas drizzled with Nutella, the chocolate spread ribboned across the fruit as if he tried to plate something gourmet. That small gesture, absurd and earnest, pushed her over the edge.

She began to tell him everything. Work hassles. Arthur's inattention and growing eccentricities. Her parents' demands. All of it spilled out, sacred no longer. Even as she spoke, some stubborn voice inside her denied it was happening—denied that she was opening up to the likes of Lester Filch. But in his current state, Lester *was* a stranger, and perhaps that was why it felt safe.

He simply listened. There were no lectures like Arthur, no interruptions, no speeches on what she ought to do. Just an occasional clarifying question, and then silence that felt—strangely—like space being made just for her. When she finished, Lester shuffled to the sink with his walker and began washing the dishes. The silence that followed was heavier than any sermon, not empty but humming. He whistled softly while he worked. It disconcerted her. She stood, restless, and walked over to him, taking the sponge and gently pushing him aside.

At least, she tried to.

"Hey," he said reproachfully, taking back the sponge, "don't worry about it. I'll do it. You just sit and make yourself comfortable."

"But you've done enough," she said softly. "Anyway, what would my supervisor say if he saw me letting my patient serve *me*? In fact—what would he say if he knew I was having dinner with you?"

"You often have dinners with me."

"You know what I mean. *These* kinds of dinners. Real ones."

Lester paused mid-scrub and looked at her with something close to gratitude. "Well, I think your boss would say you were doing your job better than anyone else could. I think he'd say you weren't just helping fix a man's body."

The silence thickened again. He kept scrubbing—though she noticed he was scrubbing the same clean spot on the pan. To spare him further embarrassment, she retreated to the living room.

The week before, she left right after their special little dinner. This week she lingered, staring at the cracked ceiling, uneasy with how natural it felt to stay. Was it getting too comfortable already? She had heard of this kind of weird relationship happening with clients. A dangerous situation. But she never saw it happening to her. She actually *liked* being here. A line was being crossed. Professional, personal—both. But then again—wasn't this still business? She only came three times a week, and he was now her last patient of the day. Getting to know someone was part of healing. Therapy wasn't always physical, after all. Sometimes it was trust. Sometimes it was company.

And who else did Lester Filch have? No friends. No family. No neighbors who cared for him. Beatrice thought of herself, realizing the list was almost the same: no friends, no family nearby, no real companionship—only Arthur, and lately Arthur had been anything but. As she stayed chatting a little longer into the night, a disquieting realization pressed in. For all her goodness, and all his badness, she and Lester Filch were pretty much the same.

CHAPTER TWENTY FOUR

Beatrice Goodie was fully prepared, in her own mind, to bring Lester Filch back to his rotten, normal senses. Over the next couple of weeks, in between her other patients, over meals, in bed before sleep, even when she was with Arthur, she thought about Lester. The plan was simple. His doctor had told her that events from his past, even recounted blandly, might help restore memory. Beatrice resolved to make that happen. It was the right thing to do. She would help him rebuild his life.

But what kind of life was it?

A singularly miserable one. A life some might say wasn't worth retrieving. Lester Filch had been a sunny-day eclipse, a true killjoy, dragging clouds with him wherever he went. Did he deserve to get that life back? Did the world deserve to receive it again?

She wrestled with the question as she parked in front of the West Lemon apartments and walked into the lobby. His warm smile, his welcome gestures, his strangely childlike eyes told her that yes—there was still a life flickering inside him. Maybe the caustic reply surfaced every now and then, the negative spin on something she did, but it was getting less and less, and compared to who he used to be, he was an angel now. This would be his chance to see where he had been and turn back, to live within those gestures, those eyes, and that fragile smile. Forgetfulness gave him a reprieve.

That was why, after their therapy session that day, she lifted the journal into her hands again. Lester straightened with excitement when she said she would read aloud. They settled in to the living room: Beatrice on the couch, Lester leaning forward in his recliner, waiting.

"Where do you want me to start?" she asked.

"The beginning, I guess."

Her eyes found the first line, and her resolve faltered:

It was Alice who ruined my life.

Beatrice shut the book. "Are you sure you want me to read this? Are you sure your eyesight isn't good enough?"

"Of course. What's wrong?"

"Nothing, it's just… it's awfully personal. You might regret letting me see it. Maybe you should wait—until your memory comes back. Or until your eyes improve. The doctor said they probably would."

Lester shook his head. "He also said recovery can be sped up by remembering the past. And there's a chance it may never get better."

"That's rare," she insisted, grasping at escape.

"Maybe. But please."

He leaned back, resting his head, already listening again. Beatrice felt the weight of it: her mouth, her choice, standing between a man and forty lost years. She opened the journal again.

It was Alice who ruined my life. I know it's stupid. She was just a fish. But I couldn't shake her. My life always had that depressing touch. My mother died soon after I went to live with my adoptive parents. For most of my childhood I didn't know how to handle it. All I knew was what I didn't have.

I always wanted a pet. Something to love. I thought anger management was a waste of time—do-gooder hippies forcing their idea of proper behavior—but I guess remembering what I was like as a kid puts things in perspective. School was miserable. The kids mocked me. My father was a communist, so that didn't help. My looks never helped either. I hated mirrors. I was pale, lanky, poor. I never tried to make friends, and I never saw any reason to. Guess that's why I wanted a pet so badly. At least at home, I wanted something that wouldn't talk back. Animals always loved you.

My father finally agreed. He brought home a goldfish. Alice. I loved her. Spent hours watching her swim. Then she was dead. I dropped her into the garbage disposal by accident. The next day I overheard my father telling a friend why he'd been afraid to let me take care of anything alive. Said I had a tendency to break things. And then I heard it: I killed my mother. She died in some freak accident, something involving the family bird and me letting it loose. It doesn't matter how. It happened. Alice was just another. It confirmed I was cursed.

    Beatrice stopped right before that final paragraph. Her eyes had skimmed ahead, and she couldn't go further. She couldn't read aloud the words about killing his mother.
    The silence stretched out.
    Lester looked up. "Why did you stop?"

"I just remembered—I have to go soon. I need to meet Arthur."

He accepted it easily, though disappointment flickered across his face. "That's fine. We can read more next week."

She rose quickly, pulling on her coat.

"Beatrice?" His voice was gentle but insistent. He leaned forward, and she looked away, suddenly afraid of his eyes.

"Can I tell you something?"

She wanted to refuse, and anxiety pressed hard against her lungs. Still, she whispered, "Sure."

"I like you, Beatrice. You're the most amazing woman I know. You deserve happiness. But I'd be lying if I said I was glad you were promised to another man."

Warmth surged in her face. She swallowed. "I'm... flattered."

"Well, don't be too flattered." He relaxed and gave a short laugh. "You're the *only* woman I know."

When she didn't join him in laughter, his expression shifted. "I'm not a happy man, Beatrice. But when you come to the door, I smile. That's real. You remind me that there's good in the world. You make it worth getting out of bed."

Tears rose in his eyes, spilling down the seams of his scarred face. She forced herself not to join in.

"I'm miserable, and I don't know why. Maybe it's not the accident. Maybe I was always like this. Can someone lose not just their memories but who they were?"

The kettle's shriek saved her. "Oh, right!" he exclaimed. "I put the water on. I just assumed you were going to stay longer."

"I'll stay," she murmured, surprising herself.

Lester smiled faintly, shuffled to the kitchen, and began rattling dishes, moving slowly but carefully, trying to be hospitable and safe.

While he worked, Beatrice idly flipped through the journal. A loose page slipped free. She hesitated, then read,

I can't do this anymore.

I don't go in for that 'goodbye cruel world' stuff. Just do the deed. But I wrote this because I know you care. You were the first friend I had, even if I paid you. In a life of very bad things, you were the only good one.

This whole exercise made me see who I was: a meaningless, useless prick, a man whose best action would be taking himself out of the world. I tried to think of a way to live it up—vacations, cars, hookers—and nothing tempted me. I've got nothing. No life. No desire left. Just the truth: the world won't miss me, and I won't miss it.

But I wanted to thank you for listening. At least that much was real.

When she heard his walker sliding back across the kitchen floor, she folded the note and put it back into the journal. She wiped her eyes and stood.

Lester was smiling, two mugs of tea steaming on the tray attached to the walker. "Tea's ready. I got cookies, too."

"I can't," Beatrice said, too sharply. Then she softened. "Thank you, Lester. But I actually *do* need to go. I'll see you next week."

She pulled on her coat and slipped out without giving him a second look, leaving him in the doorway, staring after her shadow and wondering what went wrong.

CHAPTER TWENTY FIVE

Lester Filch sat in the quiet, the mugs cooling on the table, the cookies untouched. The apartment, always foul with its cabbage-and-smoke perfume, felt fouler now, as though Beatrice had carried the air out with her. He stared at the door until his eyes blurred, then muttered, "Figures." He wasn't sure whether he meant the lukewarm tea, Beatrice's reaction, or himself.

Across town, Beatrice gripped the steering wheel as though it were the only solid thing left in her life. The letter's words clanged in her head, threatening to shatter her composure: THE ONLY GOOD ONE... BEST ACTION... TAKE MYSELF OUT OF THE WORLD. She had spent her whole life propping others up, but this was different. This was a man on the edge, and she wasn't sure if she had the strength—or the right—to pull him back. Plus she remembered what happened to all the suicidal people she had helped before. An image of Lester's splattered body lying on the street next to his apartment complex came to mind.

Beatrice Goodie realized she still held the journal in her hand when she reached for her keys to get in the car. *I'll return it next time*, she thought. *I'll just keep it in the car for now.* But she found it in her hands still when she got to her own apartment. *I'll just put it in the car tomorrow,* she thought again. Instead, at the end of the evening she found it by her bedside. *I'll just take a quick read, and then I'll return it next time I see him.* So she began reading it that night.

There isn't enough time to disclose everything she read, though much was already outlined above. Thanks to some unnamed therapist, Lester Filch wrote down all the major events in his life that conspired to make him a modern-day Ebenezer Scrooge. Where Dickens went wrong, thought Beatrice, was not explaining where Scrooge had come from. How does a man become a miser? In fiction, you can make up anything. In real life, people are sculpted into their present selves by fate and by choice. Beatrice didn't overlook this as she hungrily consumed Lester's life. To her, it read like a novel. He was no good writer—his tone was blunt, bitter, often absurd—but she couldn't put it down.

Beatrice found herself wishing she had kept a diary, that she had written down something about herself other than bland facts and philosophies. When she thought back on her own years, all she saw was a blur of goodness, of adherence to a standard she never really examined. She lived as if in a race against an invisible opponent called SAINTLINESS, never stopping to ask if she could even win.

Where did that drive come from? Her family wasn't religious. She had never set foot in a church. After all, if you needed religion to be good, then you weren't really good to begin with. And she hardly remembered anything before the sixth grade. In her own way, she was as much an amnesiac as Lester— just without a journal to guide her back.

What shocked her most was how easily she overcame the guilt of taking his journal and reading it. She told herself Lester had given her permission. Maybe his being in the room was a condition, but that was never actually specified. He had trusted her with a piece of himself, and surely he wouldn't mind if she carried that trust a little further. But her conscience raged. She knew—deep down—that she was lying to herself.

In her small, humble bedroom, she made a decision of epic proportions. The suicide note that fell out—the one exposing Lester's rock bottom—guaranteed he would never hear about his past again. Presenting it to him, after he had clawed his way free from all that, would be very bad. It would be cruel, like someone surviving cancer only to be run down by a bus the day you walked out cured.

She would do him a favor. She would give him back only the man he was becoming: the man who invited her in three days a week.

In her heart, Beatrice knew this much power broke some unspoken rule. WITH GREAT POWER COMES GREAT RESPONSIBILITY, the saying repeated itself in her mind. She had more power over Lester Filch than anyone ever had. But she knew she could wield it. She would lift him out of the pit and set him down on solid rock. The sheer magnitude of the task made her dizzy. She ran to the kitchen, gulped down a glass of water, trying to drown the doubt clawing at her insides. Who would have thought she would ever hold such a chance—to make a man better?

Beatrice had until next Tuesday. But before she began to write her own version, she wanted to know the real man she was destroying, like staring into a man's eyes before pulling the trigger. She needed to know him, if she was going to try to duplicate him, with a few slight improvements. Everything was laid bare: the abandonment by his mother, the death of his adoptive mother, the misery at school, the death of all his pets, his father's death at his own hands, his growing hatred for a world that never relented its thrashing.

A few times, when Lester stopped writing like a historian and allowed emotion to bleed onto the page, the bitterness dripped heavy as tar. Beatrice cried as she read, wiping her tears furiously, refusing to admit such sympathy for a man she was about to murder—because that's what this was, a kind of murder.

It took her just two nights to finish. He kept an entry a day for more than a year of psychotherapy. She felt grateful he had never followed through on his darker impulses; he mentioned once, almost casually, deciding not to throw himself off a bridge. She wondered if, ironically, his accident had saved him by erasing the despair that nearly undid him.

When she closed the journal for the last time, her conscience wrestled her to the ground. The decision was clear. She sat in her living room, reclined in her favorite rocker by the fireplace, which was lit for the occasion. It was late at night, almost one in the morning. Shadows danced across her walls. She shivered in the glow, the smell of smoke and wood filling the room, and looked around the room sullenly. She had been reading by firelight, but now the flames had dimmed to almost nothing.

The lights were out, and even the moon refused to contribute a glow from outside. The fire's remnant crisscrossed the walls, and shadows fought one another for their place on it. Solitude sat with her. Beatrice wished it would go away, that its presence would be replaced by someone else, someone to share the warmth of the fire with rather than having to absorb it all alone. She shivered again and closed her eyes.

It wasn't Arthur who came to mind—it was Lester, a man she never wanted to see again now vying for a position in her quiet, empty home. She wanted to hear him in the kitchen, humming as he fixed dinner or made her tea, wanted to see his body, broken as it was, lying comfortably on her couch, sharing his ideas with her or just listening to her read. He was in his forties (though he looked like he was in his fifties), but in her eyes he got younger every time she saw him. She remembered the gelatinous beer belly that hung over his belt as he would yell at her down the hallway. Now that belly was gone. The flesh around his belly had thinned, and his muscles were more pronounced.

Suddenly Lester Filch sat on her couch shirtless, bathed in the fire's amber glow. Every shadow accentuated the muscles of his stomach, the ruddy, olive complexion, the chiseled face which was, while not stunning in its beauty, somehow just right. She felt herself growing warm and shifted in her chair. It wasn't the fire.

Beatrice closed her eyes again, willing the man's mirage to disappear. This wasn't good. She can't be thinking this way about a patient, especially Lester Filch, the worst man she had ever met.

But was he really that bad?

Her mind returned to the journal. If she destroyed it, so much for accepting him for who he was. But maybe that was the gift. Maybe she was meant to erase the burden, to let him be born again. And so, after a long breath, she tossed the journal into the fire.

The leather binding curled first, shrivelling like skin. The pages crackled, the ink blackening into unreadable scars. The glue in the spine gave a sharp pop like bones breaking. She watched Lester's world disappear as his words did, each confession, each bitterness, rising up through the chimney to be forgotten forever.

Beatrice stood up and watched until the last ember glowed red, until the book was nothing but ash. "There," she whispered to the Lester in the room, "Now you can start over again."

But she wasn't sure if she was really talking to him—or to herself.

PART THREE

CHAPTER TWENTY SIX

The several writing awards that Beatrice Goodie won in college were still tucked away inside her scrapbook. She kept those, along with the pieces they represented, because she loved writing more than any other hobby. It had been a pastime that let her escape the busyness of school. While she found writing fiction frivolous and writing for money selfish, she enjoyed writing for herself. It brought her joy to express ideas simply because she loved doing it. She wrote about her social work, her ideas on world peace, on social justice—and the fact that she had no audience never bothered her. She had herself, and for a long time she thought that was enough.

In college she wrestled with the idea of using her writing for good. Not fiction, of course; there was enough real-life drama that needed addressing. Journalism seemed a possible road. She admired Barbara Walters and sometimes imagined herself writing for 60 MINUTES, though she could never stomach the supposed neutrality of journalism. All she wanted was to tell people exactly what to think and what they should be doing with their lives. If only everyone could be good, then surely the world itself would be good, too.

But Beatrice also needed to be different. The idea of publicizing problems for a world too apathetic to act seemed hollow. Her hands needed to get dirty, so she chose against journalism. Her writing stayed private, while her career followed first the social work and then the medical care work. Occasionally, she would write a journal entry with her thoughts on the day's news stories. A lot of pages were taken up by the Clinton and Lewinsky scandal, for example. That was no way to run a country. And certainly no way to use a cigar.

All of this changed when Lester Filch's journal went up in smoke. Suddenly, writing became urgent again. This time, it wasn't for herself. It *was* her job.

Beatrice's plan was simple. First, she would buy a journal that looked exactly like the one she burned. Thankfully, it had been a common, generic sort with not a lot of flourish. Very easy to find. The one she picked out wasn't precisely the same—the gold-foiled word JOURNAL was in a slightly different font—but Beatrice doubted Lester would notice. He was not the type of man who cared about fonts.

Second, she would use all her skill—shaped by who Lester was in the past, who he was now, and who she wanted him to become—to create a new story for him. She would rewrite his childhood in gentler tones, add in memories he never had, maybe even invent small triumphs, so that when he listened, he would begin to believe in himself.

Finally, she would read it to him, piece by piece, as if he were remembering his own words. If the good things she invented had truly happened—if he had been loved as a child, if he had been talented at something other than paper clip manufacturing, if he had been lucky in love—then he might have become a different man. And if he *believed* those things were true, perhaps he could still become a different man. If he acted different, he might begin to feel different.

Had Beatrice been a psychology major, she might have framed the whole experiment as a clinical study. But she wasn't. This was not science; this was art.

On that Saturday she cancelled a date with Arthur, claiming she was sick with the flu and making the congested voice sound as authentic as she could over the phone. Another lie. It paled beside the deceit she was planning for Lester Filch, but it was still a lie. Two in one week. *For a good cause*, she told herself.

She opened the new journal. There was nothing she could do about the first two entries—she had already read those aloud to him. That's why she tore those pages from the old book before burning it. She copied them verbatim into the replacement. There was no chance Lester would forget those first words she had read to him; he clung to them like a lifeline. In fact, their bitterness might even help with all of it. They set the tone, gave the story a trajectory. A life of zero problems would be unbelievable. Even goodness needs a shadow or two to be believable.

And so Beatrice bent her head to the page and began scribbling down the third entry of Lester Filch's new life—*her* Lester Filch, the one she would write into being.

CHAPTER TWENTY SEVEN

For Lester Filch the week dragged on from the moment Beatrice left him. It was an enormous grey beast trudging through the snow, day after day, footstep after footstep. By Sunday the beast had collapsed in exhaustion, only to be replaced by something worse: the anticipation of Tuesday, and her return.

She had become, to Lester, more powerful than the drugs he swallowed for the torment in his legs. The ache travelled up from his knees to his hips and back down to his ankles every morning, but her presence was more effective at calming that storm than any pill. When she walked through his door, headaches eased, his spine straightened, and though his sight remained blurred most of the time, on those days it seemed suddenly, miraculously, clear.

She was the physical embodiment of health.

Lester found himself exaggerating his weaknesses when she was around. If he limped more heavily or winced more dramatically, Beatrice would linger longer, her hands massaging him through the pain. Whatever care he needed, she gave in measured doses, neat and meticulous. But the moments he enjoyed most were when she stopped being his therapist and simply sat with him as a friend—the hours spent eating and talking. At first he wanted her voice to remind him of his forgotten life, but soon he just wanted her. Simply being in her company was enough.

Lester was falling in love. He knew it.

The strange thing was that he couldn't remember ever feeling this way before—not for a woman, and not for a man either. Given his erased past, there was a fifty-percent chance he once loved a man. *Could you forget the gay away?* he thought, amused. But it hardly mattered. In the here and now, he loved Beatrice Goodie.

Of course, he didn't remember the rules of courtship. What was he supposed to do with Beatrice on a date? Had he ever asked anyone out before? If so, how had he managed it? He couldn't remember what words might earn a *yes*. Flowers, he thought vaguely, were always a good idea. Women liked flowers—not the petals themselves, but the thought behind them: someone taking the time to choose, to buy, to hand them over. Perhaps gifts, too. Something nice, something that proved he was thinking of her.

Food was where he could start. At first, the meals he offered her were purely practical: boxed macaroni and cheese, microwave pizza, whatever he could muster. To his surprise, she sat down and ate them gladly. He told himself it was hospitality, nothing more. But soon it wasn't about practicality. It was about care. He wanted to show her, even in his clumsy, ordinary way, how much she meant to him.

The boxed dinners gave way to meatloaf, to roast chicken, to a disastrous attempt at homemade pizza. Each time her smile made the effort worth it. And yet he always feared it wasn't enough. He knew she had given up wealth for this life of service—horses, estates, all the gourmet cuisine she could ever want. What were his attempts compared to all that? Drops in the bucket. But he was determined to keep at it, afraid that if he didn't act soon, her engagement would turn into marriage, and then it would be too late.

Engaged wasn't married. But married was married. And Lester Filch had never feared finality more.

CHAPTER TWENTY EIGHT

There is no life as blessed as mine.

Sometimes, when I think about what I went through—those two days of doubt and anger—I see how small it really was. A grain of sand on the shores of the Atlantic. The sea is what matters: that vast, relentless power that pounds rock into nothing. My suffering was that grain. And now it's gone. Now I swim in open water.

"Wait a minute," Lester interrupted, straightening in his recliner, his chin sticking out with the faintest whiff of defiance. "That *cannot* be my writing."

Beatrice's stomach vaulted into her chest. Her fingers tightened on the page, and for one terrified moment she was certain he had seen through her entire deception—the burning, the rewriting, the falsification. But he leaned forward eagerly, not accusingly, and she realized his protest was half-amusement, half-wonder.

Her voice quavered, but she forced it steady. "What do you mean?" She gave a little laugh, deliberately thin and brittle. "You wouldn't remember it anyway, even if it wasn't yours."

Lester chuckled. "You're right. But still—look at that sentence. 'Swim in open water.' That's... poetic. I spent weeks in that hospital bed trying to guess what kind of a man I was. Maybe I was a janitor, or a mechanic, or some sad sack in an office cubicle at a paper clip manufacturer. But this—this sounds like something written by someone with some talent. Someone important. Someone whose life *meant* something."

Beatrice swallowed. A hot flush crept up her neck.

"Maybe I was a writer," he mused excitedly, his voice taking on a tone both dreamy and absurdly proud. "A great novelist! Some genius who churned out bestsellers. You haven't read anything in the papers about a missing author, have you? Some literary titan who disappeared, leaving a nation bereft of his great literature?" He grinned, half mocking himself, half secretly hoping.

Beatrice set the journal face-down on the coffee table, fingers trembling as she released it. "No, Lester. No famous missing authors."

He chuckled again, but something lingered in his eyes— a wistful brightness. She hated how it made her chest ache.

"Lester," she said suddenly, before she could stop herself. "Do you think I'm a good person?"

The question hung in the room like smoke. She regretted it the instant it left her lips. He blinked at her as though she had just asked whether the earth was flat.

"Are you kidding?" he burst out. "You're the most wonderful woman I've ever met! And I know that's not saying much," he added sheepishly, his finger tapping at his chin in thought, "but hey—it's the truth."

Relief bubbled up and out of her like champagne. His words mattered. Maybe she *was* a good person. She lifted the journal again, preparing to read on, but when she glanced up she caught him staring at her—not in his usual squint, not with his usual suspicion, but with a simple, steady regard that made her throat go dry.

"Why would you ever question that?" he asked quietly. "How could you doubt you're a good person?"

Beatrice's mouth opened, then closed again. She fiddled with the corner of the page, buying herself a moment. "Well, I don't go around thinking about how good I am, because—"

"That wouldn't be good," Lester interjected, smirking.

She smiled despite herself. "Yes. Because that wouldn't be good. It's just... everything always came easy for me. My parents adored me. They gave me everything—horses, cars, an education. I was smart in school, pretty, popular. You name it, that was me."

Lester gave an exaggerated sigh. "Just like my life."

She shot him a look, but his sarcasm was oddly comforting. "Right," she said softly, "just like your life. But that's the point, right? Am I good by nature? Or am I only good because everything around me was good?"

He leaned back, his scarred face peaceful but thoughtful. "Or maybe everything around you was good because *you* were. Ever think of that? Maybe you've been touching things all your life and turning them gold without noticing. Isn't life what you make of it? I mean, look at me! I'm living a new life now. It'll be what I make of it, whether the past was good or bad."

The words hung between them, startling her. Lester Filch, philosopher. Lester Filch, the man she had once called rancid cabbage, speaking with the wisdom of a monk. It made her uneasy. She lowered her eyes and stared at the pages in front of her.

He studied her a moment longer, then asked very carefully, "And what about this Arthur guy? Is *he* good?"

Beatrice looked up, startled by the question's sharpness. "Arthur? Is he good?" She had to stop and think about an honest answer, despite the temptation to lie again. "You know, I don't really know anymore. A few weeks ago, I would have said yes without hesitation, but now I'm not so sure."

She caught herself, flushing. "Listen to me. You don't want to hear about Arthur."

"I don't mind," he said. "I asked."

"You're sweet to care." The words slipped out before she could censor them. She fiddled with the journal again, turning it over in her hands. "Everyone thinks Arthur's good. My parents adore him—they've only met him once, but still. They think anyone who's handsome, wealthy, and not in jail is good. Coworkers think he's perfect. Even his family plays along with this arrangement. But the truth?"

Beatrice drew in a breath. "He's *too* good. Can you believe that? Too good. He always says the right thing. If he buys me flowers, it's always the biggest, most expensive bouquet. Sometimes I wish he'd just pick me one dandelion. Queen Anne's lace. Something ordinary. When he cooks for me—which is rare—it's never just food. It's a performance. And when he comes to my place, I try to make it simple. Just dinner. Sometimes I stay in pajamas. He thinks it's to turn him on. They're *flannel*! Who in the world was ever seduced by flannel?

Beatrice laughed, and he laughed with her, and in that moment she saw something in his smile—unguarded, crooked, a little shy—that pierced her. It was a smile not crafted to impress, not manufactured for show. It was just Lester. And for the first time, she thought: maybe that's all she wanted.

Driving home that night, she replayed the smile in her mind. If there were more Lester Filch smiles in the world, it would be a happier place. Not perfect happiness—never that—but honest happiness. She thought of her mother's voice when she was a girl: "When life gives you lemons, make lemonade." It had been said once, offhand, when Beatrice woke up with a zit on her chin. She'd never forgotten it. But the truth was, she'd been given peaches, plums, grapes—all her life. Her lemons had been rare, almost exotic.

Lester Filch, however, had been her first true lemon: sour, puckering, and unforgiving. And instead of making lemonade, she'd spit him back at the world. Yet now—watching him change, watching herself change in response—she realized something unsettling: he was no longer just her lemon. He was her mirror. Because what if, faced with the same battering as he had endured, she would have become the same bitter, twisted person? What if her goodness was not innate but circumstantial? What if she had been coasting all these years on luck disguised as virtue?

Her knuckles whitened on the steering wheel. She had always wanted to be good, but now, as she turned onto her street, she wondered whether goodness had ever truly belonged to her at all. She wondered if goodness that was not earned could even be goodness at all.

And worse—what else would Lester bring out of her, in time? What if instead of her making him good, he began to make her *bad*, a kind of reverse osmosis. The thought terrified her. She had been assuming her effect on him was greater than his effect on her, but wasn't she changing also? Wasn't she losing the goodness she thought she had, all because of Lester Filch?

As she parked in front of her apartment and sat in the cooling silence of the car, one thought crystallized, sharp as glass: Lester Filch wasn't just testing her goodness. He was exposing it, so she and the whole world could see the fraud she truly was. And sooner or later, she would have to decide whether she wanted the truth—or the lie she had been living her whole life.

CHAPTER TWENTY NINE

Beatrice Goodie arranged her desk like a battlefield. The blank journal sat in the center, its gold-foil title gleaming in the lamplight like a standard before the charge. To the left: pens and markers, sharpened pencils, a neat row of sticky notes. To the right: her teacup, refilled so many times it was now mostly water with a ghost of leaves. Behind it: a small plate with the exhausted crumbs of what had once been an oatmeal cookie.

This was her war room.

She hadn't written anything of significance in years, not since college. Her old writing trophies and ribbons still lived in a scrapbook somewhere, buried under piles of "grown-up" papers: tax returns, insurance claims, stale Christmas cards. Now, staring at the crisp pages of the new journal, she realized with a nervous thrill that she was about to use that skill again—not to entertain, not to escape, but to forge a man's destiny.

The plan was simple in design, catastrophic in implication: create a new past for Lester Filch. She had already burned the original journal, each bitter, self-loathing page curling into ash in her fireplace. That book had been a trapdoor into despair. This one would be a ladder, rung by rung, leading him into the sunlight. At least, that's how she rationalized it.

She began, as she knew she must, with the two entries she already read to him. Alice the goldfish. The early gloom. The sense of being cursed. She had copied them word for word, grimacing at how sharp they sounded in her own neat hand. Then she had written a little bit of the third entry, which she hardly got to read to him the other day. Now she would soldier on, redirecting the river of pain from his beginning towards more hopeful shores.

Her pen hovered over the next blank line. She felt the giddy fear of a schoolgirl about to cheat on an exam, except the stakes were infinitely higher. This wasn't about a grade. This was about a destiny.

> Today I remembered Alice again. But this time I remembered how she would leap toward the surface when I sprinkled her food. She wanted to live so badly she almost jumped out of her bowl once, right into Dad's hands. He caught her and laughed. For a moment I thought maybe I wasn't cursed after all.

Beatrice set her pen down and exhaled. There. The truth had been bent. Not broken, exactly, but curved toward goodness like a branch trained along a trellis.

She began to spin.

In this new life, Lester Filch's childhood was not a graveyard of dead pets but a pastoral menagerie. Alice died, sure; she couldn't change that. But before she did, she had seven children, which provided Lester with years of fishy friendship. By the time Beatrice was done with the first few entries, they had outlasted most cats and dogs in the neighborhood.

"Oh, for heaven's sake," Beatrice muttered, laughing despite herself. "I've turned him into the patriarch of a goldfish dynasty."

The absurdity made her giggle, but she pressed on. After all, she needed this childhood to feel not just less bleak, but positively inspiring. So she gave him other pets too—ones that didn't die tragically but lived long, useful lives. A parakeet that learned to whistle Beethoven. A scruffy mutt who adored him and defended him from the bullies (there had to be some negatives hanging around him in his childhood). A cat who purred loyally at his feet while he did his homework.

She wrote with relish, adding detail after detail:

> The dog followed me home. I remember I named him Samson because he was so strong. When the bullies at school pushed me around, Samson would come after them. He bit one of them in the leg, and nobody said anything about it. Even the kid's parents agreed it had been the right thing to do. Dad said every boy should have someone who barks for him like that.

Her pen raced. By the time she looked up, she realized she had accidentally written the opening scenes of a Disney prequel. Lester Filch, the boy who spoke to animals. She set the pen down again, pressed her palms to her face, and groaned. "This is ridiculous."

But she kept going anyway.

Because she knew it had to be believable, she salted the entries with modest humiliations. A cafeteria tray dropped to the laughter of classmates. A spelling bee fumbled. A ribbon lost to a smug rival. She remembered her psychology courses—however minimal they had been—and knew that too much happiness would read as fake. A completely charmed childhood would never fly. But pepper in the occasional bruise, and suddenly the narrative gained texture.

So she wrote:

> I remember the day I dropped my lunch tray. The beans slid across the floor like guts, and the whole room howled as if I'd done it for their amusement. When I dragged myself home, Aunt Maybelle told me it was better to be laughed at than ignored. Easy for her to say. She wasn't the one covered in beans. She gave me two cookies to make it better. They did, for a moment — better than the beans would have — but it didn't erase the sound of their laughter. Nothing ever does.

Soon Beatrice's living room clock read midnight. She had written nearly twenty pages of alternative Lester-history. She leaned back in her chair, flexing her cramped fingers, and reread what she created. It was absurd. It was glorious. It was fiction wearing the mask of fact, and it might just save a man's soul.

She felt a dizzy swell of pride. She was doing it—she was rewriting him. She was, in a very literal sense, playing God.

And God, she realized, had a wicked sense of humor.

For example, in this revised life, she gave him a neighbor boy named Tom who shared comic books with him. In real life, Lester probably stole comic books from neighbor kids and then ripped them up for good measure. But here, Tom was a best friend. Tom invited him to birthday parties, gave him rides on his bike, even defended him once against a playground bully.

> There was a day when Tom said he liked my drawing — a rocket ship I'd scribbled in the corner of a math worksheet. He told me I should be an artist. I laughed at him, called him crazy, because what else was I supposed

to say? But the truth is, it mattered that he thought so. Later we hid under the porch and read comics until the dark swallowed the words. Mom didn't yell at me when I came in late for supper that evening. I really miss that kid.

"There you go, Lester," she muttered aloud, "I've given you a cheerleader. Don't blow it."

She added more about that encouraging aunt, too. Aunt Maybelle, who slipped him extra cookies and told him he had "the soul of a thinker." Aunt Maybelle never existed, but Beatrice found herself liking her anyway. *Maybe I need an Aunt Maybelle*, she thought, shaking her head as she wrote another entry about her fictional wisdom.

> Aunt Maybelle used to say people were either weeds or flowers. Weeds could claw their way up through cracks in the pavement, stubborn and unwanted, while flowers needed tending or they'd wither. She told me I was a flower, and I guess I have been. Things haven't been easy, but I got watered when I needed to be. I could have been a weed — lots of people are. Pushing through the concrete of life. But thankfully, I'm a flower.

Hours slid past. The journal filled. And the more she wrote, the more she began to realize she wasn't just giving Lester a new past—she was creating an entire genre, SELF-HELP MASQUERADING. *Dear God, what am I doing?* she thought.

But it was FUN.

For the first time in months—maybe years—writing didn't feel like a chore, or like she was just keeping notes for her own moral self-flagellation, or to castigate Milli Vanilli for having tricked a generation. This was creative! This was alive! By the end of the weekend, she had written more than fifty pages. She found herself sneaking in sessions whenever she could—before work, after dinner, late at night with her tea gone cold beside her. It was addicting, all of this re-creation.

And she laughed often, because the contrast between the real Lester and the journal-Lester was so wide it could swallow West Lemon whole, peel and all.

Real Lester: cursed, bitter, a cabbage-scented troll who once told her muffins made him sick. Journal Lester: a boy who wrote poetry about lightning storms and dreamed of helping others one day.

Real Lester: smoked like a chimney and swore like a sailor. Journal Lester: nursed sick sparrows and thanked his father for teaching him honesty.

Beatrice really got a kick out of giving him his first crush: Alice Borden. Journal-Lester remembered the day he first laid eyes on her with fondness.

> There was a day I sat behind Alice Borden in class. She dropped her pencil, and I picked it up. She smiled, said thank you. That was it. Nothing more. But for the rest of the day I walked around like it meant something, like I'd been seen. Funny how a look or a word could make me feel taller. I told Samson later, and he barked. Maybe he understood, or maybe he just wanted out of his leash. But that bark gave me the courage to ask her out to Charlie's Pub, and oh, what a night that was.

Next, she made him a secret hero.

> I once saw a boy fall into the creek at the end of the street. Nobody else noticed, just me. I waded in, dragged him out by the collar while he sputtered and bawled. He lived. That was the end of it. I never told anyone. I believed in

quiet good deeds. It's what I learned in Sunday school. Better to keep it to myself. Let him breathe, and I could disappear into the woods like a guardian angel.

She put down her pen, grinning. "You, Lester?" she said aloud. "A guardian angel? Well, I used to think you were a demon."

The lies made her feel strangely light, as if she discovered some new muscle she hadn't stretched in years.

Late at night, lying in bed with the journal at her side, doubt whispered in her ear. She thought of the word FORGERY. She thought of the flames curling up around the real journal. She thought of the suicide note she had hidden away. She rolled over, clutched her pillow, and told herself the same thing every time: *this is for the greater good.* Yet she knew she was balancing on the thinnest of wires, high above a pit she didn't dare look down into. It was the pit of her own darkening soul.

She imagined herself presenting the journal to Lester, opening it to a page she had written, reading aloud some noble sentiment: I ONCE THOUGHT THE WORLD CRUEL, BUT THEN I REALIZED KINDNESS IS A CHOICE. She imagined his scarred face lighting up with recognition. She imagined him thanking her. And then she imagined him finding out the truth about what she did, and her stomach dropped through her mattress and then the floor beneath.

"It doesn't matter," she whispered vehemently into the dark, "this is for the greater good. This is what you need. Lester Filch, you're about to be born again."

CHAPTER THIRTY

The next time she visited Lester was a Tuesday. She brought dinner in a foil pan like a peace offering—a roasted chicken she over-seasoned on purpose so the smell would announce itself before she had to. The scent hit him first: thyme, lemon, something that might have been exuberance. Lester shuffled to the door in his socks. He was still using the walker, but she could tell it would be gone soon. Given all that had happened to him, it was a miracle he was walking again at all. Lester squinted past the cheerful steam.

"Smells like a good plan," he said.

"It's a chicken," she replied, stepping past him and pretending it was just another visit as usual. "And a salad, if we decide to be virtuous."

"Let's not be reckless." He left the chain dangling and led her toward the kitchen. "I'll get some plates."

His apartment had been trying to become a home for weeks now and kept failing in charming, incremental ways. A dish rack existed now, and she noticed that he must have stacked them neatly over the weekend. It was an improvement. A towel hung on its bar instead of performing its former duties as a carpet overlay. Someone had removed the flickering bulb over the stove and replaced it with a light that did not appear to have opinions about its own mortality. It was like watching a sullen teenager put on a tie.

Beatrice slid the foil pan onto the stove and took off her coat. Beneath it, the new journal lay flat in her tote bag, heavy as a secret. She would place it somewhere discreet when he wasn't looking, as if she had never taken it. *Tonight*, she thought. *Read some more tonight.* She had to do it.

Lester set plates and forks on the table with ceremony and poured water into mismatched mugs. He hesitated at the drawer with the knives. When she turned to see why he had grown silent, she saw him looking closely at a butter knife.

"Is everything okay?" she said nervously.

Lester hesitated a moment longer, and then began collecting a few other things for the table.

"Will we be… visiting with my former self?" he asked, too lightly, as he finished making the table presentable.

She swallowed. "If you like."

"I like," he said. "I'm fond of the me I'm getting to know."

They ate dinner and talked about the news, and some developments in his work situation. Lester had gotten four months leave from his job, and was using vacation time after that. He would be needing to return to work soon. Beatrice reassured him that his recovery was going well, though she was no doctor. She had no doubt he would be able to go back to work given another month. He expressed gratitude for the great insurance he had at Bor Dun and the flexibility they were giving him.

The dinner Beatrice had prepared was passable. The chicken had the dignity of a bird that had done its best in life and in death. Lester carved with surprising finesse, one hand steadying the bone, the other finding the seams like a surgeon. He made appreciative noises as he chewed, the little hums of a man who had relearned hunger and pleasure at roughly the same time.

"Not dry," he concluded.

"I accept your highest compliment." Beatrice put a piece of dark meat on his plate. "More."

They ate until the pan was full of bones, and then she cleaned the table and carried their plates to the sink. When she was done washing them, she began to wipe down the countertops, as if housework might anchor what she was about to unmoor. Lester watched her quietly, drinking a can of seltzer. He was good at watching now. Sight was a mushy thing for him— edges bleeding into edges—but attention had sharpened to compensate. He could read her nervousness by the way she set the forks down too gently, a cautious choreography, like someone returning a sleeping infant to a crib.

She couldn't avoid it forever. Eventually, she shut the faucet off, wiped her hands on her backside, and turned around with a sigh.

"Ready?" she asked.

"Ready."

They walked into the living room and sat down. The journal appeared in her lap as if it had risen there of its own free will. Beatrice opened to a ribbon she wedged at the top: entries three and four, both scrubbed of their former poisons and polished into something like hope. Lester put his head back and closed his eyes, and she began.

> There is a way some people talk about luck that makes it sound like a trick of cards. I didn't have luck. But I had the kind of blessings you don't notice until later. I had a father who showed up to every school thing even if he had to stand in back with his arms crossed and pretend it was stupid. I had a teacher who slid me a twenty dollar

bill across her desk and said, 'for the book fair,' because she saw I didn't bring money and most likely couldn't. I had Alice's kids, little fish who didn't know about any of that, but just swam around contentedly for all those years, reminding me that being blessed sometimes meant just being content to swim around in circles.

If you'd asked me at ten if I was blessed, I would have said no. But this is a journal. Here I can admit things without having to listen to anyone cheer. Yes, I was blessed. I just didn't know how to hold it yet.

She stopped. Lester was motionless, his face turned slightly away, the way he angled it when he wanted to hide the ruined side, though she was long past pretending not to see it.
　"Well?" she asked, realizing it sounded a lot like someone asking for a critical review.
　"That teacher," he said slowly. "What was the name again?"
　She had not given a name. "You didn't write it down."
　"Hm," he murmured, leaning back and tapping the recliner's arm. "Feels... true-ish. I don't have it, but I can almost remember her. Like a name on the tip of the tongue that refuses to jump."
　"Let's try another entry, ok? Maybe you'll remember that a bit better." Beatrice turned the page. "Next one's about one of Alice's babies, I think. One of the little goldfish.
　"Man, I was really into animals, huh?"

They said it was a dumb project. "You can't measure love," My teacher laughed. But I brought Alice's little baby fish, Alice 2, in her bowl anyway, along with a stopwatch. I timed the seconds it took for her to come to the side when I stood over her and then when anyone else did. Average time for me: 1.3 seconds. For others: 4.9 seconds. "Correlation," said the teacher, and wrote it on the board like a spell. I said it meant Alice 2 loved me best and that fish remember. He said that wasn't science. I said it was an observation. We compromised: I got a B and he got to keep being right in public.

Lester laughed aloud, the sound startling in the small room. "I like that kid," he said. "He sounds like he'd be good company on a bad day."

"You were funny," she said, unable to keep a certain pride out of her voice.

"Was." He rolled the word around like a pebble in his mouth. "Am?"

"Still are." Beatrice glanced down before the softness could make her reckless. "Want another one?"

"As long as there's dessert," he said, and she pushed a plate of cookies across the coffee table like an answer. She had prepared four more entries for the night—an abundance, a hedge against whichever one didn't take. Best not to do more and save some for future visits.

Beatrice thumbed to the one that made her heart kick because it was the most incredible in her mind, and therefore the most necessary. *The Day of the Tree.* A simple act with deep implications for a life well-lived and conscious of others.

"This one is about the day with the tree," she stated.

He tensed imperceptibly and then forced a smile. "Not *the* day, I hope. A different tree?"

"Oh, yes," she promised. "A good tree."

The storm had done its usual temper tantrum and left branches all over the sidewalk. People detoured into the street, shaking their heads, hoping the city would send a truck, as if trucks were saints.

A kid on a bike stopped and balanced with one foot down, staring at the branch like it had insulted him. He tried to lift it and it laughed, because wood laughs when you're small. I went out and put my hands on the other end. Together we dragged it to the grass. The bike kid grinned, the kind you can't not answer. "We saved like three seconds for everybody," he said to me. "And *that's* community service."

We high-fived. It was unscientific and entirely correct.

Lester exhaled through his nose, a sound that was either relief or surrender. "I want to remember that," he said. "Such a simple thing."

"You can," she said, and felt the tiny shiver of the lie pass through her hand and into the journal.

He plucked another cookie from the plate and studied it as if it might decide to be something else. "Do I… write anything else about school?" he asked around the crumbs. "I can't remember any of those things that were in there, none of those teachers."

"Sure, I think there's one in here. Let me see." She flipped ahead as if consulting a map. "Here's one. About sports, I think.'"

"Hit me," he said.

I am not a runner. I am a man-shaped question mark with knees that complain. But coach made me do the mile because he said character is what grows in the dirt between four laps. I miscounted and ran five laps.

Coach squinted at the stopwatch and then at me. "You didn't have to do that," he said. "Didn't I?" I said. My lungs were hot coins. My legs had written wills. But for the length of one extra lap, the world was simple: left foot, right foot, breathe, swear, repeat. When I finished I lay on the grass and laughed until my chest hurt less than my pride. The sky forgave me for everything all at once. I had done it, went above and beyond. It's what I was meant to do. Life is what you make of it, and I just made it a five-lap-run.

Beatrice felt the heat rise along her neck as she read that last line, because the room heard it too. She couldn't have made it sound more fake if she tried. Lester sat still, breathing lightly, and the refrigerator chose that moment to rattle and then fall quiet, the apartment's version of a cough.

He lifted his chin. "That sounds like something I'd do," he said, tone unreadable. "I mean, I run five laps around the coffee table with a walker."

"Heroically," she said, and the room let them be light for a beat.

"It also sounds like something you'd say," he added.

Beatrice closed the book as if dismissing a spell. "Tea?" she asked too brightly.

They brewed in silence. She moved around his small kitchen with the surety of repetition: kettle, two mugs, the bagged tea she insisted on keeping in his cabinet like a small, controllable ritual. He stayed in the living room chair and watched the steam rising up beside her in the kitchen.

"So." He cleared his throat when she set the mugs down. "How much is left?"

"In the journal?"

"In me."

She turned around to face him. "A lot," she said. "More than you think. More than I know."

He nodded as if they had agreed on a price. "Read another," he said softly.

When the tea was poured, and Beatrice was back on the couch, Lester was nodding off. She was tempted to leave and let him get some rest. Maybe then she could leave with the journal in hand. She was certain he would expect her to leave it there. It was natural, but she had more work to do.

"So," he said, perfectly on cue, "do I get to keep it for the night?"

There it was, a simple sentence carrying the weight of accusation it hadn't earned. Her mouth was ready with the careful speech she had rehearsed about cognition and fatigue and pacing one's exposure. She hated that she had become fluent in careful speeches.

"I think," she said, "it works better when we… do it together. For now."

His brow knit. "Because of my eyes?"

"In part," she lied, and the lie sprouted another lie like a Hydra that preferred the company. "And because sometimes it's upsetting, and I'm here if it is."

Lester accepted that with a reluctant nod, the way a person accepts that the medicine will taste fine, even if they know it won't. "Alright," he said. "You take the wheel."

She found herself relaxing into the rhythm—it was absurd, how quickly storytelling can become a drug. Read, watch him soften, feel forgiven. Repeat. "Last one for tonight," she said, opening the journal up again. "It's about Mr. Kowalski's garage. Do you remember that?"

"Who's Mr. Kowalski?" he asked.

"You'll see." She inhaled and pitched her voice into the cadence she discovered he liked best—wry, unhurried, a little gentle at the edges.

> You could smell the garage half a block away: oil, rubber, the sweet ghost of gasoline. Mr. Kowalski was a man who fixed things by looking at them hard until they confessed. He let me sweep and hand him wrenches on Saturdays after I turned fourteen. He paid in spare parts for a bike I pretended I would someday build.
>
> "The trick," he said, "is not taking it personally when the stuck bolt won't turn. It's not a moral failure. It's physics and rust." He handed me a rag. "And sometimes leverage."
>
> We changed brake pads on a blue sedan that squealed like a choir of mice. He let me press the pedal while he watched fluid purge from a line. "You listen," he said, "and it tells you what it needs."
>
> Later that day a woman came in with a rattle. He fixed it in three minutes with a patience that made me want to sit down. She slipped him a five. He tucked it back into her palm. "You'll have a bigger thing someday," he said. "Keep it for that."
>
> I don't know where Mr. Kowalski is now. But when something sticks, I can still hear him say it, under the swear words: it's not personal. It's physics and rust.

She set the book on her knee and watched him. While it was part of one of her best entries, it really wasn't her best work.

It was starting to read like a novel, and she couldn't tell if he would pick up on that or not. To Beatrice, it didn't sound like Lester at all. Maybe the whole thing had gotten away from her a little bit.

Lester had that far-off look again, the one that meant his mind was trying on the memory like a jacket, seeing if the sleeves fit.

"I want him to be real," Lester said.

"He is," she said softly.

He turned toward her. "Is he?"

She considered. "He is now."

He laughed once, a short bark of a sound. "I guess that'll do. I wonder if he's still alive."

A neighbor upstairs dropped something large and then apologized through the ceiling by dragging furniture twice as long. The kettle on the stove sighed itself toward silence. Time did its elastic thing; the hour stretched and then snapped back when she glanced at the clock and found it had not been as generous as she'd hoped.

"I should go," she said.

"You should not," he countered, but without heat, "but you will."

Beatrice stood and slid the journal into her bag. He watched the gesture, that smooth zip like a curtain coming down between acts.

"I'll bring it back Thursday," she said.

"You'd better." Lester shifted in his chair and then, more carefully than bravado allowed, "You're not just reading me a bedtime story, are you? This helps?"

"It helps," she said. "And it's not bedtime."

"It could be," he said. "If you stayed."

Beatrice's blood froze in her veins, but she only paused her movement for a moment, willing the rest of her to keep going, to act relaxed. She shot him a look that would have been stern if she weren't smiling.

"Behave, Mr. Filch."

"Then I wouldn't be me," he said, but he looked pleased, which was new and uncomfortable and just fine.

At the door she hesitated. She wanted to say something clean and simple—*You're doing well*, or *I'm proud of you*, or *This is working*—some appropriate, therapist-safe thing that would not taste like lemons in her mouth. Instead she said, "I like reading you."

He nodded. "I like hearing me."

When Beatrice stepped into the hall, the cold jumped her like a thief. She pulled her coat tight and told herself, with professional firmness, that tonight had gone well. The entries had landed. The doubts had not flared into questions she couldn't parry. She had fed him a day of tree-dragging and a science fish and a kind mechanic and the notion that, once upon a time, he'd miscounted a mile because he had more in him than he knew. The old journal's griefs—its darting, barbed truths—burned now in a fireplace and then in memory and then not at all.

Halfway down the stairwell she remembered Arthur. They had rescheduled their dinner from Saturday to the next evening. There was nothing she wanted to do less.

CHAPTER THIRTY ONE

Back in the apartment, Lester Filch sat for a full minute without moving, the way you do after a dream when you want it to volunteer its last details. He replayed the entries like songs he wanted to memorize: the fish nosing the glass, the kid on the bike with his righteous grin, the fifth lap that was both a mistake and a choice, the man in the garage saying it's not personal. His eyes stung. He blamed the cigarette smoke.

But what stuck out from the evening was the slight invitation for Beatrice Goodie to stay overnight. What was he thinking? But then, he was just a little proud of himself for going that far. Even saying it was something new. Maybe he really was that boy who ran the extra mile.

It was a problem he hadn't had before: wanting something soft and warm and kind. Not a pet; a person. The old wanting that he felt in his bones had been simple—leave me alone, let me be angry, give me the joy of being right about how wrong everything is. He could feel that was in there. But a new wanting had crept up, slow at first and now fast and unafraid. He grabbed his walker and took ten careful steps toward the sink and washed the two mugs and a fork with the focused reverence of a man doing the only thing he can.

When Lester went to bed he lay on his back and listened to the building breathe and the cars speeding by, throwing slush and snow out from behind their wheels. A man was yelling to someone else about money he was owed. He stared at the rectangle of streetlight on the ceiling until it softened and slid away. He dreamed that night, and the dream was not of fire or metal or sewers but of a fish in a bowl turning like a small planet, and when he tapped the glass, she came to him.

Beatrice came over the next day at around dinner time, unannounced. This was not the schedule. The chicken pan still sat on his drying rack, because he had convinced himself it was a trophy. When he opened the door to find her standing there, he was visibly surprised. "Come in," he said cautiously, and she did, with the journal in her bag and a new confidence that scared her exactly as much as the lack of it had.

"You're a day early," he said. "You just came yesterday."

"Well, I thought this couldn't really wait, and I didn't have much to do today. Thought we could get in a few more entries."

"I made spaghetti," he announced. "Nothing too special."

"I'm proud of you," she said. "Nothing too special *is* special. It's how most of us who have to cook for ourselves live our lives."

The spaghetti had ambition. It also had too much garlic, which made both of them brave but happy they were sitting across from each other and probably would be for the rest of the night. When they were done, he pushed his plate aside and set his hands, palms down, on the table.

"Before we read," he said, "I want to try something."

"Okay."

"I want to remember something without you telling me to."

"Okay," she said again, slower.

Lester closed his eyes. She watched the muscles in his jaw like she was waiting for weather. "There's a... hallway," he said. "Loud. A locker that sticks. I kick it and it cuts my shoe. And..." He paused, frowned. "And there's a... smell. Like oranges. No. Like...pencil shavings." His face pulled into a smile that surprised them both. "And chalk. It's nothing. But it's there."

She had to grip the underside of her chair to keep from clapping like an idiot. "That's something," she said. "That's good!"

He opened his eyes. "I don't know if it's real," he admitted. "I feel like I'm a psychic trying to get a good reading."

"That doesn't make it less real. It's progress."

He looked at her a long time, and whatever he saw there let him exhale. "Now read," he said, "before my courage decides to go grab another cigarette and smoke."

She pulled the journal free from her bag. Tonight's script included two more bright lies and one risky truth she had acclimated in the sun like a houseplant. The first lie was safe: an entry about the library with the orange chair (a place where the librarian always forgave fines because she said a boy who kept books past due was a boy who needed time). The second was a kindness from a stranger on a bus (the stranger giving up a seat for Lester, not to be gallant but because "we all have knees, especially handsome young men who are growing so fast."). The third lie was dangerous and necessary: his father, laughing. Just once. At a stupid joke. And then clapping Lester on the shoulder with a hand that didn't know how to be gentle but tried anyway.

She read them, and he laughed in the right places. He went quiet in the right places. When she finished, he said, very quietly, "It's unfair."

"What is."

"That I have to be told about my own life."

She put the book down. "I know," she said.

Lester stood, stretched, and winced. She set the journal down on the arm of the couch and reached, without thinking, for the plate to take it to the sink. The journal slid off the couch and somehow rolled closer to him. He bent down and his fingers closed over the leather cover before he picked it up.

"May I?" he asked.

She could have said no. She could have said later, or when the moon is right, or when I figure out how to be braver. Instead she heard herself say, "Sure."

He opened to a random page, letting his eyes blur across the words he could not quite read yet. The shape of the ink, the weight of the paper, the idea that something belonged to him— he held it like it might escape out the window.

Beatrice counted silently to sixty. When she reached the end of her courage, she put out her hand. "You can't see the letters yet, can you?"

He surrendered the book, the way you give back a photograph you weren't ready to stop looking at. "No," he said sadly. "Not yet."

"Still," she said. "You're doing so much better. And we read a lot today. So I think I'll come back tomorrow and we can do it again."

"Tomorrow," he echoed.

She left.

Lester stood in the doorway after the latch clicked and cursed himself for not asking her to stay again, for not promising to do the exercises without theatrics, for not being the kind of man who didn't need to be read to. Then he laughed at himself for promising to become someone else overnight.

Inside her car, at the curb, Beatrice pressed her forehead to the steering wheel and breathed through the slats. She had lied, again. And she would lie again the next day—gently, elegantly, medicinally. She told herself it was working. The proof was in the way he had smiled at Mr. Kowalski and in the way his voice softened at the idea that a librarian had forgiven him on principle. The proof was in the minuscule improvements of a kitchen towel, a tied bag, a plate washed before bed. The proof was in the way she had wanted to stay.

But wanting to stay was not proof of goodness, and she knew it. It was proof of a different hunger, one she had denied for years and now dared to feed on soup and stories.

Suddenly she remembered Arthur. The clock in her car said it was seven o'clock. He was supposed to come over by eight. She grabbed her blackberry and typed slowly, as if her fingers walked on a lake of thin ice.

Can't do dinner tonight. Sorry. Working late.

Another lie. The easiest kind.

She put the car in gear and pulled away from the curb, the journal on the passenger seat like a silent co-conspirator. Streetlights slid over the leather, gold briefly, then gone, then gold again. She did not look directly at it, as if it were the sun, or a mirror, and if she looked to long the word JOURNAL might turn into the word FRAUD and then etch itself into her mind.

Back in his apartment, Lester set his crutches down by the window and peered down into the street. He watched the blur of taillights that might have been hers and then weren't. He reached up and touched the scar above his collar, like a man testing the weather. Then he laughed, once, softly, and said to the empty room, "I ran five laps."

The room, not accustomed to jokes, considered this. The radiator clanked in assent. Somewhere upstairs a chair scraped the floor in agreement. And for one small, ridiculous moment, the world was simple again: left foot, right foot, breathe, swear, repeat.

PART FOUR

CHAPTER THIRTY TWO

Two nights later, on a Friday, Arthur Medlar sat in Beatrice's dining room listening to the clatter of dishes and silverware. He was at another one of those frustrating dinners. Why she insisted on having these he couldn't understand, though in his mind he tried.

They were having meatloaf. They always had meatloaf. Or spaghetti and meatballs. *So blasé.* So very middle-class. And the name meatloaf sounded disgusting, anyway. Meat. Loaf. Even the word loaf made him think of taking a dump. The smell only made it worse—steamy, grey-brown, sweating rivulets of fat that ran to the edges of his platter like grease making a break for freedom from its porcelain prison. The thing lay there on his plate like a retired boxer in a sauna, leaking out his sweat and regrettable decisions.

"Honey, what do you want to drink with dinner?" Beatrice's voice floated in from the kitchen.

A brandy, or at least a few glasses of wine, he wanted to say, but he had to respect the fact that she didn't drink much, at least for now.

"What do you have?"

"Coke, Ginger Ale, water, or milk."

Milk! Could there be anything more domestic than *milk*? Was anything more responsible? And Coca-Cola wasn't worth drinking unless it was mixed with rum and came with a buzz. Ginger ale was nothing but urine from a gingerbread man.

"I'll just take water, babe," he said sweetly. How boring.

There was nothing he wanted more than to be out at a proper restaurant, served by strangers, drinking what he pleased, eating food with names that sounded like temptations rather than bowel movements, distracted by Beatrice's beauty and the thought of ravishing her in a few months' time. In the dismal hovel she called home, they were forced to talk, and she would usually appear in pajamas at some point during the night. *Flannel* pajamas. He shuddered.

She emerged in them now, blue flannel covered in small white stars that refused to flirt. Her hair was up in an unstrategic knot. No makeup. He had heard of women "slipping into something more comfortable," but Beatrice apparently thought that meant dressing like a Mennonite on laundry day. It was baffling to him, like her choice to live simply in a one-bedroom apartment rather than in something more luxurious, as he knew she could.

"It's good to live simply," she had said to him once, when he brought up his disgust. "Arthur, don't you believe in living simply? I mean, what use can there be of excess when there are so many people who have nothing?"

"Darling," he replied with the exasperated charm of a man already imagining his next mistress, "you always do things because they're good, but you don't consider how other people live as being *equally* good."

"Well, all things can't be equally good, Arthur. After all, if everyone is good, then no one is good. There has to be *some* standard. And I happen to think mine is best."

Most men might have been surprised at her candor and matter-of-fact approach to being self-righteous, but Arthur had grown used to it. Beatrice wore righteousness the way other women wore lipstick—habitually, unapologetically. As she explained once, "It's good to be as honest as possible, even when it's disagreeable."

"Well, I don't believe living below your means is good," he had pouted. "It's not recognizing what life, fate, God, whatever you call it, gave you. It's not being grateful. It's throwing away the opportunities you have to better yourself. Isn't that bad?"

Beatrice had thought about that for a moment, ladling sauce over the sweating loaf of meat that they were also having on that night. "You have a point there, I think. I give away the money I have when I can, but perhaps I give too much. I'll consider what you're saying, Arthur. It's not good to be too hasty with one's opinions."

He had rolled his eyes and leaned back in his chair, folding his arms. So reasonable, so pliable, he thought. Yet still wrapped in flannel.

Now she set the platter down on a trivet like a proud nurse presenting a convalescent roast. "I let it rest this time," she said. "They say it's better if you let the juices set."

The loaf shivered as if it understood English.

Arthur smiled, the bright, photogenic one he had perfected for winning depositions and donors. "Looks fantastic," he lied, already calculating how many bites would constitute enough love to get credit.

She poured his water into a stout glass with light blue flowers baked into the sides, the sort of glass sold in sets of eight near grocery-store registers. Arthur missed the weight of crystal. He missed the insinuation of a stem between his fingers, the cold wink of a proper martini. He missed a city that knew what to do with him.

Beatrice slid into her chair and folded a napkin into her lap with a domestic flourish he found theatrical and yet—he had to admit—sweet. The table between them was small, the sort of table that assumed more about intimacy than the couple sitting at it did. A single candle struggled in a jelly jar, a generous compromise between romance and thrift.

"How was your day?" she asked.

"Long," he said. "Four meetings, a board call, and some... estate-management nonsense." He forked a polite wedge of loaf, wincing as a vein of what he hoped was an onion tore like a ligament.

She nodded. "I had a home visit. Some lady's knees were acting up. And Mr. Chen finally agreed to take the blood pressure meds—after I hid his cigarettes." She smiled at the memory of the small victory, then added, lightly, "And yesterday Lester tried a new stretch without his walker, so that was good."

Arthur's fork clinked on the plate. "Lester."

"Mm-hm. He's doing better." She said it in the tone people reserve for toddlers who have memorized colors. "We did heel-to-toe all the way to the kitchen. He was very proud."

"Wonderful," Arthur said, producing an agreeable noise from the region of his throat. The agreeable noise had a brittle edge. "How is—what is it—his outlook?"

"It's... improving," she responded, searching for the right word and finding that her mind brought up a slide of Lester's crooked smile instead. "He's—" She stopped herself before the word *sweet* escaped. "He's trying."

Arthur saw the warmth in her eyes at his memory and recognized it. The warmth wasn't for him. It was for the man with the walker. He took another bite of meatloaf to keep from saying something that would not play well on replay.

"You know," Beatrice went on, gently, "he asked me if goodness is nature or nurture. Whether people become better because they want to, or because they're handled with care. We ended up talking about—well." She laughed, embarrassed. "Butter on toast."

"Butter," Arthur repeated, swallowing a dry mass. "On toast."

"It's silly," she admitted. "But it made sense at the time. Some people absorb kindness easily, like warm toast. Others are cold and the butter just... skates across the top. You have to warm them up first." She cut a neat bite and chewed thoughtfully. "I think Lester's warming."

Arthur drank his water as if it were vodka and said, "How—encouraging."

She didn't register the coolness; she was watching a crumb cling to the edge of her fork and thinking of how Lester had worked so hard to make homemade pizza the other week. He had been so pleased with the crust, even though it had the texture of roof shingles. When he looked at her for the verdict, she had said "perfect" and meant it, because the real thing he made was effort.

"Do you want ketchup?" she asked.

Arthur thought of slathering the thing in Heinz until it resembled a crime scene and said, "I'll take it pure."

She smiled and set the bottle back down. "Lester thinks ketchup is a conspiracy of corn syrup to keep people docile," she said, then winced. "Sorry. I didn't—he just says these things. He's funny. In a way."

"In a way," Arthur echoed. He smiled with his front teeth and cut another bite so viciously the loaf shifted. "You mention him a lot lately."

She blinked. "Do I?"

"Since we sat down, I've heard 'Lester' more times than I've heard 'salt.' Which is impressive, considering your seasoning philosophy."

Beatrice lowered her fork. He was joking but not joking. He was always joking-not-joking, which was a way to say something true and then pretend it hadn't been said. "He's my patient," she said carefully. "You asked how work is. He's work."

"Of course." Arthur's smile widened, porcelain over iron. "I'm just keeping score."

"On what?"

"The ratio," he said. "Lester-to-Arthur."

Beatrice felt heat climb her neck. "That's not fair."

"I didn't say it was fair. Arithmetic is neither fair nor unfair."

"Arithmetic isn't your strong suit," she said before she could stop herself. It came out light, but not as light as she meant. "When was the last time you did math without an assistant, anyway?"

He leaned back, impressed despite himself. "Touché," he said, and then, because dominance dressed best in benevolence, added, "You're right. I apologize."

The apology sat between them, awkward as a third place setting meant for Lester Filch.

Beatrice took a breath, then tried to pivot. "I... got some good news today. Mr. Chen's insurance approved in-home aqua therapy for his spine. It's rare. I filled out the forms three times."

"That's great," Arthur said, genuinely this time. He liked wins. *Any* wins. "And Lester? Will he swim, or will he boycott chlorine for ideological reasons?"

Beatrice laughed. "He might. He said once that chlorine smells like every bad swim class he ever took." The laughter softened her. "But yes, I'm going to try to get him in a pool. I'd have to drive him until he can drive himself. But I know it would help."

Arthur cut the loaf again. The knife squeaked against the plate. "You're very invested," he said.

"I'm... doing my job."

"Mmm."

"And he's..." She caught herself and stared at the candle. The wax had cratered, a little white volcano around a feeble flame. "He's lonely."

"Aren't we all," Arthur said, managing to make it sound noble and bored simultaneously. He glanced around the apartment for the thousandth time and found the same catalogue of offenses: the leaning bookshelf; the thrift-store lamp with the shade a little crooked; the photo of a beach sunset that tried too hard to be scenic; the smallness of everything that insisted on being enough. He imagined replacing it all.

"How's Jasmine?" Beatrice asked, and he snapped his gaze back to her so quickly his neck almost broke.

"Who?"

"Janine," she repeated. "Your assistant at work. Her husband just started chemo, right?"

"Oh, she's good. Competent," he said, and smiled too neutrally. He took a deliberate sip of water. "And you? How is your... what is he... a supervisor?"

"He's fine," she said. "He doesn't know about the dinners." She laughed, but not entirely with humor. "He would have me sign a policy if he did. No soups after six."

Arthur watched the way she pressed her napkin to her mouth when she laughed, the way her eyes went briefly shiny, and he felt the familiar swell of possession. Beautiful, unadorned, moral—*his*. Or would be soon enough. He had been losing interest for weeks, true, but wins could be coaxed back to life with the right kind of resistance. The trick was pressure. Not too much. Just enough to shape.

"Bea," he said, softening his voice. "How are *we*?"

The question hung in the small room like a chandelier someone forgot to dust.

"We're..." She looked down at the loaf, then up at him, then somewhere just past his shoulder, as if the right answer were taped to the wall. "We're fine."

He smiled. "Fine," he repeated. The word had the nutritional value of iceberg lettuce. "Good."

She took another bite and chewed slowly. He watched her and thought, *You're drifting.* He could smell it on her like a new perfume—something faint and floral and disobedient. It didn't smell like him.

"Arthur," she said, after a moment. "Do you ever feel like... we're having two different dinners?"

He laughed. "I'm eating meatloaf. What are you eating?"

Beatrice set her fork down, and it made that particular small sound metal makes when it admits its been abandoned. She looked at him closely for a moment, and both of them said nothing. Then she sighed and began telling him about a parking ticket that made no sense that she had only gotten that morning when she went to the supermarket, about a broken shoelace, about a song that played in Sears that yanked her back to 1987 in a way she couldn't explain. He listened with half of his attention, the other half analyzing angles: how to steer her toward a better neighborhood, how to nudge her toward a better dress, how to set a wedding date that would look like a power move.

"And you?" she asked. "How was the—estate thing?"

He inhaled as if preparing a closing statement. "Dreary. A thorny little hedge of small greed. People are so predictable when money floats by. You hold it out like a bright toy and they reach with both hands and their mouths open."

She looked at him, startled, and then away. "That's… unkind. People need money to survive. Things are hard now."

"Well, it's accurate," he said, unembarrassed. "But, yes. Unkind."

There was silence again. The candle flickered on, waving between them, cheering them on. Somewhere in the building a pipe moaned like a ghost who'd just been told to keep it down.

She cleared her throat. "Lester says—"

Arthur laughed. Not loudly, but not kindly. "Of course he does."

"I'm sorry."

"No, no," he said, in a voice you might use to a child with a broken toy. "Go ahead. What does Lester say?"

"He says people don't change. They only rearrange their furniture."

Arthur's smile grew, foxlike. "And what do *you* say?"

"I think…" She trailed off, surprised by her own answer before it arrived. "I think people can change. With help."

"Ah," he said. "Rehab for the soul."

"If you want to be glib," she said, and looked him in the eye. He felt it: a small, hard click of resistance. She wasn't a doormat tonight. He sensed a different gravity about her.

"I want to be accurate," he said, still smiling.

"Maybe try being kind," she responded, then laughed at herself. "Listen to me. I sound like a motivational poster."

He tilted his head. "Is this because I don't like your meatloaf?" He speared another bite and ate it with exaggerated gusto. "Because I love your meatloaf."

"You don't," she said, amused.

"Well, I love *you*," he said instead.

The words sat there between, as heavy and overly-moist as the loaf.

Beatrice set her napkin down very gently, as if any sudden movement would startle the truth into flight. "Arthur," she said, "you always say that like you're signing for a package."

"It's a very important package," he said. "Fragile."

"Handle with care," she murmured, almost to herself, and thought of Lester again—how he tapped the edge of the bowl when he stirred soup, the small domestic tenderness of making more broth than he needed just in case she wanted seconds. She never thought she could be moved by a man rinsing a spoon. She was learning very bad things about herself.

Arthur watched her drift and reeled her back. "Do you love *me*?"

Beatrice hesitated. He saw it, too, and he felt his chest go hot. And with what, anxiety? Anger? His smile stayed put.

"I think—" she said.

He laughed once. "You think."

"I think yes," she said quickly, and hated the way the word felt. "I'm trying."

"Trying," he repeated, and his smile chilled. "Love is not a try. It's a *do*."

"Well, I know that," she said softly.

"And I've done a lot to show that I love you, don't you think?"

"Yes…" she hesitated, and took a drink to wash the dryness out of the response.

"I've done my best to provide, to help you with this place," he continued, "to help improve this place."

Her eyebrows lifted. "You mean improve *me*."

"Refine," he amended. "Polish."

"I'm not silverware," she said, and smiled so he could pretend she was joking. But he knew she wasn't.

They ate in small sounds for a while: knife, fork, glass, breath—a small rhythmic world where everything meant more than it should. Twice she almost said Lester again and caught herself; once she didn't. In fact, she decided to say the name on purpose, because he was trying to improve her. A part of her wanted the name said, wanted it to hurt. She tried to sound as casual as she could.

"Lester said he used to hate Christmas because snow looks like dandruff. Doesn't it, though? I can't stop thinking about that. It's... horrible. And funny. And sad."

Arthur put his fork down and folded his hands. "Beatrice," he said, "do you know how many times you have said his name."

She swallowed her food and a gloating smile. "Too many?"

"Correct."

"Well, to be honest, I'm worried about him," she admitted. "He has no one. Really. He's just some guy with no family, a future on the line, injuries that will leave permanent scars."

"You're someone," Arthur said, and the smile thinned. "Or are you no one now, too."

"That's unkind," she said again, but there was no heat in it.

He leaned in. "I'm asking you to be here, with *me*. Not there." His finger made a small circle over the meatloaf, as if the loaf itself were the other man.

She nodded. It was easier to nod than to describe the shapeless ache in her chest, the sense that something true was calling to her from a shabby living room two towns over, something she had always claimed to want: a simple, stubborn goodness that didn't know it was good. Arthur, by contrast, had a goodness with a résumé.

"Tell me about the wedding," he said, pivoting into safer terrain he could pave. "Dates. Venues. Colors. I favor Navy. You, perhaps—ivory? And we'll move you into the city after the honeymoon."

"After," she echoed, as if the honeymoon were a distant planet. "Arthur... I like my apartment."

He laughed gently. "Bea, it's a starter apartment."

"I started a long time ago," she said. "The other place was my starter apartment. On the other side of town. This is a step up."

"No," he said, the smile back to full wattage. "This is a step sideways. New York is a step up."

Beatrice felt suddenly, viscerally tired. She could have put her head down on the table and slept through his sentences like a child in a pew. "I need to clear," she said, standing. She gathered plates, grateful for the small reprieve of rinsing, of the hot water's steam. Arthur watched her move—the easy efficiency, the kindness even in the way she stacked forks—and felt the old surge again: want braided with conquest. He would fix this. He would fix her. He would make her stop saying Lester the way a person talks about her favorite pastime.

She returned with two slices of something that wanted to be cake and wasn't. "I tried a new recipe," she said. "Yogurt loaf."

"Loaf again," he said cheerfully, and managed not to wince. "Wonderful."

She set it down. The candle offered its last brave light and then sighed out, unwilling to cheer for them anymore. They were left with the hum of the refrigerator and the faint squeal of a radiator that most-likely pre-existed God.

"Arthur," she said suddenly, surprising herself, "*why* do you love me."

He spread his hands. "Because you're beautiful. Because you're good. Because you're—Beatrice."

"Those are... adjectives," she said. "Well, except that last one. I want verbs. What do I *do* that's worthy of love to you."

He stared at her for a moment, his brain racing for the right answer, and then he laughed. "I love you because you love me," he said. "I love you because you're good to me, you cook for and are there for me when I tell you about my day. Things like that."

"That's it?" she said, not quite a question.

"And the rest," he said, magnanimous. "Everything you do."

She looked at him for a long, unblinking moment and then glanced at the window. Snow dusted the sill, glittering like a cheap necklace. She thought of dandruff and laughed, and the laugh came out wrong.

"What?" said Arthur.

"Nothing," she said. "Just... a joke."

He nodded, the way men nod when jokes aren't for them. "Eat your dessert, sweetheart."

Beatrice lifted a forkful. "Arthur," she said again, because she had to puncture the heavy quiet or it would harden into something habit-shaped, "did you notice that we never talk about... us. We talk about me, or your work, or my patients—"

"Lester," he interrupted, and smiled.

"—but not us," she finished. "What we want to be. Together."

"I want us to be married," he said promptly. "I want you in the city. I want a decent caterer and a band that doesn't play *Shout* or *Dancing Queen*. I want—" he paused, managed a tender note, "—you near me when I come home."

She waited. Nothing about her. Not really. "Okay," she said softly.

"Well what do *you* want?"

Beatrice opened her mouth, then closed it. Her mind, traitor that it was, offered an image: a scarred man at a chipped table, blowing on a spoonful of soup so he wouldn't burn his mouth. Ridiculous. She set the fork down.

"I want—" she began, and then the phone by the counter sang its bright, merciful note. She stood too quickly, scraping the chair. "Sorry."

He leaned back and watched her cross the tiny kitchen, watched the way she tucked a strand of hair behind her ear before she answered. "Hello?"

Beatrice's face changed. "Oh—hi," she said, voice pitched in a careful middle. She pulled the telephone into the hall, and Arthur watched the phone line stretching from the wall. He couldn't make out the words, but he could read the name on her mouth before she disappeared. Lester. Suddenly he imagined that phone line wrapped about that stranger's neck.

"Everything okay?" Arthur asked when she returned.

"Yes," she said, sitting, and felt the lie slide across her tongue like a slug. "Mr. Chen. He—um—needs help with the forms again."

"Of course," Arthur said blandly. "Mr. Chen."

She picked up her fork again. The yogurt loaf waited, untroubled by human drama. She pushed it around, drawing a map to nowhere.

"You're distracted," he said.

"I'm tired," she said. "It's been a long week."

He reached across the table for her hand again. "I love you, Beatrice" he said, precise and final.

She looked at him. She looked at their two hands on the cheap wood of the kitchen table, his just as delicate as hers, if a bit bigger. She looked at the extinguished candle, the crater of wax. She thought, absurdly, of butter again—how it melts when it's wanted.

"I know," she said, which was not an answer and was all she had.

He squeezed her hand harder. "Say it," he said firmly.

The room felt too small for both the truth and polite fiction. She gathered the fiction first. "I love you," she said, and the sentence clinked like the water glass beside her.

Arthur smiled, victorious. "Good," he said, and the word landed with the dullness of a stamp. He stood, went around the table, and kissed the top of her head, holding it there for a second longer than she liked. "You'll see," he murmured. "You and I—we're perfect for each other. It's just nerves."

Nerves. Sure, that's what it was. Just nerves.

Beatrice kept her eyes on her plate. In the reflection of the jelly jar, she saw a small, warped version of herself, candleless and utterly depleted. She thought of a different reflection: a window in a shabby apartment with smoke marks on the sill, a man tapping ashes into a novelty mug and trying—God help him—to be better today than he was yesterday.

"Coffee," she said brightly, standing because standing is sometimes a kind of courage. "I can make coffee."

"Not tonight," said Authur, slipping back into his chair. "Let's keep it simple."

Simple. She smiled and nodded and set the fork down. It made that small, resigned sound again. Across the table, Arthur studied the yogurt loaf, the plates, the woman. He smiled at her, and his mind was on the woman she would one day be, the woman he would eventually upgrade.

"Here, Arthur," she said, placing the last slice of yogurt loaf onto his plate.

He traded her a grin for a loaf. "Thanks, babe," he said, as cheerfully as he could muster. Of course, Arthur Medlar always grinned at whatever it was that he intended to upgrade. And if something didn't improve after he was done working on it, well, he would simply throw it away.

CHAPTER THIRTY THREE

Arthur Medlar had never once lowered himself to visit a man like Lester Filch. Men like Lester belonged to the background hum of the world, wallpaper people—the cough in a movie theater that ruins the best line. But now Beatrice Goodie, who ought to have been choosing dinnerware patterns and practicing her married signature, had begun saying Lester's name with softness around the edges, and to Arthur's mounting disgust the cough had become the competition.

The day after the meatloaf incident, he stood outside Lester's dingy apartment building in West Lemon, rehearsing his cover story in the reflection of a cracked glass door. He adjusted his tie, admired the sharp angle of his jaw, and produced the business card he printed the night before at Kinko's: CHARLES CHESTERTON, ESQ.PERSONAL INJURY, EMOTIONAL DAMAGES, RESTITUTION FOR THE SOUL. Unhinged? Slightly. He invented the tagline while shaving that morning. Beatrice liked that word—soul. Well, this card had it in gold foil.

The buzzer didn't work but the door was unlocked, which was good for drama. Inside, the lobby smelled of boiled cabbage and a thousand bad decisions of a hundred tenants.

Arthur pressed two fingers beneath his own nose as he climbed the stairs, because the elevator was jammed. He couldn't believe Beatrice had once stooped to this level. He had heard it was bad, but experiencing it was another thing. This was unacceptable. He understood now more than ever where her parents were coming from. This wasn't a marriage. It was a rescue mission. She was out of her mind.

On the third floor, he paused to smooth the lines of his coat, fixed his smile into something between benevolent and victorious, and walked over to Lester Filch's apartment.

Lester opened the door in a t-shirt that had surrendered long ago. He was both the same man and a slightly rearranged version—stitched, puckered, the left eyebrow permanently sceptical. The apartment behind him was a museum of old furniture, rusty appliances, and stale air.

"Mr. Filch," Arthur sang, gliding inside as though Mr. Meeks had personally invited him to inspect the apartment, as if he had every right to be there. "Charles Chesteron, attorney-at-law," he said, extending a hand towards the obviously surprised tenant. "But you may call me Chuck. I specialize in personal injury and, ah—" he checked the card "—emotional damages."

"A lawyer?" Lester repeated, taking his hand and shaking it politely.

"Yes." Arthur made a sympathetic mouth. "And you, my friend, are sitting on a goldmine."

"I am?"

"A catastrophic accident, trauma, burns, broken bones. You deserve compensation! Dignity! Respect!"

Lester considered that and then said, flat as a highway, "I'm happy the way things are. I'm getting better. And I don't like lawyers."

Arthur's smile hiccupped, then recovered. "Nonsense. I'm here to help!" He gestured toward the sagging recliner. "Shall we? Start at the beginning. The accident—what do you remember?"

"Nothing."

"Well, surely—family, friends—"

Lester's laugh became a cough. "To be honest, I don't have too many people in my life. Only person who tells me anything is my home health aide. She's been reading me my life out of some journal I kept. It took a while to talk her into doing that, though. Apparently, I used to write."

Arthur didn't blink, because blinking would concede surprise. A journal. He was curious, and of course Beatrice would have been, too. She loved books and paper the way other women loved diamonds; she believed truth arrived in tidy paragraphs. If she was reading Lester his own past, she was truly getting to know him. That was an unfair advantage Lester had over Arthur. He had never written anything in his life, except for filling out a bank check, and even that was usually done by his secretary. He had wanted to meet the man who was competing for Beatrice's attention but realized the only way to truly get to know his enemy was to take this little detour.

"And the journal?" he asked lightly. "Where might that be?"

"My aide took it home. She brings it to read to me after our appointments."

"I see," Arthur replied cooly. He was thinking on his feet, but he was sitting calmly on the sofa, trying not to think about how dirty the upholstery must be. He should have worn his least favorite pants.

"Mr. Filch, aren't you worried that she might lose it?" *Or that someone might steal it?* he thought, laughing internally. Because that was exactly what he going to do. Surely there was something in that journal he could use against the man.

"Well, sure." Lester said. "But she wouldn't lose it. She's very capable, and anyway, if she did there's a copy with my old therapist." He waved in the direction of downtown. "Dr. Klein, a head-doctor type. Made me write it, and I think he kept a copy. I used to see him pretty regularly, but I can't remember how long. All I remember is I stopped seeing him shortly before the accident."

Arthur stood, and automatically wiped the back of his pants of whatever might have clung to them. "Mr. Filch, you should know that you are entitled to money. I'm sure you could win a case, and I'll look into it to see if that's true, free of charge. Don't be surprised if you see me again soon."

"You're a funny lawyer," Lester said. "Didn't ask me to sign anything. And I never heard of one working for free."

Arthur flashed his teeth. "I don't get paid unless you do," he said. "It's the good thing to do." He let himself out before the smile cracked.

As Lester's door closed behind him, Arthur wasn't sure if they would actually see each other again. If he could find out something juicy about Lester from his journal, then he wouldn't need to come back. But if it was a dead end, he would certainly have to return in order to snoop around.

Arthur Medlar never thought of himself as the sneaking sort. Men like him were supposed to stride through doorways, not slip through them. But there he was, sliding Beatrice Goodie's spare key into the lock of her apartment, heart steady, hands sure. She had pressed the key into his palm months ago with that radiant, unsuspecting smile. "Just in case of an emergency," she said, as though Arthur were the sort of man who would rush to fix a burst pipe or rescue a stranded kitten. He had nodded solemnly, grateful for her trust, and thought: *should have been for emergency booty calls, but okay.*

Her door opened on silence. He lingered a moment, listening for movement, even though he knew the apartment would be empty. She was at work, as she should be, ferrying soup and tenderness to the sick and half-dead. He shut the door gently behind him and let himself breathe. The place smelled of lavender and bleach, irritating in its purity. He hated how everything in Beatrice's orbit was so infuriatingly clean, everything except Lester.

The journal, he reminded himself. He was there for the journal. Lester had said that Beatrice was reading from it aloud, turning the thing into a bedtime story for that miserable wreck of a man. Arthur intended to see for himself what secrets it held, what filth Lester had scrawled in the dark.

He moved down the hallway and into her bedroom. At once he stopped, startled by the mess on her desk. It wasn't the clutter of a careless woman (Beatrice was *never* careless) but the frenzy of a purpose. Papers covered the desk and the floor immediately around it: drafts, sheets, ink-blotted scraps. Pens lay like discarded weapons, caps popped off, their tips bled dry from overuse. He bent over the desk, picking up a page.

The handwriting was neat, *painfully* neat. A date at the top, then a few paragraphs written in a voice that wasn't Beatrice's at all. He flipped another page, then another. His smile tightened.

It was the journal, yes — but not Lester's. These were imitations, fabrications, and—dare he think it—lies. A fiction of Lester Filch, smoothed and polished, as if the brute were being dragged onto a stage to play the part of a better man. "When I dropped my lunch tray," one entry read, "I thought it was going to be the worst moment of my school life, but Aunt Maybelle said sometimes it's better to be laughed at than ignored. I took that to heart. After that moment, I learned to make jokes and would laugh at myself usually. People loved that. I gained a lot of friends." Arthur chuckled. The words were too positive, too good. Lester couldn't have written them. The man barely spoke without dripping bile.

He set the paper down and closed his eyes, considering. Beatrice wasn't preserving Lester's voice — she was *creating* it, line by line, forcing him into a mold she could love. For her to do something this bad, his actual journal must be that much worse. It was laughable, grotesque. And it was dangerous, because if she succeeded, Lester might start to believe the fiction, and a reformed Lester could become a true rival.

Arthur paced the room, trying to recall his encounter with Lester Filch. It was obvious he was going to have to tell the poor man he'd been duped. But how? He needed to do it without Beatrice knowing he was involved at all. There was something Lester said that tweaked his interest: the mention of the therapist he used to go to, a Dr. Klein. Yes. Lester said the man probably kept a journal of their sessions in his file. Made sense. And it would be untouched by Beatrice's sanctimonious hand.

Arthur's grin returned. That was it. Forget these pretty lies. He would find that journal, pry open the real Lester Filch, and expose him for the miserable fool he really was. It would be the end of Beatrice's ridiculous experiment. He closed the drawer, left the papers as he had found them, and slipped out of the apartment as silently as he had come, already plotting how to break into a doctor's office.

Dr. Jerome Klein's waiting room smelled of chamomile and the optimism of people who bought notebooks to fix their lives. Arthur presented himself to the receptionist—a young man with purple hair that stuck up like a startled dandelion.

"I'm Charles Chesterton, attorney-at-law. I need access to the records of your patient Lester Filch."

"Do you have a release form?" the receptionist asked.

"I have a business card," Arthur said, placing it down as if it were a court order.

The receptionist eyed it suspiciously, and then looked up in disbelief. "This isn't going to be enough. We need a release form. If you get Mr. Filch to come in, then we can give you the documents you need."

"But he's injured, and he can't leave his house."

"Have a seat over there, and I'll let Dr. Klein know you're here. Maybe he can help you."

Five minutes later, Dr. Klein emerged in a corduroy jacket that sounded like dry leaves when he moved. He held a mug that read TRUST THE PROCESS. Arthur immediately distrusted both.

"Mr. Chesterton," Klein said with polite bafflement. "I hear you're looking for Mr. Filch's records. I'm afraid we would need a release form. I heard that he was in an accident, and I meant to send him a card but it slipped my mind. Won't you come in?"

He gestured to his office door, and they both walked past the receptionist and into the first door on the left.

When the door closed, Dr. Klein sat down and looked up at his guest. "Is Mr. Filch okay?"

"He's just fine, considering," said Arthur, sitting down across from him. "But he suffered catastrophic injuries. Somewhere in your files is a journal that will help us pursue justice and maybe give us a clue as to who was coming after him. Brakes don't get cut on their own, you know."

The doctor's eyebrows raised. "Were they really cut? Wow. That's awful. Who could have done that?"

"That's what we're trying to find out."

"Isn't that the job of the police?"

Arthur stumbled a bit at that. A lie got knocked together somewhere in the back of his mind, and he barely found the words. "Well, yes, but police already called it an accident. You know how they never admit they're wrong. But we suspect foul play. He had a lot of enemies."

"I can believe that," Klein replied. "But I'm sorry. I can't help you without his release form. Patient records are confidential. Without Mr. Filch's signed consent—"

Arthur leaned forward, dropping his voice to a courtroom whisper. "Doctor, I am offering you the chance to assist in a case that could change Mr. Filch's life. The truth is, he barely remembers who he is. He remembers things that just happened right before the accident, such as his job and his relationship with you, for example. But his past is lost to him, and he told me he isn't really comfortable signing any sort of documents without legal representation."

"Well, aren't *you* legal representation?"

Arthur blinked at him for a moment. "Right...Yes. I am, but—"

Klein sipped his tea, then said, "The way to change someone's life is usually not through their garbage can." He slid two pamphlets across the desk, as if issuing medicine. SO YOU FEEL YOU NEED TO SAVE THE WORLD. And, for garnish, WHY YOU FEEL THE NEED TO CONTROL.

Arthur stood up, not hiding his anger and crushing the pamphlets into a ball. "This isn't over."

"I recommend that exact same sentiment to most of my patients," Klein said kindly. He reached into his desk again and pulled out a third pamphlet: PERSEVERANCE AND THE NEED FOR GRIT.

Arthur parked his Hummer across from the office that night, as inconspicuous as a rhinoceros in a bowler hat. Through the first-floor windows, lights still glowed. Arthur made a list in a notebook labelled OPERATION TRUTH.

- Disguise: cap and sunglasses from a gas station (both so aggressively generic they were suspicious on principle).
- Tools: a new crowbar (he bought it with a thrilling sense of criminality—truth was, he missed the thrill of this kind of underhanded deed) and a flashlight.
- Alibi: networking (which could mean anything and nothing).
- Time: between 9:30 and 10:00.

It was 9:42 when the last light winked out. Arthur pulled the cap down over his face and sunk lower into the driver's seat. He saw Dr. Klein come out the large wooden doors, lock them behind him, and walk home in the opposite direction. The door, which had a large glass rectangle cut out of the middle, gave an annoyed shiver but did not open when he tried it. No surprise there. Next, he worked the crowbar into the lock. The metal groaned. The mill building the offices were in must have been at least a hundred and fifty years old. Still, his heart was jackhammering in his chest, and he looked up and down the snowy street. No one was walking out there. No one was driving by. But could there be a police officer somewhere? A camera, perhaps? A passing raccoon with a conscience? West Lemon wasn't famous for its patrols, but it *was* famous for nosy old women.

He breathed. He pried. The lock surrendered with a pop like a cork.

Inside, the hallway carpet tried to choke his shoes. He switched on his flashlight and instantly a red light blinked awake on the wall. An alarm? He froze. The light blinked again, indifferent. *Probably a far-off smoke detector begging for a battery*, he thought and kept moving. Past the receptionist's desk was a hallway that held a long line of therapy offices, but the only one he needed was the first one to the left.

The door marked DR. JEROME KLEIN had a keypad. But he was prepared for this. People used birthdays, anniversaries—numbers that meant something, so he tried 1-2-3-4 for the sport of it and, offended, the keypad blinked orange. He tried 0-0-0-0. Orange again. He put his ear to the door like a thief in a Victorian novel, as if the numbers would whisper themselves. He needed a hint.

Right outside the door, The hallway held framed diplomas and, crucially, a photo of Dr. Klein at a 10K charity run. His bib number was 1014. It couldn't be so easy, could it? He typed in 1-0-1-4. The light went orange. No, it wasn't so easy.

Arthur thought about breaking the glass or forcing his office door with the crowbar. How would he ever figure out the code to get in? He brought the crowbar up and started to push it into the crack between the door and the wall. As he did, he leaned against the handle and heard a click. He looked down in disbelief. His hand leaned on the handle again, pressed it down, and pushed it open. *Of course*, he thought, rolling his eyes. *Why would he lock a room full of confidential files?* It turned out easier than he could have ever imagined.

Dr. Klein's office smelled like old paper and coffee. A filing cabinet stood at the other end of the room, behind the therapist's desk. It was just as unlocked as the office door. *Man*, he thought, *with therapists like these, who needs enemies?*

Arthur ran his finger along the labels—A, B, C—until he reached F. FILCH, L. He lifted the most recent folder in there and quickly found what he was looking for: a photocopied journal. He pulled it out and placed the pile of papers on the desk. Arthur wanted to laugh—the universe was cooperating for once. He read by the light of his flashlight.

The first entry was tidy, deliberate, and venomous. It did not read like the floating bromides Beatrice had quoted lately over meatloaf. This was the voice of a man who had sharpened himself on grudges. Arthur skimmed some more. Names. Dates. The relentless march from petty bitterness to outright malice. It was everything he had hoped for and then some.

He thought about photocopying the packet, but then feared taking too long and being caught after he had gotten so far. He decided paper was better, and since Lester was a former client, there would be no reason for Dr. Klein to check his file. It would hardly be missed. He put the journal under his arm and closed the filing cabinet.

When he slipped back into the hallway, Arthur was almost giddy with adrenaline. He closed the door, feeling thankful that he didn't have to figure out how to lock it with the keypad. He moved toward the front door, locked it before closing it again, and hoped no one would notice the slight damage to the wood he had caused with his crowbar. Outside, a slight flurry of snow fell peacefully around him.

When Arthur got inside his Hummer he breathed hard, laughed once, and pulled out the journal from under his arm to assure himself it hadn't evaporated. It hadn't. He hugged it like a child who had just adopted a pet. It was his ticket to freedom. Beatrice Goodie would still be his.

Arthur drove to a hotel—never bring a crime to your own home, even executives knew that—and checked into a suite under the name C. Chesterton, which delighted him privately. He ordered room service: a steak, asparagus, a bottle of something French, and some chocolate lava cake for dessert. It was well-deserved after all that. He laid the journal out on the bed and began to read.

The entries marched from childhood humiliations to adult pettiness with the inexorable logic of a falling anvil. There was Alice the goldfish—less lovable in Lester's own telling, more obsession than innocence. There were teachers whose names he still remembered in the voice of a curse. There was the day he had beaten a neighbor's mailbox to death with a hammer after that neighbor had threatened to call the police when Lester had taken one step onto his lawn. He spent a paragraph describing the sound of metal crunching metal. The journal was not merely unflattering; it was an indictment written in the author's own blood. Lester Filch was a very bad man.

Arthur's heart swelled with relief that he mistook for righteousness. Beatrice would see. She would see that love is for men like him—capable, clean, in control—not for damaged animals who keep hammers for company.

He took a pen and began flagging passages with the small sticky notes he found in the hotel's stationery folder, writing helpful summaries like: LATENT CRUELTY, RESENTMENT TOWARD WORLD, POSSIBLE PYROMANIA? The more he annotated, the more noble he felt. He was, after all, saving Beatrice from a life of mopping up another man's brokenness. He ate his steak in triumphant bites.

By midnight he was crafting the speech he would deliver over dinner at Beatrice's apartment, something gently devastating. DARLING, I WANTED TO BELIEVE AS YOU BELIEVE, BUT THE FACTS ARE STUBBORN THINGS. BAD PEOPLE DON'T CHANGE, EVEN IF YOU TRIED TO CHANGE THEM. He practiced the tilt of the head he would use to signify empathy. He practiced the pause before he slid the journal across the table, the way she would lift her eyes and understand, and forgive him for the burglary because heroes often had to do ugly things.

No. *What was he thinking?* Beatrice could be brought around, eventually, but she needed time, that was all. He knew she wouldn't like this if he sprung it on her. She might end up forgetting Lester *and* him if he wasn't careful. He had to come out of all this squeaky clean. The relationship with Lester had to unravel by itself. And there was only one thing he could do to make that happen.

Arthur fell asleep at midnight with the journal under his pillow like a smothered prostitute. Or, like he *imagined* a smothered prostitute, to be clear. A smile was plastered on his face. It was the most peaceful sleep he had had in a very long time.

CHAPTER THIRTY FOUR

Arthur Medlar had never worn a disguise before. He didn't count Halloween costumes or the silk masks at charity galas; those were accessories, enhancements. This was different. *This* was degradation.

He stood in front of his bathroom mirror under the uncompromising white light, dabbing at his jaw with a sponge soaked in cheap foundation. The wig—"chestnut brown, synthetic, heat resistant," the tag had promised—sat lopsided on his head. Every time he adjusted it, the elastic snapped back and made his ears stick out like a barn door in a windstorm.

"You look like a pervert," he muttered to his reflection. Then, more generously: "Actually, you look like a professional."

It was not the face of a CEO, a man accustomed to bespoke suits and corner offices. It was the face of a middle-aged "care worker" trying very hard not to look like Arthur Medlar. He added oversized glasses with smudged lenses, a zip-up sweater that smelled faintly of mothballs (borrowed from his driver, to the man's horror), and plain khakis he would never have been caught dead in. His Italian loafers peeked beneath the hems, gleaming incongruously, but he wasn't about to destroy his arches in bargain shoes.

Name, he thought. *I need a good one.* All good disguises had a name and Charles Chesterton was already used up. The first thing that floated to him was Gary. Bland, helpful Gary. He tried it out in the mirror.

"Hello, I'm Gary."

Pause.

"Hello, I'm Gary. Replacement home health aide. How do you do?"

He looked like he was auditioning for a cheap spy movie. Still, it would have to do. From what he gleaned from Beatrice's explanations and the little he interacted with Lester, the man couldn't see too well past a constant blur.

By the time he reached West Lemon, his confidence had returned. It was a fine costume. His Hummer loomed like a tank outside the dreary row of apartments, but he parked it around the corner to avoid suspicion. It was another morning, and he was pretty sure Beatrice didn't come until closer to dinnertime. But only a fool would associate a man named Gary with a vehicle that could flatten mailboxes by accident. He wanted to be as inconspicuous as possible. Arthur straightened his wig in the rearview mirror, practiced a smile that said *trust me*, and patted the briefcase in the passenger seat. When he walked towards the apartment doors, he shuffled with the sad gait of a man who spent his entire life attending to other people's bedpans.

Lester answered on the third knock.

The apartment was worse than Arthur remembered from his first reconnaissance: the smell of boiled cabbage, cigarette ash, and something indefinably sour, like wet plaster, lingered around his nostrils. A mountain of newspapers were slumped in the corner. The wallpaper peeled in strips that looked like old bandages. Arthur's lip curled, but he forced it into the approximation of a smile.

"Mr. Filch," he said, pitching his voice low and nasal, "my name is Gary. Gary Garrettson. I'm your temporary aide. Miss Goodie has taken ill. Nothing serious, mind you. Just a flu. But I'll be filling in for the week until she recovers."

Lester squinted at him, as if trying to adjust a blurry television channel. "Beatrice is sick?"

Arthur nodded gravely. "Yes. Like I said, not serious. Just a flu, but we can't have our clients get sick on our account."

"Of course." Lester scratched the side of his face, which still bore the corrugated scars from his burn. "You don't look like an aide."

Arthur's heart stuttered. "What do you mean?"

"You're too tall. Most aides are short. Easier to wheel people around."

"Oh." Arthur adjusted his glasses nervously. "Genetics."

Lester's eyes lingered on him a moment longer than Arthur liked. Then, with a grunt, he shuffled aside to let him in.

Arthur breathed shallowly as he entered. The air was thick enough to slice. He made a mental note: Beatrice was one hundred percent crazy. Only a lunatic would be caught spending time there voluntarily.

"So," Lester said, lowering himself into his recliner. "What do you *do*, Gary?"

Arthur produced the prize he smuggled in from his briefcase: a copy of the journal. He held it up like scripture. "I help with… memory therapy. Miss Goodie told me she's been reading to you. It's a wonderful idea. I thought we might continue."

Lester leaned forward, eyes narrowing. "That doesn't look like the same book."

"Of course it isn't. Beatrice has the original. She brought it in to the office, and we made a copy."

"Seems like an invasion of privacy, if you ask me," Lester said, shifting in his seat uncomfortably. "I didn't give her my consent to show anybody else."

Arthur felt a pulse of glee but made himself refrain from looking too happy. "Well, that's Beatrice. She's so dutiful, even to the point of being untrustworthy. She'll do whatever it takes to help her clients. Whatever it takes. In fact, Beatrice may have… modified things a bit. She mentioned that to me also. For your comfort." He softened his tone, trying for sympathy. "She meant well, of course."

Lester stared at him, and for a moment Arthur felt the full weight of the man's suspicion. Then Lester leaned back again and closed his eyes. "Well, I don't know what you mean, exactly, but go ahead. Read, then."

Arthur exhaled, smoothed the first page, and began. He read the pages with a kind of contemptuous relish, inflecting each line as if to say, *Can you believe what a pathetic creature you were?* He sneaked glances over the top of the page, expecting Lester to crumble, to beg him to stop, or to ask for some reassurance that this wasn't the original and the other one was. But Lester just listened, brow furrowed, lips pressed tight.

When Arthur finished reading through the third page, Lester spoke up. "That doesn't sound like what Beatrice read."

Arthur smiled tightly. "Because she was protecting you. Editing, perhaps. She wanted you to see yourself as… softer."

Lester's mouth twitched, almost a smile. "She's good at that."

The remark landed on Arthur's chest like a stone. He bristled. "Yes, well, good intentions can be dangerous. They can keep you from the truth. And the truth, Mr. Filch, is right here." He tapped the journal with a flourish. "This is you. The *real* you."

He launched into another passage, one about the constant bullying at school, the bitterness that grew like mildew, the hatred of cheerful people, especially the cheerleaders. Arthur's voice grew theatrical, almost gleeful, as he narrated the spiral into despair.

Lester shifted in his chair again, fingers worrying at the armrest. He was listening, but not in the way Arthur wanted. His expression was not devastation; it was puzzlement, as if he were turning a puzzle piece over in his mind and seeing whether it fit. Arthur kept going, sweat beading under his wig. His glasses slipped down his nose; he shoved them back up with an irritated finger.

Finally, Lester said, "What did you say your name was?"

Arthur froze. "Gary."

"Gary what?"

Arthur's mind blanked. For a man who had argued high-profile lawsuits, he could not summon the surname. "Gary... Garret."

"Gary Garret?" Lester rolled it around like a marble in his mouth. "Funny. I thought you said Garretson before."

"I did!" Arthur said hastily. "Gary Garretson."

"You don't look like a Garretson."

Arthur forced a laugh. "What does a Garretson look like?"

"Shorter."

The wig itched. Sweat prickled down Arthur's temple. He turned back to the journal, rattling off another paragraph, hoping to drown out the scrutiny in words.

> My father said I was cursed. That misery followed me like a shadow. That if I ever married, I'd ruin her life, too.

Arthur slowed deliberately on that last line, savoring it, not least because he *may* have added that one in for good measure. "See? Even your own father thought you were cursed. Does that sound like the man who wrote the journal that Beatrice read from?"

Lester's eyes opened slowly. He fixed Arthur with a gaze that was half fog and half lightning. "Maybe. Maybe not. But it doesn't sound like the man I am now."

Arthur snapped the book shut. "That's because you've been living a lie." His voice rose, tight with frustration. "She's been feeding you sugar when what you need is medicine. You think she cares about you? She cares about her PROJECT. That's all you are to her—a project!"

Silence filled in the gap his words had chiselled out of the atmosphere. Lester sat back, his scarred face unreadable. Then, after a long pause, he said, "You sound jealous, Gary."

Arthur nearly dropped the journal. "Jealous?"

"Yes." Lester tilted his head. "Of Beatrice."

Arthur's throat went dry. He had gone too far. He needed to get out of there. "Don't be absurd," he said chuckling. "Beatrice is just a coworker. And I'm a professional."

Lester gave him a look that was not quite disbelief, not quite amusement. "A professional what?"

Arthur stood abruptly and moved towards the door. "Enough for today. We'll continue next time." He made sure to leave the journal on the coffee table. Let Beatrice find it there. He didn't care. His wig slipped precariously as he fumbled for his briefcase and jacket.

Outside, in the thin winter air, he yanked off the wig and hurled it into the passenger seat of his Hummer. His scalp steamed with sweat. He gripped the steering wheel so tight his knuckles whitened.

"He bought it," he told himself. "He had to. He's half-blind and half-brain-dead. He *had* to."

But behind him, in the dim apartment, Lester Filch sat in his recliner, a faint smile tugging at the corner of his mouth. He might not have remembered his past, but he knew a liar when he heard one. And Gary Garretson had lied through his teeth.

CHAPTER THIRTY FIVE

Lester Filch waited all day for Beatrice, the weight of anticipation pressing against his chest like a sandbag. He didn't tell her, in the halting phone call the day before, about the stranger who sat in her chair, basically pretending to be her, reading from the journal in a voice that dripped with smugness. Lester hadn't even bothered to ask her if she had been, in fact, sick. He knew she hadn't. But then, he wondered, maybe she *was* a little sick, in her own way.

He had let Gary's words burrow into him like worms, let them stir up things he had not wanted stirred up. But he wanted to see her face, as best he could, when he asked her to read the journal again. He wanted the truth to walk through his door on its own two legs, carrying her tote bag and her bright professional smile, and then he wanted to see whether it could survive the weight of his suspicion.

When she knocked that evening, he did not leap to his feet or call out a cheerful "come in" the way he sometimes did. He waited a beat too long, as though considering whether to open at all, before muttering, "It's open." Beatrice stepped inside, brushing the snow from her coat sleeves, cheeks pink from the cold. She looked like goodness itself incarnate, a walking sermon in flannel-lined virtue. But Lester watched her differently now—measuring, suspicious, like a man watching a magician's hands instead of the hat.

"Hello, Lester," she said, setting her bag on the counter, her voice composed, practiced. "How are we feeling today?"

"Feeling," he said slowly, "is complicated. Sit." His hand gestured stiffly toward the couch opposite him. She blinked, smiled nervously, and complied.

Beatrice knew instantly something was different. This was not how their sessions usually began. Normally she coaxed him to stand, to stretch, to walk the hallway with his ridiculous walker, to practice his exercises. Today he kept his weight sunk into the recliner, his body arranged like a barricade.

"You look tired," she ventured, unpacking gauze and tape. "Rough night?"

"Rough morning," he replied. He let the words dangle in the air, heavy with implication.

"Is it your scars? Are they still weeping?"

When she moved toward him, he raised a hand. "Not yet. Before you start fussing—there's something else." His voice carried an unusual authority, the brittle edge of a man daring himself not to tremble.

Beatrice tilted her head. "Something else?"

"The journal."

The two words landed like stones on the table between them. She froze, her hand halfway to the bandages. Her eyes flicked to her bag, as if making sure the forged diary was still tucked safely inside. "The journal?" she repeated, carefully neutral.

"Yes." He leaned forward, his blurred gaze trying to pin her down. "I want you to read to me again. Today. Right now."

She gave a small, uncertain laugh. "Lester, I don't think…"

"Humor a cripple, won't you?" he said sweetly.

"But Lester, we—"

"Read." His tone cut through her hesitation, harsher than he intended, but he didn't soften it. "Open it. Pick up where we left off."

For a moment she seemed to consider refusing outright. Every nerve in her body was suddenly on edge. There was a trick somewhere. She knew it. Her fingers hovered over the tote bag, then closed on the spine of the journal, of *her* journal. She drew it out slowly, like contraband.

Lester's breath came shallower. He felt the trap he had set for her closing in and some part of him hated it even as he longed for it. If she went through with this, if she read even a little bit, he thought he would scream. She would be just as much a liar as Gary Garretson, or Arthur Medlar, as Lester was certain it was. She would be just as much a liar as every other person in his life.

Beatrice opened to the next neat, careful entry she forged. Her voice, calm and deliberate, began to read: "There were days, when I was young that the world seemed brighter, almost forgiving. I remember walking home from school with my friends—"

"Stop." The word cracked from him like a whip. Beatrice startled, nearly dropping the book. "Friends?" he barked. "I had friends?"

Her throat worked as she searched for a reply. "It's what you wrote, Lester. It's here, in your own words."

"No." He shook his head violently, as if to rattle loose the words he needed from inside his skull. "That's not right. I *know* I didn't have friends. You see, I don't have any friends now, and people who make friends usually keep them. So that's not a memory, that's fiction." His hand curled against the armrest, nails biting into the fabric.

"But Lester, how can you—"

"Try again," he demanded.

Her voice faltered as she flipped a page, then resumed. "My mother would wait at the window for me. She always said I had the brightest smile."

A sound erupted from Lester's chest, half laugh, half growl. "My mother? My mother is *dead*. Who waited for me at the window, her ghost?"

"Lester, she—"

His voice rose, scraping raw. "You think because I can't see clearly you can paint me pictures I'll believe? Don't you realize my memories are ugly? Don't you see that I can feel them underneath my skin. I don't need a so-called journal. I don't need your help to see that."

Her eyes widened, panic surfacing at last. She stood up and took a step towards him. "Lester, calm down. I only—"

He slammed a fist on the table. The mug beside him rattled, water sloshing over the rim. "Don't tell me to calm down, dammit! I've swallowed your medicine, your soup, your goddamn bedtime stories. But I remember now! Do you hear me? I remember!"

And he did. The truth was he started remembering again when Arthur came in to feed him his reality like gruel. Fragments clawed their way out of the dark: a classroom, children pointing, the word "Commie" spat like venom; a fish bowl shattered, orange scales circling the drain; his father's voice heavy with disappointment; the long nights alone, nursing hatred like it was the only warmth available. His chest heaved. The memories were jagged, cruel, but they had the taste of iron truth.

Beatrice's lips trembled. "I thought—I thought I could help."

"By lying?" he rose to meet her stare across the coffee table. "Is that what you call help? You thought you could rewrite me," he spat, "make me into some saintly project for your collection, but I was never your project. I was a man. A wretched man, maybe, but a man all the same. And you stole my life from me."

"I wanted to give you a chance!" she cried, tears burning in her eyes. "A second chance!"

He laughed bitterly, the sound scraping at her brain like glass. It was the sound of contempt. "*You* don't give chances. *Life* doesn't give chances. It gives bruises and burns and losses, and we either rot or we crawl. You think covering it up makes me new? It makes me nothing! A ghost! Your puppet!"

Lester's eyes glistened, but tears didn't fall. He wouldn't let them. His eyes burned instead. "Better to be the monster I was than the doll you want me to be."

Beatrice's hands shook the journal. She set it down as though it might bite. "I only wanted you to be happy," she said, voice breaking.

"Happy?" He barked the word like a curse. "I don't even know what that means, but I know one thing: I was never happy. And pretending I was won't save me." He turned away and walked towards the window, the white crest of his anger having broken onto sand. There was only sadness now. He stared into the blur of the frosted glass. Snow fell outside, soft and indifferent. "Get out, Beatrice," he said softly. "Get out and don't come back."

She staggered back, horror filling her. "Lester—"

"No," he said firmly. "You're not going to tell me who I am. You're not going to tell me how to live. Take your false gospel and your pity and just leave me alone. I've had enough of saints. Enough of liars." His voice dropped lower, ragged. "Enough of you."

For a moment Beatrice stood frozen, tears streaming silently down her cheeks. Then she gathered her bag with clumsy fingers, pressed the journal shut, and turned toward the door. At the threshold she paused, looking back one last time. He did not look at her. Lester's eyes looked straight out the window, his hand closed into fists that rested on the windowsill. It was the first time she noticed he didn't need a walker anymore. She opened her mouth, but no words came. With a strangled sob, she fled.

The door closed. Silence smothered the room, broken only by the hiss of the radiator and Lester's uneven breath. He stood motionless, every muscle coiled, his chest a cage of fire. Slowly, as the quiet deepened, the anger began to curdle into something heavier. Shame. Grief. And underneath it all, the sickening recognition that she had been right about one thing: he did not want to go back. He remembered the misery, the cruelty, the corrosive joy he had taken in making others suffer. He remembered—and he recoiled.

He thought of memory the way the doctor had described trauma: there are injuries that heal into the shape of what they were, and injuries that heal into something new. His memories—the ones that were returning—felt like the second kind. They were not bringing back the man he had been; they were helping to build a different kind of muscle around the same skeleton. He could feel the old Lester, his habits like a suit still hanging in the closet, pressed and ready, but every time he reached for it, his arm remembered pain. He did not want to put it on.

From the hallway came the old building's nocturnal chorus: a pipe's hard cough, the baby's thin whimper that turned—already—into a child's toddlerish whine, the hiss of someone boiling water at an hour that suggested loneliness. These were the sounds he knew how to hate. He was good at it. There are men who can change a tire in five minutes in the rain; there are men who can describe the habits of migratory birds by their shadows alone; he could hear the shape of a neighbor's happiness and aim his grievance like a stone.

He waited for the old instinct to return, but it didn't. Under the chorus he heard something else: a quiet shape, an absence shaped like someone not at his table—no small clinks of a spoon against a mug, no mild bossiness telling him to drink water first, then swallow, not the other way around. Damn her for making the empty space articulate.

Lester turned from the window and limped back to his recliner. He grabbed another cigarette from the pack on the coffee table and lit it, his hand trembling a little. He sucked until the smoke scratched his throat. The scratch was good; it was a feeling that obeyed cause and effect. Too much of his life lately had refused the dignity of logic. You bleed out but don't die because fire cauterizes you; you forget everything but remember how to loathe yourself; you detest a woman and then discover you prefer breathing in rooms where she is.

"Do-gooders," he muttered as he sat down, letting the ash lengthen indecently before tapping it into the tray. "They come with casseroles and scissors. They trim and feed and call it love."

He could see them all—he'd seen them his whole life—people of projects and committees, the professional empathizers, faces smooth with certainty. They arrived with pamphlets and phrases and left with praise. People like that believed the world was a series of misapplied bandages and that, if they could only get their hands on your wound, they would show you the proper wrap. They delighted in diagrams. They used verbs like uplift and empower. And he had let one in. He had watched her count pills into a ceramic bowl and remind him that mercy comes in milligrams. He had let her point him toward the shower and tape a square of plastic over his bandage while joking about Napoleon and Waterloo. He had allowed soup—soup!—to become an instrument of meaning. He, Lester Filch, who had once called a landlord at 2 AM to complain about the tone of a neighbor's sneeze, had sat docile while a woman with a ponytail reorganized his despair into a treatment plan.

But not anymore. She was gone for good, along with her so-called medicine. He pressed a palm to his chest, the way you do when you mean to swear something to yourself and want your heart to notarize it. "You are not clay," he said, low, to the scarred sternum beneath the threadbare T-shirt. "You are not a project. You are not fixable."

The words should have comforted him. Once upon a time they would have. There is freedom in declaring yourself unredeemable; you are excused from the soft labor of hope. But the sentences felt—he groped for the word and hated himself for it—outdated. He had been edited. His body had forced revision upon him. He could not pretend to be the original draft.

"What do you even want from me?" he asked the empty apartment, which, to its credit, did not pretend to answer. He knew what he wanted from himself, at least for tonight. He wanted not to call her. He wanted not to write something meant to hurt and call it truth. He wanted not to pace the rooms rehearsing speeches that, if delivered, would close a door he might want open later. He wanted to wait, which was a skill no one had ever accused him of owning.

The building settled around him with its usual complaints. A neighbor laughed once, a sound like cutlery in a drawer. Outside, a car crept by, tires whispering on old snow. He thought—not for the first time—that if love were a sound it would be that: a car refusing to go faster than the road allowed.

"I love you," he said into the room, softly, because even just practicing those words hurt a little. "And I don't forgive you." The sentiment was true enough to sit with him without protest. Love and forgiveness could live on separate chairs for awhile, nodding at each other across the coffee table like men who refused to shake hands but had agreed to share the same air.

Lester rubbed his eyes. His vision, never great since the accident, blurred even further, as if the room were suddenly underwater. For a moment he saw the hospital ceiling again, the way the fluorescence flattened everything into a single color; he felt the helmet of bandage, the straps at his wrists; he heard the nurse whispering kielbasa outside the door and the priest who had nearly sent his soul to the wrong room. He smiled at the memory despite his irritation then.

Lester pressed his scarred hands against his face, the tears finally sliding free, hot and salty. He did not weep loudly. The sound was low, guttural, the noise of a man who has seen himself clearly and cannot bear the sight. He remembered who he had been. And he knew, with dreadful certainty, that he could never be that man again—because if he was, there was no reason left to live, and he had already been down that bridge before.

CHAPTER THIRTY SIX

Beatrice Goodie left Lester Filch's apartment with her hands trembling on the steering wheel, but it wasn't the tremor of fear. It was something more corrosive, something that began in her chest and burned its way outward, until even her fingertips ached with it. Rage at herself, despair at herself, shame that felt bottomless. By the time she parked in her driveway she could barely breathe. She sat in the car as if bolted to the seat, unwilling to climb the steps to her apartment because she didn't know what version of herself would be waiting inside.

She had always prided herself on being steady. When she was a child, her mother said she had been born composed, a baby who rarely cried, a girl who rarely disobeyed, a teenager who never rebelled. Teachers adored her. Old ladies praised her. Friends called her the one they could rely on when their lives fell to pieces. Beatrice Goodie, the good girl, the dependable saint, the one who always did right, who always gave, who never asked for anything in return.

And now? She pressed her forehead to the cool steering wheel. Now she was a liar. A thief of memory. She had stolen a man's life and rewritten it, all because she thought her version of him would be better than the one that really existed. It was breathtaking in its arrogance. Worse, she had told herself it was kindness. Necessary evil, she had named it, like the great moral philosophers she once admired. Lies for the sake of love. Deceit for the sake of redemption.

But when Lester's eyes turned on her—sharp, narrowing, seeing her not as his savior but as his betrayer—she felt the full collapse of her illusion. He had asked her to read, and she had done it, fumbling, her throat dry, her voice cracking. He had listened. Listened with a quiet that was more terrifying than rage. Then he had told her she was lying. Told her the words she fed him were not his. Told her she had tried to shape him into something he was not, and he hated her for it.

And he was right.

She had walked out weeping, but the tears weren't only for him. They were for herself, for the death of the only story she had ever truly believed: that she was good.

Beatrice stumbled into her apartment at last, dropping her keys on the table, and collapsing onto the couch without bothering to take off her coat. She covered her face with her hands. What was she, stripped of her goodness? She saw herself as she had been for years, working in the shelter, handing out muffins, folding blankets, soothing strangers. Always giving. Always perfect. And always secretly proud of it. The woman who had once believed that goodness could spread like butter across the world—soft, melting, filling every empty corner—now realized she had been holding a knife the entire time, carving her vision into others without asking.

The word *hypocrite* rose in her throat like bile.

She sobbed, then bit her lip hard, furious at herself for sobbing, furious at herself for everything. She was no martyr, no saint. She was a coward who lied to a man too broken to defend himself. She was a manipulator who burned the truth because it offended her sense of justice. She was, at bottom, just like Lester Filch had always been: someone who bent the world to her misery, only cloaked in prettier clothing.

Her tears slowed eventually, though the ache in her chest did not. She stood, pulled off her coat, and began pacing the apartment in restless loops. The same thought returned again and again: if I'm not good, then what am I?

She had no answer.

Beatrice drifted into her bedroom and sat at the vanity. The mirror reflected a woman she hardly recognized: eyes red, cheeks blotched, mouth twisted. Not the serene Beatrice, the angel everyone had adored. Just a woman, broken like any other.

It was almost a relief.

She studied her own face, leaning close. "What if you've been wrong your whole life?" she whispered to the mirror. "What if goodness isn't the point at all?"

The mirror, faithful to its role, did not answer. But something else stirred within her—an image of Lester, his scarred face crumpling as he realized who he had been, the tears pooling in his eyes when he spoke of misery as if it were his only inheritance. He had not been condemned to evil, not truly. He had simply never been loved. Not *really* loved, not for who he was. His parents had failed him. The world had failed him. She had failed him. Maybe this was the point of religion, the point of God. To be loved by something when everything else in the world fails.

And yet—even now—she could choose to turn this around not by being good but by being honest.

The thought settled into her like a stone sinking to the bottom of a dark, murky pond. She remembered the way his hand trembled when he signed the insurance forms, the way he secretly smiled when she told him he smelled better after his first proper shower, the way he ate her soup grudgingly but completely. None of it was dramatic. None of it was saintly. But it was real. It was Lester Filch as he was, not as she wanted him to be.

And maybe that was enough.

She pressed her palms flat to the vanity table, her breath steadying. She had spent years telling herself that goodness was about rejecting evil, about never being tainted, about being pure. But purity without love was brittle, an external façade of behavior modification. It wasn't real. It cracked the moment life pressed too hard. Love, on the other hand—*real* love—was not about staying untainted, helpful as that might be. It was about walking into a tainted mess and staying there as long as it took to make things right. It was about sitting across from a man whose entire life was defined by bitterness and saying, *I'm here for you, no matter what.*

The revelation was terrifying. But it was also liberating.

Beatrice rose and began to undress for bed, her movements deliberate, as though each garment shed was a piece of her old life. She was not Saint Beatrice anymore. She was simply Beatrice, flawed, guilty, and strangely freer than she had ever been.

She slid under the covers, staring up at the ceiling. Her tears dried on her cheeks, leaving her skin tight. Sleep did not come quickly, but when it did, it was not the dreamless sleep of the righteous. It was the restless, fractured sleep of a woman who had chosen to face herself in spite of everything, and who knew tomorrow would test her all over again.

She whispered a prayer into the dark, half to herself, half to a god she wasn't sure was there. "Show me what goodness is. I want to know." Lester's face flashed in her mind, along with the thought, *Goodness starts with men like these, men who know who they are, even when they're bad.* It sounded counter-intuitive. She couldn't understand it. But she had to receive it by faith. The man who had destroyed her sense of goodness, a man the world could not accept and could not understand, was the beginning of what was truly good. "You are not condemned, Lester Filch," she said aloud. "You are not condemned."

Beatrice closed her eyes, and the night folded around her like a difficult but honest embrace.

CHAPTER THIRTY SEVEN

Arthur Medlar prided himself on checking his mail with the air of a man opening a stock portfolio. It was, after all, beneath him to acknowledge that most of the envelopes belonged to credit card companies, charity solicitations, and coupons for frozen dinners he wouldn't touch with tongs. But there it was: the ritual of sifting through society's paper offerings, like a king who stooped once a day to see what his subjects had left at the palace gate.

That morning, tucked among the banal, was an envelope in Beatrice Goodie's hand. He knew her handwriting instantly. After all, he had seen it in that fake journal of hers. Beatrice's script was painfully upright, each letter properly formed, a schoolmarm's handwriting that believed good penmanship still mattered in a world of AOL and blackberries. It radiated effort, moral effort. And there, in the return address, was her name spelled out in full—**Beatrice Goodie**—as though anyone would confuse her with another Beatrice in the vicinity of West Lemon, New Jersey.

Arthur's chest swelled. Finally, he thought. At last she'd realized what she had in him: wealth, charm, the opportunity to be associated with the Medlar name. She was probably writing something sentimental, perhaps quoting Jane Austen or Emily Dickinson, asking forgiveness for her stiffness lately, pledging herself once more to him and his vision of the future. Women had a way of doubting themselves, of letting small grievances cloud their perspective, but eventually they came to their senses. He was sure she received a good tongue-lashing from his unfortunate competitor and that whole fiasco was over with. Arthur may be whatever was left over, like her meatloaf, but at least he was on the plate. Lester Filch was in the trash.

He slit the envelope open with his silver letter opener—an ostentatious piece shaped like a sword he'd bought from a shop in Vienna to remind himself he was always armed, even during correspondence. He unfolded the pages with a flourish. And then he read. The opening line was polite enough, but it landed like a slap: ARTHUR, YOU ARE A VERY GOOD MAN, BUT I DON'T THINK WE ARE GOOD TOGETHER.

Arthur froze. His eyes darted over the words, rereading them twice, three times. NOT GOOD TOGETHER. He imagined her rehearsing it, her lips pursing as she told herself how honest she was being. The letter continued:

> I tried very hard to admire your way of living, but I find myself more exhausted than uplifted by it. Your gestures are large, Arthur, but they leave me feeling small. I prefer smaller gestures—like a cup of tea, or a conversation that doesn't end in a business metaphor. I'm sorry, Arthur. I know you will find another woman who will see you the way you want to be seen.

Arthur's mouth fell open. BUSINESS METAPHOR? He slammed the paper down on the counter and paced, muttering. That line alone was enough to convict her of treason. He *lived* on business metaphors. They were the oxygen of his success. "That's how you explain life," he growled. "That's how you win at it! A conversation without a business metaphor is just gossip!"

He picked the letter up again, scanning.

> I hope you won't take this personally. Truly, it is not you as a man—it is us together. I simply can't pretend to be happy, and it would not be good of me to let you think otherwise.

Not take it personally? He barked a laugh that startled the neighbor's dog into yapping down the hall. Not personally? She had written a breakup letter stuffed with personal grievances, each sharpened like a knife, and then had the gall to call it NOT PERSONAL.

The worst part, though, was the tone. It was relentlessly kind. Every sentence wrapped in apology, every insult delivered with the frosting of decency. Arthur could practically hear her voice: earnest, patient, as though explaining to a child why he couldn't have dessert before dinner. It wasn't a rejection, she seemed to insist—it was a LESSON.

He reread the letter, this time slower, and the humiliation spread across his skin like fire ants. Beatrice Goodie, of all people, was dismissing him as though he were some intern she'd decided couldn't handle her filing system.

He crumpled the letter in his fist, then smoothed it out again, unwilling to lose the evidence. His jaw locked. The humiliation spread across his skin like heat rash.

Arthur Medlar had never lost. Never. In his forty-five years, he had not once walked away empty-handed. He had not once been denied what he wanted. He was captain of his high school football team, editor of the law review at NYU, youngest partner at his firm, CEO before forty. Every room he entered bent itself around his gravity. Women bent themselves around him too. And here was Beatrice Goodie, a woman who wore flannel pajamas at dinner, telling him he was TOO MUCH.

Arthur could not even process the absurdity.

His mind, hot and erratic, conjured images. Beatrice writing the letter at her little desk, fussing over margins, proud of each moral flourish. Beatrice reading it aloud to herself, nodding, smiling that pious smile. Beatrice sealing the envelope with her thin, chapped lips, convinced she had been merciful.

He thought of tearing her lips off.

The thought came unbidden, and it shocked him with its clarity. He saw her mouth open to scold him, to lecture him on simplicity, and he saw himself tearing the words right out of her throat, along with her tongue. Or maybe he would shove the letter opener into her mouth as it lectured him, and he would push, push, push until it came out the other side, right through her spine.

Murder bloomed in him like a flower.

He imagined her locked in a room, her sermons muffled by gags, her composure shattered. He thought of fire, of knives, of what a woman looked like when stripped of her righteousness. It was intoxicating.

But then, more deliciously, he thought of Lester Filch.

Filch, the broken man she doted on. Filch, with his scars and walker and pathetic drool. Filch, the charity case. Arthur's hand clenched into a fist. Filch was the real enemy here, wasn't he? Beatrice might have written the letter, but Filch handed her the ink. Even if the man had excoriated her for what she did, he had done enough damage to make her realize she really wasn't that happy with Arthur Medlar. And she was just a stupid woman, anyway. As dumb as she was good. Could he really blame her for being such an idiot?

Arthur pictured Lester dead: slumped in that filthy recliner, cigarette fallen from his lips, the acrid smell of cabbage finally drowned by the smell of rot. He pictured Beatrice finding him, her face collapsing in horror, realizing her little project had expired, not knowing that she would be next.

But no, that would be too easy, too blunt. Arthur Medlar was not a blunt instrument; he was a scalpel. Killing them would end the game. And anyone could end a game by flipping the board, but Arthur never ended games; he won them.

So he would win this.

He wasn't going to kill Beatrice. He was going to marry her. He would bind her to him, publicly, legally, permanently. He would make her smile at the wedding while remembering this letter, this foolish attempt at leaving. Every day afterward she would look at him and know she had failed to escape. She would sit across from him at their perfect dining table, in their perfect home, and she would see her own powerlessness mirrored in his smirk.

That, he thought, would be better than murder.

But first, something not so extreme.

Arthur paced his apartment, the letter trembling in his fist. She had played her move. Fine. He would play his.

The question was how.

He poured himself a scotch and sat at his desk, the glass desk that reflected his own face back at him like a boardroom god. Whether Beatrice and Lester were speaking or not after his little game didn't really matter. Even if the journal tore them apart, she was still going to leave him. *What could he do now?* Arthur banged his head on the desk several times, hoping it would shake his brain up a little bit and give him some good ideas other than murder. At that moment, his computer screen turned on like a dare.

That's it! he thought. *Destabilize her.*

She thought she was honest. Well, he doubted that, after what she pulled with the journal. And how honest was she really being with her parents? Did she tell *them* she didn't want to marry him after all the money they already invested, all the plans and rentals? She prided herself on never lying, on being good. But Arthur knew goodness was just a brand, a label slapped on choices to make them palatable. He was sure she never told her parents about Lester Filch.

Beatrice was already troubled, and if Lester had told her off, she was alone. If her family turned on her, she would fold, like every woman eventually folded. Maybe her parents could talk some sense into her, or yell some sense into her. Soon she would smile again by his side, this time because he forced her to. And if she didn't? Then maybe the locked room fantasy wasn't so far-fetched after all.

Arthur leaned back, sipping scotch. He felt calmer now. Purpose steadied him. Murder could wait. Torture could wait. Winning could not.

He smoothed the letter flat on the desk and read it again, slower this time, savoring every line as fuel. By the time he finished his drink, he knew what he would write to her mother, and Hell hath no fury as a woman scorned. And Mrs. Goodie was *definitely* a woman, or maybe more like a demon in high heels. There would be fury indeed. This would not go well for Beatrice.

Arthur smiled and then began to type.

CHAPTER THIRTY EIGHT

Arthur Medlar believed words could bend the world. He had built his fortune, his reputation, even his charm on them. A clever phrase in court could ruin an opponent; the right toast at a party could win an ally. Words, when selected and sharpened, were weapons; when softened and sugared, they were bait.

Tonight, words would serve him again.

He sat at his desk, the snow pressing in at the window, a glass of scotch warming his hand. His laptop glowed like a stage spotlight, waiting for his performance. Arthur cracked his knuckles, leaned forward, and began to type.

The first draft was a snarl. YOUR DAUGHTER HAS BETRAYED ME. SHE'S CHOSEN A BURNED CRIPPLE OVER A MAN OF WEALTH AND LOYALTY. I WON'T STAND FOR IT! He read the lines aloud and grimaced. Too coarse. A tantrum, not an argument. Delete.

The second draft was melodrama. SHE CAVORTS WITH A MAN UNWORTHY OF HER PRESENCE... SQUANDERS HER PURITY ON HIS DECREPIT SOUL. Arthur sneered at himself. Cavorts? Purity? He sounded like a disgraced preacher. Delete.

The third draft had potential. I AM WRITING TO YOU AS A SON. NOT YOUR SON YET, THOUGH I HOPE ONE DAY TO BE. BUT I

FEAR BEATRICE IS LOSING HER WAY... That had promise. Humility. Heartbreak. Noble suffering. But it needed more sweetness, more sanctimony. He would wrap his poison in lace. He typed furiously, polishing each phrase until it gleamed.

The final product oozed sincerity:

> I NEVER IMAGINED I WOULD WRITE SUCH AN EMAIL. MY HEART IS HEAVY, BUT I MUST SHARE WHAT WEIGHS ON ME. BEATRICE HAS WRITTEN ME A LETTER STATING THAT SHE NO LONGER WISHES TO BE MARRIED TO ME.
>
> I LOVE YOUR DAUGHTER. I HAVE ALWAYS LOVED HER, FROM THE MOMENT WE MET, AND I WANT ONLY WHAT IS BEST FOR HER. BUT LATELY, I FEAR SHE HAS BEEN MISLED. SHE NOW SPENDS HER TIME WITH A MAN WHO, THROUGH NO FAULT OF HIS OWN, IS BROKEN IN BODY AND, I FEAR, IN SPIRIT. I RESPECT HER KINDNESS—WHO WOULD NOT?— BUT KINDNESS HAS BECOME CAPTIVITY. SHE GIVES HIM WHAT BELONGS TO YOU, TO ME, TO HER FUTURE.
>
> I BEG YOU, GUIDE HER BACK. REMIND HER WHO SHE IS. REMIND HER WHERE HER TRUE HAPPINESS LIES. I WILL LOVE HER FOREVER, NO MATTER WHAT. BUT I CANNOT STAND BY WHILE SHE THROWS HERSELF AWAY.
>
> PLEASE—HELP ME SAVE HER.

Arthur read it twice, then three times, admiring his craftsmanship. It was perfect: pity masquerading as devotion, judgment cloaked as concern. He imagined the Goodies reading it aloud in their parlor, Mrs. Goodie clutching her pearls, Mr. Goodie pacing with rage. He clicked SEND and raised his glass in silent triumph.

The storm struck Beatrice the next afternoon. She was folding towels in her apartment, contemplating the best moment to spring herself on Lester again, when her phone rang. Beatrice set aside the last one, walked over to the kitchen, and answered.

"Beatrice Anne Goodie," her mother shrilled, without preamble, "what in heaven's name are you doing with that man?"

Confusion quickly led to realization. Her letter had gotten to Arthur. Arthur had gotten to Mom and Dad. Beatrice braced herself for another wave.

Her father's voice thundered in from the background. "Don't you dare pretend ignorance! Do you think we raised you to disgrace this family? To leave everything we provided for you and consort with some invalid? Some... some... *parasite?*"

Beatrice's throat tightened. "You're talking about Lester?"

"Of course we're talking about Lester!" her mother snapped. "Arthur told us everything. After we got an email, we called him right away. Arthur, who has done nothing but love you. Arthur, who has given you gifts, devotion, stability. And you—you betray him for some wretch in bandages."

Her father piled on. "Do you even realize what you've cost us? Arthur's father pulled out of a major deal this morning. Millions, Beatrice! Millions gone because of your stupidity! Your selfishness has ruined our family!"

Beatrice gripped the receiver hard, her pulse pounding. They were circling her like hawks, talons of shame and obligation outstretched.

"If you walk away from Arthur Medlar," her mother continued, her voice trembling with fury, "you *will* be cut off. No inheritance, no support, no family name. You'll be alone, disgraced! Do you hear me? Alone!"

Something inside Beatrice snapped at that moment. A lifetime of obedience, of being the dutiful Goodie daughter, collapsed under the weight of their threats. The reality was, she had always been alone. Just like Lester. She had never really had parents. In fact, it seemed that Lester's father had been better than both her parents combined. They were threatening to take away what she never even had.

Her voice shook, but it rang clear. "Then cut me off. I don't care. I will *not* marry Arthur Medlar."

Her mother gasped, horrified. Her father shouted something indistinct. Beatrice pressed her thumb to the button and ended the call.

A few minutes later, she sat rigid at her kitchen table, the phone still buzzing faintly on its cradle as if it hadn't quite finished spitting her mother's voice into the room. She had pressed END mid-sentence, mid-threat. Disinheritance. Disgrace. Words as old as every argument she'd ever had with her parents, dusted off from some locked trunk of family intimidation and hurled across the country as though they could still stick. Her mother had cried. Her father's voice had risen in the background like a stage cue. And Arthur—Arthur's fingerprints were all over it.

She sat trembling, the echo of the call clanging in her head. For one stunned moment, she felt like the obedient girl she had once been, toeing the family line, promising to be perfect. Then something inside her had broken. Not dramatically, not loudly, but with the quiet finality of glass cracking under heat. Earlier she had been contemplating when to make her move. But there was no time like the present. She grabbed her coat, slammed the door, and drove.

The streets of West Lemon blurred past. Stoplights glowed, and she didn't remember if she stopped at all of them. Snowbanks slouched against the sidewalks. Houses huddled, lights winking through frosted windows. Her hands clenched the wheel as though she were clinging to the last solid thing in her life.

She tried to remember what her mother had said, word for word. Something about Arthur being the only respectable man she'd ever bring home. Something about family honor. Something about disgrace if she didn't straighten herself out. It was always disgrace. Always the family name, the legacy, the expectations.

But what about her? What about her own name, her own life? For forty years she lived between obedience and rebellion, never quite one, never quite the other. She left California for independence but found herself shackled in Boston by the same invisible leash. She only said yes to Arthur because it seemed good, respectable, safe, and that *Yes* had soured in her mouth every day since.

Now, at last, she had said *No*.

The word thrilled and terrified her. She had hung up on her mother. She had broken something that might never be mended, and for once, she didn't have to fix it. She could almost hear Arthur's laugh when he found out. He would gloat. He would push harder. He had never lost in his life, and he would make this a war. But Beatrice wasn't driving toward Arthur. She wasn't driving toward her parents. She was driving toward the one man who had looked her in the eye, scars and all, and shown her both his weakness and his strength. The one man who, for all his cruelty in the past, had wept in front of her. The one man who had told her the truth, however bitter it was.

Lester Filch.

The car rattled over a patch of ice, and she steadied it, muttering aloud, "This is insane." But her heart knew better. It wasn't insanity; it was inevitability.

She pulled up to the familiar curb in front of the West Lemon Apartments. The engine ticked as it cooled. She sat there for a long breath, hands still clutching the wheel, forehead against the leather. Then she whispered, "Beatrice Goodie, this is *your* life. Not theirs. Not Arthur's. Yours." And she got out.

Lester heard her before he saw her. The knock on his door was soft, hesitant, the knock of someone testing whether she still had the right to come in. He had been smoking again—half a cigarette in the ashtray, another smoldering in the mug that had become his personal ash urn, WORLD'S BEST DAD now lacquered with tar. He thought of ignoring her. He thought of telling her to get lost, that he didn't need more of her charity, her muffins, her lies.

But he didn't. He shuffled to the door and opened it.

There she was. Wind-bitten cheeks, hair frizzed from the cold, eyes tired and sagging. And despite himself, despite the bitterness in his chest, he stepped aside.

"Come in," he muttered.

She did. She closed the door behind her and leaned against it, her breath coming fast, as if she'd just outrun the cold like it had claws. For a long moment they didn't say a word, just looked at each other. The apartment smelled as it always did, but she breathed it in as if it were air she had been suffocating without.

"I'm sorry," she said finally. "I was an idiot. It was the worst thing I could have ever done. And I'm sorry."

Lester expected denial, excuses, her saintly spin on everything. Instead, she gave him a blunt apology. For once, Beatrice Goodie didn't dress her goodness up in ribbons.

He half-hopped, half-shuffled back to his recliner and lowered himself into it, wincing at the pain that still dogged his hips. She stayed standing, her hand pressed flat against the door as if she might need to bolt at any second.

"You read me fairy tales," he said finally, his voice low. "You rewrote my life. You thought you could fix me."

"Yes," she said, "I did."

"And you thought I wouldn't notice."

"I hoped you wouldn't."

Silence fell again. The refrigerator groaned. A radiator hissed. Somewhere down the hall, a neighbor cursed at a sports game. Lester stared at the space on the couch across from him that she should have been occupying. Beatrice stared at the back of his head.

Finally, she crossed the room and filled the space on the couch. Her hands were clasped in her lap, white-knuckled.

"Lester," she said, "I have spent my whole life trying to be good. Not just decent. Not just kind. Good. Perfect, even. I thought if I gave everything, if I lived simply, if I never hurt anyone, then maybe I could be worth something. But it wasn't real. It was just…an act. A story I told myself." She swallowed hard. "And with you, I thought I could make someone else good too. Rewrite you. Rewrite myself. But it was a lie. And I'm sorry."

He looked up then, his eyes sharp, scarred face illuminated by the lamplight. "And what do you want from me now? Forgiveness?"

"No," she said. "I don't want forgiveness. I don't blame you if you never want to trust me again. But I *do* want to start building again. As friends. As ourselves. No lies. No rewriting. Just…two people, trying to get to know each other."

The words hung in the stale air. Lester leaned back, the recliner groaning beneath him. He felt the weight of her gaze, the sincerity in it. And for the first time in weeks, he let himself soften, just a fraction.

"I was a bastard," he said. "All my life, I made people miserable. Especially you. I can remember that now. I can remember hating you just for being good. And I don't want to be that man anymore."

"You don't have to apologize for who you were," she said quickly, leaning forward. "Not to me. The only thing that matters is what you choose now. Today. Tomorrow. Going forward."

He studied her, as if trying to decide whether she was real or just another fiction. Then, slowly, he nodded.

And in that moment, though no one said the word, though there was no kiss, no embrace, no declaration, something shifted. I personally would call it a contract, or an engagement, or maybe simply the moment two broken people decided to bind themselves to each other. But I guess, in reality, it was quieter: two scarred hearts, recognizing that they might beat more steadily in tandem.

Beatrice sat back. Lester lit another cigarette, but this time he didn't turn away from her. Smoke curled between them, but for once it didn't feel like a wall.

And that was how it began.

The world would see only neighbors. Friends, perhaps. Patient and aide. But in truth, in that dingy apartment that smelled of cabbage, Lester Filch and Beatrice Goodie had already decided. They would marry each other—not in ceremony, not yet, but in the stubborn, secret resolve that binds people tighter than vows.

Neither of them spoke it aloud. They didn't need to.

CHAPTER THIRTY NINE

Arthur Medlar always considered himself a man of action. He never lost anything in his life—not a race, not a contract, not a girl worth taking seriously. Winning was his religion. Losing was for other people, the unwashed, the mediocre, the men who wore brown suits and thought Oldsmobile was still a luxury brand. And yet here he was, forty years old, a Hummer in the garage, bespoke suits in the closet, the CEO of a company with its name in lights on Times Square—and he was losing to Lester Filch.

Lester Filch, of all people. A man who smelled like cooked cabbage and unemployment checks. A man who had to be carried out of his burning car like a sack of spoiled meat. A man with scars where cheekbones used to be. Lester Filch: human mildew. And somehow, Beatrice Goodie—Arthur's fiancée, his prize, his possession—had drifted into Lester's orbit.

Arthur had followed her the day before, just to be sure, after getting off the phone with Beatrice's mother. She had told him the horrible news through tears. According to her, she had a daughter no longer. He could hardly believe it, so he got in his car and drove all the way to West Lemon. He parked two blocks down from Lester's apartment, his Hummer squatting among the sedans, and he waited. Sure enough, there she was: Beatrice, halo-haired, carrying her tote bag of mercy, stepping across the cracked concrete path into Filch's cave. He knew the look on her face. It was the look she used on their first date together—the look that told him she was happy.

Something had to be done.

At first, Arthur toyed with ideas, extravagant and operatic. Hire a private investigator. Catch her in the act. Publish photographs in the society pages: HEIRESS GOODIE SLUMMING WITH INVALID. He pictured her disgrace, her parents' continued tears, her running back to him, grateful for his forgiveness. But the flaw was simple: Beatrice wasn't afraid of disgrace. She had always sneered at reputation. She had officially cut ties from her family. He couldn't figure out how Lester Filch could have forgiven her for what she did to him, but it was apparent that he had. They were two peas in a pod once again.

No, it was quite simple. Lester Filch must be removed. Permanently.

Arthur didn't leap immediately to the word *murder*. He was not, in his mind, a murderer. Murder was crude, reckless, pedestrian. But then again, so was Lester. And to fight mildew, one sometimes needed bleach.

But how does one *murder*? He had thought about it so many times, but he'd never actually done it. If he was going to, it might as well be well-planned and, above all, elegant, in keeping with his persona.

POISON.

The word came to him like an advertisement. Elegant, invisible, silent. A gentleman's solution. Poison killed kings and left no fingerprints. Best of all, Lester was already half-dead. No one would bat an eye when his ticker gave out. He would just be one more casualty of bad luck, nothing more than a sorry statistic.

Arthur smiled in the driver's seat of his Hummer. It was the kind of smile you saw in mob movies right before the piano wire came out. He sat back and laughed. It wasn't a maniacal laugh, mind you. Not *really*. It wasn't the laugh of a comic book supervillain. It was more the laugh of a man who had told himself a very good joke.

This was going to be great.

The first obstacle, as with most of Arthur's plans in life, was reality. He had no idea how to acquire poison. In his mind's eye, he imagined a velvet-lined shop, perhaps in Chinatown, with glass jars labelled HEMLOCK and BELLADONNA. Or a shadowy dealer in an overcoat whispering "cyanide, arsenic, take your pick" at the back of a jazz club. But this was the mid-90s, not a dime novel, and Arthur Medlar had never set foot anywhere seedier than a midtown cigar lounge.

So he did the only thing a man could do in that era: he went to the library. The West Lemon Public Library was a brick cube squatting beside a parking lot. It smelled like paste and the dying breath of old men. It was a nursing home for books. Arthur had not been in a library since law school. He entered like a spy crossing enemy lines, collar up, sunglasses on.

"Can I help you find something?" the librarian asked—a woman with glasses that magnified her eyes until she looked like an owl.

"Chemistry," Arthur said. "For... ah... research."

"High school or college level?"

Arthur cleared his throat and adjusted his tie. "College. Let's say college."

She pointed him to the science section. Arthur stalked through the aisles, feeling ridiculous. Each step squeaked. Each title he pulled from the shelf was wrong: PRINCIPLES OF ORGANIC

CHEMISTRY. WATER QUALITY AND YOU. HOUSEHOLD CLEANING SOLUTIONS.

Finally he found it: TOXICOLOGY, AN INTRODUCTION. He carried it to a table by the window and opened it gingerly, as if the paper itself might accuse him. The pages smelled of mildew. He guessed it hadn't been used in quite some time. *There's not enough murderous intent around here*, he thought.

But the book wasn't really that helpful. More like overly-complicated, at least for Arthur's mind (although he would never admit it). It was filled with graphs, LD50 numbers, case studies. He skimmed one page: *A 42-year-old male ingested two grams of cyanide and expired within minutes.* Expired. As if the man were a carton of milk. He shuddered. How horrible — and how obvious. Cyanide was for amateurs. Cyanide reeked of an announcement.

He copied down a few names in a leather notebook he carried for appearances: cyanide, arsenic, strychnine. Just a few ideas—the classics. Strychnine appealed to him. It had flair, but flair was suspicious. He needed subtlety, something that could be mistaken for fate.

Arthur flipped another few pages. There was a section on PLANT ALKALOIDS. Hemlock, deadly nightshade, oleander. He had heard of those — staples of tragedies, but then a line caught his eye. *Digitalis (Foxglove): used medicinally in small doses to strengthen heart contractions. In larger amounts, causes nausea, dizziness, arrhythmia, and cardiac arrest.*

His eyebrows lifted. A medicine that was also a poison. A flower that pretended to heal until it killed. How interesting.

Arthur read the paragraph twice, then again, savoring it. Cyanide was crude. Rat pellets were vulgar. But *foxglove* — foxglove was poetic. Imagine slipping a dose of medicine across the table and watching it undo a man. A flower with two faces. After all, Beatrice was foxglove herself.

He flipped through to see if there was more. There was an anecdote buried in the text: a nineteenth-century physician named William Withering had "discovered" digitalis' medical use when he noticed village healers brewing foxglove tea for dropsy. He started experimenting with it himself, but lost some of his patients. Too much of it and they died. *Woops*, he thought. *Some doctor.* The same cup that saved one heart had stopped others. *Nowadays he would have gotten sued faster than you could say* foxglove digitalis.

Arthur sat back in the library chair, fingers drumming the book cover. That was it. That was elegance, a treatment that became a toxin, a flowered executioner. He could picture it already: Beatrice brewing Lester a cup, coaxing him to drink, never realizing she was the accomplice. Nightshade, arsenic, strychnine — they all looked guilty. Foxglove looked innocent until the last minute. Arthur closed the book, wrote the word DIGITALIS in capital letters in his notebook, underlined it three times. In the margin, he jotted: *Dropper. Herbal disguise. Tea.*

He checked out three volumes under an alias, signing the cards with a flourish: AL ALFREDSON. Back at his apartment, he spread them across his dining table as if he were an academic in the middle of a thesis. He spent the next night paging through them with a tumbler of brandy at his elbow. Most of the text was dull: binding sites, dosage tables, metabolic pathways. But every so often a phrase gleamed. *Visual disturbances. Irregular heartbeat. Collapse within minutes.* He underlined those.

By the end of his studies, he was an expert. *Foxglove Digitalis.* A flower that killed politely.

Arthur Medlar smiled at his own genius. The library had given him the key. The rest was procurement, though therein lay the problem. How does one get such an herb? The internet was still a blinking dial-up connection that screamed when you logged on, good only for emails. You couldn't order strychnine from Amazon in those days.

Arthur's break came not at a velvet-lined shop or a shadowy dealer but, absurdly enough, at a Manhattan herbalist tucked between a laundromat and a psychic. He had walked past it a dozen times without noticing — a narrow storefront with dusty window jars labeled things like *Valerian Root* and *St. John's Wort*. Normally he would have sneered. But now, with the word DIGITALIS burning in his notebook like a spell, the place glowed like a revelation. As soon as he remembered it, he ran down his apartment stairs, not even wanting to wait for the elevator, and briskly walked the four blocks to the store, aptly named *Thyme Square*.

The bell over the door tinkled when he entered. The shop smelled of old wood, dried flowers, and too much mildew. Behind the counter stood a man with hair down to his shoulders, the kind of man who believed in energies and vibrations. Arthur despised him instantly.

"I need foxglove," Arthur said, with the confidence of a man who thought saying the word made him educated.

The clerk blinked, then nodded slowly. "Digitalis tincture," he said, pulling a small amber bottle from under the counter as if it were nothing more exotic than cough syrup. The label was handwritten in looping script: *Digitalis – 20 ml*.

Arthur felt giddy. "Yes," he said, his voice coming out too fast. He pulled a fifty from his wallet and slapped it down. The clerk raised an eyebrow but made no comment. No questions, no hesitation, just business. He couldn't believe how easy it was to obtain. *This stuff should be illegal!* he thought. But he said nothing and left the shop with the bottle tucked safely in his coat pocket, walking taller, as if possession alone made him a man of destiny. He ducked into an alley and pulled it out, admiring the neat glass, the small black dropper. It looked innocent. It looked medicinal. It looked perfect.

Arthur Medlar understood deals, not patience. He was used to signatures that moved money and doors that opened because his card said so. But murder, he discovered, obeyed smaller mechanics: hands, steam, seconds. It was a dance of sorts. You didn't bludgeon your way into it. You learned a choreography.

At home, he cleared his kitchen table and built a stage: two mugs, a kettle, a battered thermos, the amber bottle of Digitalis Tincture. He set a cheap kitchen timer by his elbow like a metronome and told himself the only dance step he really needed to memorize: *Precision, Arthur. Precision.*

The first move was the uncap–dose–recap. He palmed the dropper, cap between ring finger and thumb, bottle tucked in the heel of his hand, a magician's grip. With the kettle on and its steam rising, the stage was set. He practiced the motions a hundred times—cap, squeeze three neat droppers into the cup without a splash, cap again, bottle gone. The timer punished him; he punished it back. Twenty-three seconds became twelve. Twelve became ten. He shaved it to seven with the satisfaction of a man landing a deal below asking.

Steam, he learned, was an ally. It curled over the cup and masked small sins: a tremor, a micro-splash, the tiny sound drops make when they touch water. He tested angles. From directly above, too conspicuous. From the side, safer. Standing, riskier; seated, smooth. He marked his favorite spot on the table with the pad of his finger and said it aloud like a stage direction: find your target, and hit the mark.

But, he thought, *I do have a helper: Beatrice.*

Somewhere between practice attempt number eight and practice attempt number twenty five, he remembered Beatrice telling him about all of Lester's pills and how stubborn the man was, because he never wanted to take them. What came to the forefront of his mind was heart medication, some powerful stuff. Lester had to take them every morning at the same time. Beatrice would often have to coax him. Those pills, coupled with the foxglove, would be a sure win. Even if he didn't manage to get the full dose into Lester's mug, he was sure an added jolt to the heart by his meds would finish the job, and it would look even more like a simple heart attack. It was almost *too* good.

Arthur auditioned mugs the way directors audition actors for movies. There was no way for him to know what kind of mugs Lester had in his apartment. Thick diner crockery swallowed sound but demanded a bigger pour to hide the taste. Bone China sang at the slightest touch. He settled on what should have been an obvious choice—his favorite mugs, worthy of the occasion: one-of-a-kind porcelain Williams-Sonoma designer mugs. That was definitely the best fit.

Arthur also studied his own hands until they obeyed. The dropper disappeared between index and middle finger when he shook Beatrice's imaginary hand. It rested along his palm when he reached for a napkin. It hid behind the thermos as he poured. He taught himself eye-line control: say a name and people look up; say, "Careful, it's hot" and they look at the steam. While they looked, the hand worked.

He rehearsed entrances. Thermos in the crook of his left arm, bottle palmed in the right. Place the thermos first—people respect containers that promise heat. Offer to pour, and host mentality disarms suspicion. Keep the bottle's neck below the rim of the mug; steam makes a curtain. Squeeze three droppers, cap, pocket, talk.

He even practiced spills—on purpose. A little slosh of tea on the saucer gave him an excuse for the cloth, the reach, the misdirection. "Let me get that—sorry—" was a spell. While they laughed or waved him off, his fingers did their separate work. The taste worried him, though. He knew it too well now: a biting metallic green, a venus-fly-trap that learned how to hold a gun. He ran tastings the way sommeliers do, except the goal was not to savor but to smother. Ginger beat mint; honey beat sugar; lemon helped, but announced itself too brightly. Of course, he would only take very small sips during these experiments—hardly enough to cause a hiccup. In his notebook he wrote a list that made him proud:

- Maskers: ginger, honey, strong black tea
- Distractions: conversation, apology, heat
- Allies: steam, speed, patience

Speed really mattered. He practiced on two of his porcelain Williams-Sonoma designer mugs, always two. When there are two of anything, people believe in fairness. He learned to center them like a ritual and to move them as if they had already belonged where he placed them. He choreographed who gets which cup without appearing to choose. Left hand for Lester, right for Beatrice—and he would grab whatever mug was around the place for himself. Then, a toast of *by-gones* between him and his new friend, Lester.

He trained his timing against other people's movements. He set a chair across from him and imagined Lester requiring help, Beatrice reaching past, someone knocking, a phone ringing. He learned that the safest window was the hand-off moment: when a person accepts a cup, their eyes go to the rim, not your hands. He learned to build the hand-off: pour, remark, offer; let the social machine do the rest.

He tested covers in public. At a café he dosed his own tea—water in the dropper, not poison—and watched a pair of strangers at the next table. Neither saw him. At a hotel bar he practiced palming the dropper while ordering coffee and left a tip large enough to erase the bartender's interest. He wanted frictionless invisibility, and money was oil.

Arthur timed himself to a metronome, the tick-tick of inevitability. Uncap—one; squeeze—two; squeeze—three; squeeze—four; cap—five; pocket—six; stir—seven; and smile. He could do it now while speaking about the weather. He could do it while shaking his head sadly at the state of modern medicine. He could do it while telling a joke. He was, he told the mirror, born for this.

CHAPTER FORTY

The lamp over Lester's table hummed like a tired insect. The glass shade was the color of nicotine and cast the kitchen in a faint yellow haze, as if everything in it had been smoked. On the table sat his favorite chipped mug, steam rising in stubborn curls, and his morning pills were set squarely in front of him.

Lester was sitting there with the *New York Post* in hand, reading the latest headline: KISS YOUR ASTEROID GOODBYE. Apparently there was a rock the size of Mt. Everest heading for earth. Wonderful.

Beatrice was preparing breakfast in the kitchen. That was their latest switch in rituals, especially on her days off. She glanced at the wall clock. The hands were certain: 9:00, but her wristwatch said 8:50. Beatrice rolled her eyes. His clocks were always wrong. Lester said it was so that the clocks could match his watch, which was always wrong. And always cheap. Why he couldn't buy himself a better watch, she would never know. But she *did* know what she was getting him for Christmas.

Well, she thought happily. *Maybe the world could use catching up to Lester Filch.*

"Don't forget your heart meds, Lester. It's almost nine."

"What do you mean *almost*," he muttered, head still buried in apocalyptic prophecies of doom. "It's already nine o'clock."

"Your clock's fast, remember?"

"Right." He flipped the page over to the comic section. And he *had* been more open to laughing lately. It took him a few days to win back whatever joy he had lost after "the incident." He had softened considerably, as if he'd misplaced his bitterness somewhere and wasn't sure if he wanted to find it again.

Beatrice kept frying the eggs. Lester kept reading the newspaper. And the pills just sat there, waiting.

Lester shifted in his chair and closed the paper. He had read enough about the crazy world out there and suddenly appreciated being cocooned in his little apartment, small and dirty as it was. He took a sip from his mug. "You changed the tea," he said.

"Ginger."

"Because my stomach won't shut up."

"Because it's good for hearts and nerves. And for men who think too much at night."

He huffed, which in Lester-speak was a pretty close approximation to a laugh. The house huffed with him. Steam rose, the radiator popped, branches scratched at the window. Life was pretty normal again, all things considering. He was glad about that. Of course, he had to complain anyway.

"Well, I don't understand why you think suddenly all I can handle is grass and water. Coffee is *just* fine, thank you, and beside that—"

The phone rang.

It startled Beatrice enough that she laughed. "Saved by the bell," she said, taking the eggs off the stove. She grabbed the receiver and placed it to her ear.

"Hello?"

"Beatrice." Arthur's voice was rounded, practiced, carrying that old courtly tone. "Beatrice Goodie."

She froze. The towel went slack in her hand. "Arthur?"

"Yes. I hope you don't mind me tracking you down. I tried your apartment and you weren't there. Then I thought, well, perhaps you're with him, and I had the bright idea of checking the phone book."

She looked over her shoulder at Lester, hunched over his mug, half-reading the newspaper again, half-listening to her. "What do you want?"

Arthur sighed in a way that suggested a hand pressed to his chest. "Only to apologize. For everything I've done. To you. To Lester."

"To *Lester*?" she asked before she could stop herself. Lester's head tilted slightly.

"Yes," Arthur said quickly. "I've been dreadful. Pride, jealousy, bad behavior. All of it. You don't know the half. I thought about you early this morning, and it struck me — what use is any of it? What good comes of bitterness?"

Her brow furrowed. The only thing he'd ever really done to her, as far as she knew, was tell her parents about Lester. And hadn't that been almost... reasonable? She had left Arthur high and dry only months before their wedding. It would have been natural for him to run to her family, licking his wounds and trying desperately to convince them to interfere.

"I just... I miss you, Beatrice," Arthur continued. "Even after all this. If we can't be married, can't we at least be friends? That would be something."

She swallowed, her mouth dry. "Arthur—"

"I'm nearby, actually," he interrupted, tone brightening as if a thought had just occurred to him. "Drove down this morning, foolishly, not sure what I was looking for. And then it came to me — why not call? Why not ask? Could I… come up? Say hello?"

"Arthur…"

"I even brought a thermos and a couple of mugs for us. Tea. Our favorite kind, remember? For old times' sake. But there's plenty for three, of course." His chuckle was thin, rehearsed. "No reason not to share."

The towel twisted in her hand until the threads strained. She should have said no. She *wanted* to say no. But the part of her that still strained toward goodness, that reflex to forgive and make room, rose up before her reason could anchor it.

"All right," she said softly. "Come up. I can buzz you in."

Arthur's relief rushed across the line. "Thank you, Beatrice. Truly."

She hung up slowly, as though realizing she had just eaten something rancid and was going to vomit. Turning, she found Lester's eyes on her — puzzled but also slightly amused.

"He's coming by," she said, her voice apologetic, small. "I couldn't… I couldn't say no."

Lester blinked, leaned back, and snorted. "Of course you couldn't."

"I'm sorry," she said, looking down at the stained linoleum. "I don't know why I do that."

"Don't be sorry," he said, a man used to disasters arriving at his doorstep. "This ought to be good."

Arthur Medlar had been parked outside for about half an hour. The Hummer squatted at the curb like a giant cat, ready to pounce. The windows were fogged from his breath. He scraped a little circle in the frost with his thumb so he could watch the building. From the third floor, light glowed in the kitchen window — warm, domestic, insulting.

He hated that glow. Hated that she was up there with him.

Arthur rubbed his hands together, more from nerves than cold, though the cold had its say. His gloves lay on the passenger seat beside a folder of papers, half-crumpled from his impatience. The folder contained nothing important — old drafts, receipts, scribbles about legal strategy. Props, really. He liked to keep things that made him look busy, official. Nobody trusted empty-handed men.

But today was not a meeting or a consultation. Today was an intervention, and when he had called them with his cellular, Beatrice had played her part beautifully. He knew she was too good to say *No*.

Nine o'clock had finally arrived, and Lester would be taking his heart medication, the little backup to make sure the foxglove made its mark, should his hand waver. Arthur checked his watch. Actually, it was nine-oh-five. Good. It was time to go up. He had given them enough space between the call and his visit to make it seem like he really *was* just driving by, not like he was stalking them right outside the apartment. Soon, it would be all over. The next time he got in his Hummer, Lester Filch would be dead.

He felt a fierce, private joy at the thought of it: Lester's heart laboring under foxglove, his body betraying him, Beatrice realizing too late that love could not rewrite chemistry. Arthur smiled in the driver's seat and looked at himself in the rear-view mirror. His smile deepened. For a moment, he had almost pitied her. Almost.

Beatrice belonged to him. Not in the sentimental sense—he had no illusions about hearts and vows—but in the sense of credit. He had invested years in her, propped up her ideals, worn the mask of her lover while she played the saint. He had given her his presence, the opportunity to take his name. He had even written her into his will as soon as they got engaged. And now she traded all that trust and investment for poor, sad Lester Filch.

Arthur's jaw worked. He imagined Lester's face contorted in confusion, Beatrice's tears, his own voice calm and reasonable as he called the police on their behalf, knowing the heart attack before them was completely his doing.

The thought steadied him. He reached for the thermos in the passenger seat, unscrewed the cap, and inhaled the bittersweet fumes. Soon it would be more bitter, still. Digitalis, his private sacrament. He had measured the drops again and again until the routine became muscle memory. One swallow and a man might believe he had taken nothing more than strong tea. By the time his stomach told him otherwise, his pulse would already be rewriting itself.

Arthur capped the thermos and slipped it into his coat pocket. His fingers brushed the small amber bottle, cool and promising. He patted it like a lucky charm.

The knock came sooner than Beatrice expected — sharp, practiced, like a man who had rehearsed it on the walk up the stairs. She startled, smoothing her skirt, wiping damp palms on the fabric. Lester hadn't moved from the kitchen table. It was only for a passing second, as she got up to open the door, that she realized Lester hadn't taken his medication. But that would have to wait now. She grabbed the bottle from the kitchen table and put it on the counter with his other prescriptions before she opened the door.

Arthur Medlar stood in the hallway in his overcoat, scarf knotted just so, brown hair immaculate despite its length and the bitter wind. He held a silver thermos cradled in one hand like an offering and a brown paper bag with two identical porcelain Williams-Sonoma designer mugs in the other. His smile was polished, brittle, the kind of smile that cracked if you looked at it too long.

"Beatrice." He said her name as if it were a prayer, or a line of poetry he had practiced in the car mirror. "Thank you. I was half afraid you'd send me away."

She stepped aside automatically, her body obeying a script older than her suspicions. "Come in, Arthur."

The warmth of the apartment hit him. He inhaled, smiled wider. "Cozy," he said, as if complimenting a stage set. "Just as I imagined it."

Lester didn't rise. He stayed slouched at the table, and his eyes tracked Arthur like a cat tracks a bird — without blinking, without moving, with the certainty that the other creature would eventually slip.

Arthur cleared his throat, and set the thermos and mugs on the table. "Hello, Lester. I'm Arthur Medlar." He held out his hand, but Lester didn't receive it.

"I know," said Lester dryly.

"Well, then you must have heard how awful I've been to Beatrice, and how things went down between us. I know you two have things to do, medicines to take and all that, but I thought we might share tea and possibly get acquainted. It's your favorite, Beatrice. *Ours*, once." He laughed too brightly. "But I've brought enough for three, of course. No one left out."

Beatrice stood awkwardly at the kitchen counter, a safe distance away as the impromptu tea party unfolded. She twisted a dish towel in her fingers. "That's... thoughtful."

Lester finally spoke, his voice gravel. "What are you doing here?"

Arthur looked at him, then away, as if eye contact might soil his suit. "I came to make amends. To apologize for everything I've done. To Beatrice." He paused for a moment and looked sideways at his former fiancé, who was still standing in disbelief a good distance away. Then he looked back at Lester and said quietly, "To you."

Lester's eyebrow climbed. "Apologize? To *me*? Whatever for?" He held Arthur's gaze until the other man's eyes gave way.

Arthur pressed on, voice smooth but urgent. "Yes. I've been foolish. Jealous. Cruel. And I can't take it back. But I can say sorry. I miss… what was good. If marriage is impossible, can we not at least be friends? That would be something, wouldn't it?"

"I—" Beatrice began, but Lester cut in.

"You don't know the half of it, Beatrice," he said softly, his eyes on Arthur Medlar.

Arthur met the look at last, and for a moment the room throbbed with unspoken things. The realization hit him. Beatrice didn't know what he had done. Lester hadn't told her. *How perfectly gentlemanly of him*, he thought, straightening his tie. *What a good man! It's too bad he has to die.* He gestured to the thermos.

"Shall we?"

Beatrice swallowed, glanced at Lester with apology in her eyes. "It's only tea," she whispered, as though that excused it.

Lester gave her a look of amusement. "Sure," he said, voice low. "Let's have ourselves a nice cup of tea. I'm sure that'll fix everything."

Arthur unscrewed the cap with a flourish. Steam rose, fragrant and sharp. He pulled over Lester's mug and tilted his head in mock surprise. It read WORLD'S BEST DAD.

"Oh, well you can't use *this*," he said. "Not for a tea party."

"But I *like* my mug," Lester said dryly. "It's a nice mug."

"Well, it's already full. We can't have you drinking out of that when I've gone to the trouble of bringing you the good stuff."

"I'll drink out of my own mug if I want to," said Lester.

"Nonsense," said Arthur, gathering Lester's mug in his hand along with the two mugs he had brought, and carrying them to the sink. "No offense, of course, but let's start fresh. Proper cups for a proper visit. Beatrice, could you fetch some cookies? I remember you always kept those little butter ones in a tin. And plates, napkins, something to make it feel civilized. We deserve civilized, don't we?"

She hesitated, caught between suspicion and that lifelong compulsion to be good, to host properly. Arthur's tone made it sound like a harmless request, like the polite thing, but with Arthur she could never be sure. There were always strings attached with him. She pressed her lips together, then nodded. "All right."

As she moved toward the cupboard, Arthur emptied the horrid-looking mug into the sink, letting the weak tea swirl down the drain, talking the whole time. "You know, Lester," he called, "there was a time I thought you and I could be friends, the way Beatrice talked about you. Imagine that. Two men with so little in common, joined by the same extraordinary woman. Life is funny that way."

With a flourish, he retrieved the amber bottle from his coat and uncapped it with a snap masked by running water. He grabbed the tea kettle when it started to squeal and placed it beside him by the sink, making sure to slosh some of the water out of it, spilling it on the counter to create a bigger fuss. Arthur's heart raced as with one hand he reached for the sponge to clean up the mess and with the other he squeezed the little amber bottle into the designer Williams-Sonoma porcelain mug to his right. Four droppers squirted in, oozing threads of oil coagulating at the bottom. One more dropper-full than he had planned. His breath caught. Even without the pills, even without anything else, it was enough to kill. He capped the bottle and quickly shoved it back into his pocket. It all took less than ten seconds.

"Arthur," said Beatrice, holding three plates and a pile of napkins, "you brought your own thermos, remember? Why are you boiling more water?"

He jumped around and laughed nervously. "Of course! Silly me." Arthur palmed his forehead in feigned embarrassment. "I'm such a dolt." He turned and poured the tea from his thermos into all three mugs, making sure to carefully remember which one of the two porcelain Williams-Sonoma designer mugs he planned for Lester. Then he brought them all to the table.

"Beatrice," he said, raising his voice jovially, "don't fuss. Simple will do. A plate, a napkin, a smile. That's all the world needs."

She returned a moment later with a tin of cookies, her face set but obedient. He met her eyes, smiled that brittle smile, and pushed both mugs across the table, one towards her and the one with the foxglove towards Lester.

"There," he said, grabbing the WORLD'S BEST DAD mug in his hand. "I'll drink from this one. But only the best for you! Aren't they lovely? They're Williams-Sonoma, you know." He smiled at Beatrice, his voice softening. "You and I, we always had tea, didn't we? Those quiet evenings. I thought — why not bring it back? For all of us."

Beatrice sat down in her chair, uneasy but bound by the script of politeness. She slid the napkins out, laid the cookies on a plate. The domestic rhythm asserted itself, and for a moment the room felt absurdly ordinary. Arthur's heart leapt in his chest as he looked around. Beatrice's face was tight, uncomfortable, though beautiful as always. Lester looked like he was waiting for the other shoe to drop. *Oh, yes. And what a shoe this was going to be*, he thought gleefully. This was the stage. This was the scene he rehearsed so many times before.

"Now then," he said, grabbing the mug and raising it high, steam caressing his face. "How about a toast?"

Lester barked a dry laugh. "And what, exactly, are we toasting? World peace? The war in Iraq? My heart condition?" His eyes widened slightly at that. "My heart condition! I didn't take my pills today."

"I'll get them!" yelled Arthur, as he sprang from the chair, leaving both his hosts staring in disbelief. He could not believe his good fortune. So Lester *hadn't* take his medication yet (not that it mattered). Instead, Arthur would be watching Lester take a double dose of heart-stopping chemicals. This couldn't be better.

He grabbed the first bottle he saw on the counter and brought it back, but Beatrice shook her head and told him it was the wrong one. It then took him a minute to find the right one nestled in a pile of about twenty almost-identical prescription bottles. How Lester Filch wasn't already dead from poisoning himself, Arthur couldn't understand.

When he returned, Lester took the bottle from him and poured himself a pill. Arthur watched hungrily as he downed it with a swig of tea. He grabbed his mug and spread both arms out in a magnanimous gesture of conviviality. "To truth!" he proclaimed. "To forgiveness! To a new season of friendship!"

Arthur drank with pride, as if he were, in fact, the WORLD'S BEST DAD. As he drank the tea, he tried very hard to ignore the fact that he had *never* drunk from anything other than a porcelain Williams-Sonoma designer mug. The tea tasted even worse in that horrible mug. Poverty made everything taste worse. Arthur decided to down all of it in one gulp, since he saw Lester finishing up his. The faster he was done, the faster he could get out of there if he needed to.

"There," he said, setting down his mug. "Shared together. You see? We're all friends now."

Silence stretched out for far too long. There would be no friendly conversation, despite all of Arthur's best efforts. Beatrice looked at him and thought he looked rather sad and somewhat pale. What was he trying to accomplish with all this? More importantly, what did she ever see in him? She didn't know how she was going to get him out of her life, but this fake friendship stuff really had to go. Beatrice downed her own mug to get it all over with faster. But it was as she placed her mug back down on the table that she noticed the sweat beading up on Arthur's forehead.

Arthur didn't quite know what everybody was staring at, but his body knew. His throat tightened, the bitterness rising metallic at the back of his tongue. It was awfully hot in that apartment. *If Lester doesn't have money*, he thought, *how can he keep the heat on so high?* He forced a smile wider.

"Delicious," he said. "Isn't it?"

Beatrice kept staring at him. "I suppose—"

Arthur's hand shot out, catching hers. Too fast. Too desperate. "No, let me—let me pour you more. Plenty to go around." His voice wobbled.

Beatrice frowned. "Arthur? Are you alright?"

He laughed, sounding small and brittle. "Nerves, that's all. Haven't we all had nerves this morning?"

Arthur tried to rise, to move back toward the kitchen, but the floor tilted under him. He placed his hands on the table to steady himself. "Just nerves," he said faintly. The sweat began to flow like rain down his face. He wiped at it with the back of his hand. "I don't understand. How is *he* okay?" He was looking at Lester but talking to himself.

Lester leaned forward, suspicion dawning slow and grim. "What do you mean, *how is he okay?*" he asked cautiously.

Arthur blinked at him, face tightening, then loosening, then tightening again, as if every muscle was undecided. "How do you look fine?" he asked, incredulously. "I put it in your mug." He wiped at his sweat again, and then looked at his wet fingers. "Didn't I?"

"Arthur," Beatrice said slowly, rising from her seat, "what did you do?"

But Arthur wasn't listening to her anymore. "The cup. I put it in your cup...But how?"

"Well, actually," Lester explained grimly, "I drank the tea from *your* cup, which is really *my* cup. When you had your back turned. When you were looking for those pills."

"Nonsense," Arthur gasped. "Why would you do that?"

"Because nobody tells me not to drink from my own mug. I told you I would."

"You're crazy! How can a man be *that* stubborn? I—" He reached for the WORLD'S BEST DAD mug and missed it by an inch. His hand trembled on the table again. "But the mug was full when I drank from it!"

"I know!" said Lester. "I poured my mug into yours."

And that's when the great Arthur Medlar collapsed.

Beatrice was on her feet and by his side in a second. "Arthur, what did you drink?"

Arthur wheezed, trying to sit up in her arms. "Only... what I meant for him." He patted the pocket of his coat, which he still had on.

She jammed her hand into the pocket and pulled out the amber bottle, grimacing as she opened it. The faint bitter tang released into the air. Her stomach lurched. "Foxglove," she whispered, reading the label. "*That* can't be good."

Arthur sagged back onto the floor, trying to smirk but failing. "No," he rasped, "it's actually perfect. Really a flower, you know. Thought it would be... poetic."

His body betrayed him again — a stumble in his heartbeat, a skip in his breath. He reached up for Beatrice's face and missed, grasping only air.

Lester stood, slow and stiff, and shuffled over to the phone. "I guess I should call an ambulance," he said casually.

Arthur's eyes flashed, furious now. "I *never* lose," he hissed, but the words cracked. He tried to raise himself, to reclaim his dignity, but he collapsed a third time. It was the last time he would.

Beatrice crouched beside him, two fingers at his throat. The pulse bucked, dragged, bucked again.

"Call 911," she said firmly.

But Lester was already on it.

The sirens came fast, red light painting the snow outside. The EMTs burst in, efficient, unstartled, attaching wires and noting arrhythmia. Beatrice handed them the amber bottle without ceremony. "Digitalis tincture," she said calmly.

Arthur's eyes fluttered as they strapped him to the gurney. "Didn't... want... to lose," he whispered, the words collapsing under their own weight.

"But you did lose, Arthur," said Beatrice sadly. "Sometimes, we have to."

The EMTs wheeled him out, and the door shut behind them, leaving Beatrice and Lester staring at it, speechless. They both slumped down at the kitchen table. Her untouched mug of Arthur's tea was cooling between them. Beatrice had the feeling that soon this nondescript little apartment would become a crime scene. She had just handed them the murder weapon, and there was no doubt in her mind that Arthur Medlar would not survive the night.

Outside, the snow fell down again, cleaning up the streets of West Lemon, working its best lie. Down the street the Hummer sulked under a film of it, a monument to a lone man's crazed insecurities. Upstairs, Beatrice was putting together her tote bag, gathering her coat, and making plans to head out before the police got to them. And they would, eventually, get to them. How could they not?

Lester had told her not to worry, that it was a simple mistake born from his own stubbornness. They could explain what happened, and surely they would see that they had never meant to kill Arthur Medlar. Of course, nothing with Lester Filch was simple. But she didn't say that as she headed for the door.

Beatrice paused for a moment before turning around and giving him a hug, almost without meaning to—quick, awkward— like the kind you practice in a mirror and finally try on a person. He returned her hug with a simple kiss on the cheek. It was the best he could muster with the lingering memory of death still in the room. Anything more would not have been appropriate.

"See you tomorrow?" she said, then added, "Of course, if the police don't get us first."

"Of course," he answered, "see you tomorrow." And he heard inside his own words the small, stupid miracle of a future.

EPILOGUE

Epilogues are for tying bows. This one is for tying knots—sailor knots, Gordian knots, stubborn knots you chew with your teeth when your hands give up. Most stories shut the door on life with a neat blessing: they lived happily ever after. This one leaves the door ajar, the draft whistling through, the hallway light flicking on and off. Beatrice Goodie and Lester Filch were married, yes. Whether they were happy depends on the day you asked, the angle of the sun, the humidity, and the number of children currently gluing breakfast to the cat.

The wedding had all the pomp of a county recycling drive. The organist had bronchitis and performed the bridal march in wheezes, the way an accordion might sound if it had emphysema. The church flowers were plastic carnations from a closing sale; some still wore their tiny stickers like price-tag freckles. The priest—on loan from a funeral home and smelling faintly of lilies and disinfectant—mispronounced Filch as Finch and then, realizing he'd accidentally improved it, stuck with Finch all the way to the paperwork. Welch's was decanted into Styrofoam cups that squeaked when you pinched them. Guests held their breath through the vows because the HVAC seemed to blow only dust.

And yet, there in the shabby aisle, Lester tried very hard not to cry and almost succeeded. Beatrice didn't try at all and cried like a garden hose. The congregation, a coalition of sceptical neighbors, misfit cousins, and twenty home health aides who insisted on hugging everyone, felt the strange tug that attends unlikely victories: a little awe, a little dread, the sense of witnessing a miracle cobbled together from spare parts.

Immediately after the service, the State brought them back down to earth. Beatrice and Lester were charged with the murder of Arthur Medlar. The indictment read like a bitter limerick: they had motive, they had opportunity, they had porcelain Williams-Sonoma designer mugs. But they maintained their innocence with the fervor of people who were, in fact, innocent, though innocence looks shabby in court next to wealth and outrage. Arthur's parents, dressed like a libel suit, sat in the front row and practiced fainting. Beatrice's parents weren't even there.

The trial—if one could call that meringue of objections and gossip a trial—was a parade of people trying to sound reasonable while describing wildly unreasonable events. The prosecutor presented Arthur's will as Exhibit A: he had left Beatrice a tidy sum. The defense countered with Exhibit B: common sense. Jurors took notes like they were learning a new board game. The judge, caught between a statute book and a headache, finally dismissed the case on evidence so technical the clerk had to explain it three times. The short version: Arthur never returned his library books. They were found in his New York apartment, used, perused, and marked with yellow highlighter.

The public objected. Arthur's parents yelled their threats. The law shrugged. Beatrice and Lester walked out into daylight blinking like houseplants shoved onto a stoop, and the tabloids—disappointed but adaptive—declared them PROBABLY GUILTY IN AN INSPIRING WAY.

They made for the nearest travel agent and bought a honeymoon cruise because nothing says "new life" like buffets engineered to remove the will to live. The ship, named something hopeful in Italian, was large enough to have its own weather. For two days it played the role of a floating mall admirably: the endless carpets, the air that smelled like fruit-scented detergent and old money. On the third day, the ship elected to stop being a ship. No storm, no iceberg, no drama. It just… retired. Somewhere between the midnight chocolate fountain and the sunrise stretch class, the rivets reconsidered their vows, and the hull breathed in a sigh and then a little more and then too much.

Announcements came in the captain's calm voice, which was calming only until you noticed it kept getting closer, as if he were walking toward the lifeboats while speaking. Crew members did their best imitations of calm ducks: gliding on the surface, paddling like hell beneath. Lester and Beatrice—two seasoned survivors of domestic disasters—grabbed a deck chair, a bag of pretzels, and each other. They bobbed in the sea for a couple days like a tragic snack for a lot of hungry sharks.

Fate, drunk and sentimental, threw them a beach before the sharks could figure out they were available. They crawled ashore, coughed up the Pacific, and were promptly surrounded by islanders who did, in fact, wish them ill but had a flair for theater to go with that, making their intentions at first unclear. A cooking fire. A very large pot. A ring of faces that said *Sorry, but we have our traditions*, and *Also, this is mostly for the tourists.* Beatrice instinctively thanked everyone for their hospitality while bound at the wrists; *please* and *thank you* carry surprising distances over a jungle clearing. Someone's grandmother, scandalized by politeness, declared them too well-mannered to stew. The tribe fed them roasted yams instead and a lecture about sunscreen. No one was eaten. Everyone got a story.

A helicopter—its pilot a man who had been bored for ten years and was overdue for something to talk about—hoisted them into the sky when he saw the word HELP spelled out on the sand in palm fronds. For a couple of hours, at least, they were joyful and happy to be heading home. But they clung to each other as the helicopter coughed, reconsidered, and fell neatly into the ocean directly beside a passing cruise ship, also heading home. Fate had gone full slapstick now: rope ladder to life raft, life raft to gangplank, gangplank to all-you-can-eat buffet.

They returned to West Lemon with island tans and the faint aura of the blessed or cursed—no one could decide which. Their first act was to shower. Their second was to nap. Their third was to discover that their new house was burning down.

The fire began humbly, as so many disasters do: a sullen cigarette smouldering in a kingdom of old magazines. The blaze ate through Lester's memories first—the broken recliner that he brought from the old apartment and held a dozen apologies, the laminate kitchen table where soup had done so much heavy lifting, the wall where the calendar hung, filled with pencil promises. Neighbors lined the sidewalk, trading theories and lemonade and looking on as the not-so-happy couple stumbled from their house, coughing and wondering if they were still napping. The fire chief, who had seen every human folly twice, nodded at Lester's explanation of "spontaneous combustion" and wrote down "ashtray."

Insurance, which had never liked them but feared them a little, cut a check so generous it felt like hush money. They built again, but bigger: a house with a porch that could seat a baseball team, a kitchen with a moral obligation to host Thanksgiving, four bathrooms in case someone had a number three and needed some privacy (if you don't know, don't ask). The new fireplace had a glass door. Lester taped a sign on it that read NO CIGARETTES; beneath that he taped another sign that read I MEAN IT.

They wanted children like some people want peace treaties: desperately, without proof it was possible. Nature kept her own counsel. Doctors, gentle and practiced, said the phrase "advanced maternal age" as if handing over a parking ticket. Beatrice cried once, in a laundromat, into a pile of warm towels that smelled like other people's lives. Lester stood beside her not knowing where to put his hands. Then bureaucracy threw open a side door and twenty children poured in.

They adopted so many that the postman began delivering the mail in a sack labelled BEATRICE & LESTER & ET AL. Boys who spoke six languages and none. Girls who had never seen snow and then saw too much of it at once. Babies who arrived with instructions in three-ring binders. Teenagers who arrived with instructions written on their faces: DON'T FAIL ME. The living room became a United Nations of plastic blocks. The refrigerator door groaned under art that attempted to rhyme animals with fruit (Rhinoceros/asparagus . . . close enough!).

Money ran away in shoelaces and snacks. Time ran away in permissions and apologies. The upstairs hallway smelled permanently of shampoo battles and bubble gum. Someone was always losing a sock; someone else was always hiding it for science. Lester discovered that he could fall asleep standing up if he leaned against something moral, like the washing machine. Beatrice discovered she could remember twenty names, twenty shoe sizes, and which kid liked peas and which believed peas were fascism. Both of them aged ten years in two. They softened where it helped and hardened where it mattered. The house could have been chaos. It was, instead, a country.

Disaster did not retire with this new arrangement. It developed new tactics. There was the Year of the Roof, during which the roof learned to leak at different places depending on the strength of the rain. Lester ascended ladders in a harness Beatrice called his "martyr costume" and stapled tarps to the heavens. There was the Week of the Stomach Bug, when the washing machine prayed for death, not least because it had to be used as a communal emergency toilet, and Beatrice sterilized the air with Lysol. And yet, disasters—dutiful as they were—paired themselves with miracles like polite dance partners. A neighbor with a nail gun. A librarian who waived the late fees on a thousand dollars' worth of dinosaur books. A doctor who laughed and said, "They're all normal. This is what normal looks like."

Beatrice realized, slowly and then all at once, that Lester's worst qualities had origin stories. He had been sharpened by loneliness until he could cut people by accident. He recognized malice because he had entertained it; he recognized grace because he had been starved for it. This recognition was, in some sideways way, its own goodness. It made him a better critic of himself than any saint she'd ever met. Meanwhile she, the woman who had tried to staple halos to strangers, had to confront the rot inside her charity—the habit of loving people as projects, of fitting them into hypotheses. She had burned a book and called it mercy. She had tried to script a man. Control is not a fruit of the Spirit.

Lester tried to hate her for the lie, the way a man tries to hate sunlight after a sunburn. He discovered that forgiveness is less a single decision than a thousand small ones, the way a path is less a road than a million stones that agree to lie still. That lesson kept on giving long into their marriage.

On the ten-year anniversary of everything—the trial's dismissal, the wedding that sounded like a funeral, the cruise that drowned politely, the house that went up like a journal—Beatrice and Lester sat on their porch in their fifties, wondering how they made it.

They watched the sky try on different reds. Lester lit a cigarette and then, looking sideways at her, thought better of it, not because he was a reformed man but because the porch repairs were new and probably easily flammable. The children were inside inventing a game that sounded like upholstery dying bravely. Their new cat, Sushi, stared through the screen with the face of a monarch who disapproves of democracy.

"We should have been dead a dozen times," Lester said, as if reporting the weather, brushing back his greying hair.

"We did die in a way," Beatrice said, "but then again, here we are." Her voice had changed over the years. It had kept its warmth but acquired grain, like wood that survived a winter.

"People keep asking me if this"—Lester waved at the house, at the chorus currently arguing about who had eaten all the meatloaf—"was worth it."

"And?"

"I tell them no," he said, deadpan. "I tell them it's exhausting and loud and everything is sticky. Then I tell them I can't imagine not being here for it."

He paused, and she slipped her hand into his the way you slip a letter under a door after midnight. They stood like that for a while, two ridiculous saints of a tiny parish no one ever heard of, and watched a raccoon the size of a carry-on-bag make an ethical decision about their garbage. The porch light hummed on. Somewhere a child asked the moon a question in a language only the night understood.

They did not become model citizens. They did not even become a concrete example of success to many who got to know them. But they *did* become a rumor of hope told by people who wanted to believe that wreckage and resurrection often share a fence. Their porch gained chairs for neighbors. Their mailbox filled with thank-you cards written in clumsy crayon. Their Christmas tree collapsed annually under the weight of ambitious ornaments and was often propped up with a hockey stick and a threat.

When I asked Beatrice what she had learned through all this, she said something honest and unhelpful like, "That goodness is not a personality trait." When I asked Lester, he said, "That no one, not even me, is as terrible as his worst thoughts." Then he added (because he could never resist the symmetry), "or as noble as his best."

On a Tuesday evening, unremarkable except for the way ordinary evenings sometimes become perfect for a moment, Beatrice set bowls of stew in front of three small children, one teenager, a traveling nurse who was staying with them for a few weeks, two neighbors, and a man who claimed to be there to check the smoke detectors. Lester tasted the stew and nodded solemnly, as if acknowledging a treaty. Beatrice dropped a pitcher of water, and though four hands moved to rescue it, they failed. But the glass fell and did not break—an omen of modest mercies. The cat, who believed in good omens only when they involved tuna, leapt onto the counter and was negotiated down with a speech about boundaries.

I was the traveling nurse at dinner that night. It was how I met them, and over those few weeks I got to hear their story. It stayed with me, begged me to write it down, and so finally I did after many years. I would visit them every year like clockwork, until work became leisure, and convenient hosts became good friends. I told them I was going to write a book about them, but they didn't seem to care. "As long as it's good," Beatrice would say with a smile. But mainly they just kept on keeping on, with all the craziness of life, with the good and the bad.

And if, years later, you caught them at the right hour—long after bedtime, when the dishwasher sang and the house held its breath—you might have seen Beatrice and Lester sitting on the floor against the kitchen cabinets, leaning into each other in that practical way exhausted people do, sharing the last peach from a bowl. He would take a bite and hand it to her, and she would laugh because he would mutter that peaches are socialist fruit, and she would kiss juice from his wrist and say that socialism tasted pretty good to her.

Neither of them lived happily-ever-after. Nor did they live unhappily-ever-after. They just lived deliberately-ever-after—spilling, mending, arguing, apologizing, cooking, rebuilding, ferrying small humans from tantrums to sleep, occasionally remembering to look up at the sky and pray.

Whether all this was a bad thing or a good thing, nobody could tell. I certainly couldn't. Which, between us, is probably what goodness looks like when it's busy—too busy to pose, too busy to be pure, too busy to be anything but true.

ACKNOWELDGMENTS

Every writer knows that a book is never really written alone. Even the most solitary late nights at the desk are carried on the shoulders of those who encourage, tolerate, and sometimes simply endure the writer's obsessions. This novel, which began as a manuscript more than twenty years ago, and was put aside to complete another novel, was kept alive by the patience and love of many people in my life, and now that it is finally finished, I cannot help but feel more gratitude than words can properly contain. But words are what I have, so I will do my best.

First and foremost, I want to thank my wife, Juliana. To say that she puts up with me is an understatement of operatic proportions. She has endured me talking about my writing, *not* talking because I'm too busy writing, obsessing over my writing, and then obsessing over why I'm obsessing about my writing. She has lived with my secret manuscripts, odd mutterings of characters and plots, and random speeches about the greatness of some plot twist that would either fix a book or break it further. Through all of this, she has remained my biggest encourager, the person who reminds me why I do this in the first place. Without her patience, her gentleness, and her willingness to listen to me explain (again and again) the difference between a draft and a final draft, this book would still be languishing as a collection of half-baked ideas. She is a very good thing that happened to me, despite the very bad things that happened before she came along.

I am equally grateful to my children: Sofia, Ezekiel, and Isabella. They have a Dad who gets easily distracted, especially by them, and decides to go out and add writing novels to his already multiple jobs. They sometimes find him hunched over his desk late at night with his keyboard, and I'm sure they wonder if they ever really want to grow up. I don't make it look appealing. And yet, they never complain, they let me do my thing, and they support me. In fact, they ask questions. They want to know what I'm working on, what characters I'm creating, and why I look so tired all the time. They have pretended to be interested in literary discussions that most children would have fled from, and for that I am deeply touched.

Sofia deserves special mention. At sixteen, her enthusiasm for literature and books is infectious. She reads voraciously, debates passionately, and constantly reminds me of the joy that first brought me to the page myself. To have a daughter who loves books as much as I do is more than just encouraging—it feels like a quiet confirmation that stories really do matter, that they still have the power to move, shape, and inspire across generations.

To my mother, Cecilia, I owe more than I can say. She has always been my first encourager, my first audience, and in many ways my first muse. As an artist herself—though her medium is paint rather than words—she understands the restless itch to create, the compulsion to bring something into existence that wasn't there before. From her I inherited not only a love of the arts but also the stubborn belief that they are worth pursuing, no matter how impractical they sometimes seem. She knows what it is to lose yourself in a work, to wrestle with it, to despair of it, and to finally step back and see something that somehow justifies the struggle.

Finally, I can't forget my good friend of over twenty years. Robbin Bergfors is a very good thing, indeed. She journeyed with me as I lived through much, both good and bad, and she was there when I first showed her a preliminary draft of *Very Bad Things*. If I remember correctly, Robbin was the first one to read it. Over the years, she mentioned several times how much she wished I would finish it. I had her in mind as I closed this book out, and I was eager to give her a copy, with gratitude for a friend who gently nudges you to finish what you start. I don't know if what I created stuck the landing; time will tell, but I do hope that for Robbin, reading the full novel will be an experience that brings her joy and more than a few laughs.

And while I do not believe in the pagan gods of old, I cannot help but nod toward the Muses—if only to admit that inspiration is often a mystery. Ideas come unbidden, out of nowhere, and sometimes they are so surprisingly good that I look back and wonder where they could possibly have come from. If I were an ancient Roman, I might chalk it up to the whisper of a Muse leaning over my shoulder. But since I am not, I can only give thanks to the Creator Himself. After all, He is in the same business that I'm fumbling my way through: creation. Any spark of imagination that finds its way onto the page is, in some small measure, a reflection of His larger work. So to Him be the final thanks: for life, for words, and for the stubborn grace that saw this story through from its beginning to its end.

And to all of you reading this, who picked up this book and gave it your time: I am very grateful. Writers write to be read, and readers complete the circle, however few they may be. If you laughed, or cringed, or saw a glimmer of yourself in these pages, then it was worth the work. Thank you.

AUTHOR'S NOTE

This book was written over the span of two decades, which means it took me longer to finish than most marriages last. It began as a single idea scribbled in the margin of a notebook, the kind of idea you're sure will change the world. I think I had read one of Shakespeare's work, from the funny ones; I can't remember which. And I decided to write a silly story, with silly characters, and silly plot points that come together nicely. Of course, as I wrote, it became much darker and much more personal. I realized it reflected the deeper truths that so many of us are wrestling with: discovering what is truly good in life. At twenty three, that was a tall order for me. I didn't have much good during that time. In fact, I faced a lot of very bad things. So life happened, another novel—a murder mystery—happened, and this idea just sat there, quietly judging me every time I tried to start something new. I would revisit it on occasion over the years.

You should know up front: this is not a moral fable. If you finish these pages and think, "I have learned how to be a better human being," then I either failed as a satirist or you failed as a reader. What you have here is a comedy of errors, full of people who are better at messing things up than fixing them, which means it may feel strangely familiar.

A note on the characters: if you recognize yourself in these pages, that's not my fault. Everyone has a neighbor like Lester. Everyone knows a Beatrice, who thinks she's better than she is and has life served to her on a silver platter. And everyone has met an Arthur, who most people think should be legally prohibited from living. These are universal types. If you find yourself offended, it's probably because you have something in common with them. Don't worry—I do, too.

There is also no guarantee that anyone in this story lives "happily ever after." In fact, it may be just the opposite, as you read in the epilogue. But they do *live*, and sometimes that's the more interesting miracle. Believe me, Lester could just up and die one day. Maybe they took a cruise on their twentieth anniversary, and he was stung by a Man-O-War. Or Beatrice's luck ran out, in the form of a school bus careening into her (she was always so careful to look both ways!).

But whatever happens to those two, even if they both live to be a hundred, we all know that life doesn't *really* end neatly. Some of us are deeply in touch with the fact that true meaning, true goodness in life, cannot be found in any one person. Everything is ephemeral, including relationships. Our lives will pass away, and then we will pass into the next realm, standing before God and looking back trying to make sense of it all. Life is rarely neat, never perfect, and almost always a mixture of very bad things and the occasional very good one. This novel is my attempt to capture that tension—with more than a little exaggeration, grotesquerie, and dark humor.

Finally, I should mention that while I have made fun of just about everything in this book, I take writing itself seriously. Words matter. Stories matter. Even the ridiculous ones. *Especially* the ridiculous ones. If they didn't, you wouldn't still be reading this.

So thank you for reading. And if you don't like the book, remember: satire isn't for everyone. Some people prefer meatloaf.

ABOUT THE AUTHOR

Seraphim George has been writing for so long that he sometimes wonders if his earliest drafts belonged on stone tablets. Over the years he produced poetry, plays, half-finished novels, and more than a few forgotten manuscripts. Some of these he released into the world; others remain safely hidden away.

His first published novel, *Mariner's Hollow*—released under a different name—earned awards and readers way back in 2014, proving that the late nights at the keyboard weren't wasted. His current work, *Vera*, explores literary horror and vampires without sparkles. He began writing through poetry, and has recently released his poetry in three collections: *Milkweed for Monarchs*, *A Swiftly Tilting Shore*, and *Dear Seamus Heaney*. All three collections were also published in a full-length book of poetry, *The Floating World*.

By day, Seraphim works as a Communications Director for nonprofit organizations, helping people who do good things explain them better. This allows him to indulge in journals he'll never fill and pens he'll inevitably misplace. Outside of writing, he spends time with his wife, Juliana, who patiently endures his constant talk about plots and drafts, and with his children—Sofia,

Ezekiel, and Isabella—who occasionally pretend to be interested. Seraphim enjoys traveling, helping out at church, swimming whenever he can find water, and venturing outdoors, where he insists mosquitoes should count as real life vampires.

Asked once why he writes, he answered, "Because I can't *not* write. Also, therapy is expensive." He continues to create new novels while revisiting old ones, determined to keep shaping words into stories. Whether anyone is reading or not, he'll keep at it, because stories have a way of insisting on being told. To find out more about him, visit www.seraphimgeorge.com.